W9-BGJ-033

The Trilisk Ruins
Michael McCloskey
Copyright 2012 Michael McCloskey
ISBN: 978-1466393844
Cover art by Howard Lyon

Prologue

Kirizzo fought while curled around himself inside the round control module. In this position he looked like a mottled ball of gold wrapped in dozens of thin legs. At his mental command, a salvo of antimissile drones shot out of the belly of his metal walking machine. The drones circled as they ascended, forming a defensive perimeter in the spiny alien trees. It wouldn't be long until the enemy war machines returned from the last diversionary trail and found his real escape route.

The spider-legged walking machine shot forward through another group of trees and came to a halt in a slight depression in the landscape. A warning in his mental interface informed Kirizzo the walker's stored power waned. And those had been the last of his drones. A thin layer of cells covering his analog of a spinal cord pondered his next move. The decision arrived with a cool clarity: Abandon the walker and try to lose the robotic hunting machines in the alien forest.

Kirizzo felt immensely lonely. There were no others of his race to help him now. He was undoubtedly the only Gorgala within many light years. Nevertheless, he did not waste time lamenting the situation. Kirizzo's electronically augmented mind gave a command that caused his walker to open, allowing egress. Uncoiling his flexuous body from the control nest, he flowed out of the walker on a quick stream of thin legs.

Kirizzo took stock of the alien forest. His world was utterly silent, as he lacked any sense of hearing.

He felt resistance where his spiked legs met the surface. Dead plant spines covered the ground, causing it to give slightly as his sharp legs sank in.

Bundles of fibers under a flat, wide protuberance rising from his body fed Kirizzo signals from light that impinged upon them. These organs allowed him to see the native canopy of frills and spines above that shaded out most of the sunlight. The smooth hulls of trees rising upward surrounded him.

Kirizzo moved his upper protuberance side to side rhythmically, collecting information about the mass densities in all directions out to his sensory range. From this, Kirizzo constructed a mental mass-map of his surroundings in three dimensions. The tree roots, trunks, and limbs formed a dark web in Kirizzo's mind. There weren't any threats within his sensory limits, but that was little comfort. Most Bel Klaven weapons could strike from great distances.

He deployed a personal screen, a group of floating metal defense modules that followed his every move. Four of his forty limbs held guided projectile launchers. He used these to shoot four seeker bullets into the sky, where they patrolled for the Bel Klaven machines that hunted him. Then he burst into the forest, his legs a blur, mapping his route well ahead using his mass sense.

Kirizzo topped the next rise and was deep into the forest when the first of the hunting machines penetrated the drone defense to assault his abandoned walker. The ground shook and the sky flashed momentarily as one of them blasted the walking machine. The robotic Bel Klaven constructs were not very smart, but they made up for that drawback with firepower and numbers.

Kirizzo hoped the machines would stop to investigate the wreckage and leave him to slip away in the cover. He moved on tirelessly, churning through dense foliage. He descended another ridge and started up its far side.

Suddenly masses whirled around Kirizzo rapidly. His personal defense modules intercepted three hunter-seeker projectiles and destroyed them before they could embed themselves in his exoskeleton and explode. Smoke filled the area and debris flew about, ricocheting against nearby trees. The close miss caused a chemical release of stimulants in Kirizzo's body. For Kirizzo, this was fear: his legs twitched, his vision became sharper, and his mind raced.

He launched four more seeker rounds into the sky and continued on course. Back in the walker he had detected a power emanation in this direction. A power source meant some kind of civilization, which presented a chance for escape.

Long seconds passed until Kirizzo sensed something in the forest ahead: an artificial construct. He perceived it as a large uniform shell of mass covered with natural growth. He didn't have time to hesitate. He ran forward to get a view of the site.

An opening beckoned beyond a thick covering of vegetation. Only his mass sense allowed Kirizzo to detect the flaw in the shell of the building. Kirizzo pushed aside the plant growth and entered the breach. The building interior contained complex machinery that had begun to degrade once exposed to the elements. Mud covered most of the floor. A layer of dust clung to the old machines. A few light-starved plants struggled to exist amidst the wreckage. In the center of the chamber a huge circular tube rose from the floor.

Kirizzo determined that the large white tube descended in a spiral, leading deeper under the surface. The tube was empty as far as he could detect. There was no other way to go except down or back out into the forest. Kirizzo's race had its origins in subterranean lairs, and so the choice was perhaps as instinctual as intellectual.

Still quite aware of the looming pursuit, Kirizzo scuttled into the tube. He made his way rapidly down, searching for the end of the passageway.

After five or six complete revolutions, the smooth white walls came to a terminus at a circular portal that seemed to be the barrier of a blackfield. No detectable radiation came from inside the circle.

Kirizzo guessed it was a security gate. His race had mastered enough science to create a field that allowed passage of EM radiation in one direction only. These were often used for controlling entrances to important facilities. From beyond the blackfield, the defenders of the complex could remain hidden but still detect intruders approaching.

But this time, more than his sight remained blocked. Kirizzo could not feel any mass behind the portal. This would not be indicative of an active defense in a security checkpoint of his own race, since it was important in Gorgalan warfare to have many points of constantly moving mass to confuse the mass sense of attackers. With many masses in motion, it became difficult to mark enemy positions and attack them.

Kirizzo worried about unseen dangers but continued toward the circular blackness anyway. As he neared the flat plane of the blackfield, he still couldn't detect any mass beyond. This was a very eerie feeling. It reminded him of the first time he had approached the outer shell of a space cruiser and felt the emptiness beyond the bulkhead, reaching out as far as he could feel, cold and unchanging.

There were other situations in which the mass detectors of a Gorgala could fail. Massive physical trauma, the effects of certain sonic weapons employed by his race in more primitive times, and certain illnesses were known to deprive his kind of the mass sense. As far as Kirizzo knew, however, it could never happen selectively as it did beyond the strange inky blackness in the circle. Still, it was consistent with the blackness. Whatever had created the portal didn't want any information about what was beyond to come out.

Kirizzo wrapped up into a ball to consider his options. Usually the ball position made him feel safer, but it was inadequate this time. The enemy might have already detected the building. He could run out now and hope the Bel Klaven servitors thought he had gone deeper inside. On the other hand, it might be safer on the other side of the field. It certainly didn't seem to be safe out in the forest. His exoskeleton could withstand a vacuum for a short time if it turned out the area beyond really was completely empty.

Kirizzo uncoiled his long body and approached the gate on forty nervous legs. He flicked a slender limb through the blackness and then retracted it. The leg was unharmed. Certainly a good sign.

Suddenly a small mass came clambering down the tunnel behind him. Kirizzo sensed its dense outer shell filled with some lighter material.

Probably an explosive drone.

Kirizzo bolted into the blackness and was swallowed by the portal.

Chapter One

Telisa Relachik stood in front of the mirror in the transport station bathroom. The reflection showed a fit woman in her early twenties with straight black hair and a clear complexion. She wore a black business suit, a one-piece garment with a fake button-up front that showed off the contrast between her slender waist and athletic shoulders. Her link picked up a service for an appearance evaluation from a microcomputer embedded in the mirror, and she considered running it. She had to look right for her interview, but she decided against running the service. She could keep her own counsel on her looks.

Still, she felt anxious. Her interview would be in person, instead of the virtual link interviews she'd already had. It shouldn't make any difference, but some trace of instinct in her felt more nervous about a real face-to-face.

It's not that unusual, she told herself. With the government ever encroaching on communications, probing the data streams with snooper programs designed to flag suspicious messages, more and more businesses were starting to protect themselves by conducting important meetings incarnate. It was an odd reversal back to old traditions, the rejuvenation of the real office.

One of the nightmares of the real office was the commute. Having to appear physically for a meeting proved time-consuming and expensive. Already Telisa had spent a good fraction of an Earth Standard Credit, all charged through her link for public transportation.

Telisa found her way out of the station, buffeted by bodies moving in all directions. She inhaled the Colorado air. It smelled the same to her as on the coast, although it felt colder. She ordered an electric cab through her link and walked up to the curb. She looked over the sprawling buildings across the way. They looked pristine with an expanse of perfect grass. A cat sauntered out from behind a tree and dared to approach the concrete.

"Don't do it," Telisa warned playfully. The cat looked at her, then darted across the street.

Telisa raised an eyebrow. If the cat had a link, it would have been turned away from the street, but apparently it was feral.

"Never mind," she called after the receding feline in a singsong voice. A low hum announced the arrival of her cab. Impatient, she walked toward it as it slowed and moved to the curb. She slipped into the compact one-person contrivance and sent it a map pointer from her link. The engine whirred back to life and accelerated her back onto the street. Telisa thumped her foot and fidgeted during the ride. The streets seemed a little rougher here than in California. Perhaps a byproduct of the weather, she thought.

Finally the cab deposited her at Parker Interstellar Travels and charged her account. She dismissed it and walked up to a metal gate. Evergreens lined the road, hiding a low wall.

The estate looked sharp. A well-trimmed lawn bordered the house and the office, which were joined by a second-story walkway. She wondered if the grass was real. If so, it was wintergrass, since it had doubtless already snowed a couple of times up this high.

The gate opened for her and offered her link a map to her interview. She saw the pathway in her mind, marked by a red line on a bird's-eye map. Kind of old fashioned, she thought. Most location finders these days just superimposed red arrows over a person's regular perspective view. Less chance of getting mixed up that way.

She followed the map through the front yard and into the building. She stepped through a sparsely decorated atrium and toward the office highlighted in her mind. A man in a suit met her at the open doorway.

"Come on in, Ms. Relachik."

"Thanks. I appreciate you calling me in for this interview, Mr. Parker," Telisa smiled and followed the man into the office. He looked about forty, with short, straight brown hair. She thought his face looked a little rough and too thickset, but his smile softened it a bit. Telisa thought she detected a confidence in dealing with people.

"Please, call me Jack," he said. "Would you like a drink?"

"No thanks, Jack. Telisa. Call me Telisa, I mean," she said nervously.

"Okay. Just relax," he told her. "I can see why one might be a bit nervous for an interview like this. Hard times, I hear, for xenoarchaeologists," he said. "Please don't take that wrong. I'm only commenting on the way things stand in general."

"That's true enough," she replied. "You must be interviewing many people." Telisa made the comment to probe about her competition.

"No, actually you're the only one," he said, smiling widely and leaning back in his chair.

Telisa raised her eyebrow at him. "The only one? Why's that?"

"I've checked you out," Jack told her. "I read your stuff. I was impressed by what you had to say, and I think you're just what we're looking for."

Telisa looked at him for a moment. "That's incredible," she replied, somewhat stunned. "I didn't know my papers were being read by potential employers, unless I gave them out myself."

"I also know that you were rejected by the UNSF patrol, and that you've been speaking against their policies rather strongly." As Telisa bristled, he held up a hand and continued. "Please don't take offense at my probing of your personal business, Telisa. But you must understand my position. I can't afford to hire someone with connections to the space force. As a private collector of alien artifacts, you must know I'm sometimes…at odds with the government."

"You're a smuggler." It was a statement, not a question. If true, Telisa realized that meant Jack operated against the tight controls set out by the United Nations Space Force.

"I investigate alien cultures. I collect artifacts. If I do it without the government's permission, and you feel that makes me a smuggler, then you may call me that. But you're like me, in that you place your fascination of things alien above all else. That's why I know I'm safe in extending an invitation for you to join my team. This may be your only chance to get your hands on real artifacts, do real work, without being in the UNSF."

"That explains a lot," she said. "Like why a guide business is interested in hiring someone in my line of study. And why the real face-to-face interview." Telisa had checked the official disposition of the company before showing up. Parker Interstellar Travels was supposed to be an agency providing guides for hunting and tourism expeditions to undeveloped planets, as well as providing freelance mapping of faraway places for potential property buyers and planet information directories.

"Well, I think the job is a perfect fit. And I don't think you'll find a better opportunity anytime soon because of the shutdown on harvesting new artifacts," Jack said. "Officially, we have a side business of trading artifacts discovered in past years, all registered and found to be harmless by UNSF inspectors, of course. On the record, your expertise is needed to help us avoid the rampant fraud by identifying real items from fake ones."

"Looks like you make a good living at it," she said, pointedly taking a look around the room. The office was lavishly furnished, and there were a few artifacts in the room sitting on the desk and the bookshelves. "I assume I'm supposed to point out that this Talosian on your desk is fake?"

Jack smiled. "I was hoping that you might notice that, yes. How could you tell, without even picking it up?"

Telisa grabbed the fake and squeezed it in her slender hands. "Talosian stuff is always concave.

They made everything thinner in the middle of the piece than at the top, unless that would make the item functionally useless."

"Ah yes, of course. That's very observant of you. The job I have to offer, though, is considerably more exciting than merely identifying fake artifacts in our offices."

"Is the money good?"

"The money can be good, if you know what you're doing. But I'm not trying to lure you with money, Telisa. I'm guessing that the chance to get your hands on real Trilisk artifacts is more of an incentive."

"Trilisk artifacts! How could you—"

"I can. A lot of them, and ruins that no one has been to yet. You'd be breaking new ground, and who knows what we can find? Get back to me and let me know your decision, but make it quick. I can't sit on this for long, and the expedition is going out very soon."

"I'm interested. But I'll need more details to make my decision," Telisa said.

Jack nodded. "If you link in, I have an information package ready for you."

Telisa activated her link just by thinking about it. The device in her head connected with the office computer and received the file that Jack had referenced so that she could look it over later.

"The position starts at 4200 ESC per year," he told her. "And your duties, outlined in here, are as I've already mentioned."

Jack paused for a second, then continued.

"Your real duties, however, include advising my team on the probable function and value of artifacts we find, as well as helping us identify and navigate alien facilities. We have limited cargo space, and so I have to be choosy about what to bring back. Also included is a small personal cargo allotment for anything you might want to recover for yourself."

"How shall I contact you?" Telisa asked, somewhat overwhelmed by the suddenness and enormity of what he offered.

"Voice is fine; my numbers are in the brief," he said simply. "If you have additional questions of a mundane nature, just send them along and I'll answer them quickly. If you have more delicate questions, about your actual role, then please just come back in, no appointment necessary, and I'll answer them before you give us your final decision."

"Thank you, Jack. I'll get back to you tomorrow. I trust that's not too late?" she smiled, half joking.

"That'd be fine, Telisa. If you decide to come on, we can meet again and discuss our first expedition."

"That sounds great. Thank you."

Jack escorted her to the door, and they shook hands again. Telisa left on a high of new ideas and possibilities.

***

Jack watched Telisa leave with a hop in her step. He could tell she would have to digest this for a while to absorb all the implications. She would be full of questions tomorrow.

Thomas was in Jack's office as he walked back in. His friend was taller and thinner, wearing a worn leather jacket in contrast to Jack's impeccable business suit.

"Jesus, Jack, you have balls. I can't believe you just told her all that. The daughter of a UNSF captain."

"I know what she thinks about the patrol already. She never talks to her father, the whole family has been permanently fragmented. It's so obvious that it couldn't be a trap. The UNSF would never select someone clearly connected to the military to be a spy. Besides, I didn't admit to doing anything illegal, just alluded to it."

"Well, I hope you know what you're doing. Don't let her good looks cloud your judgment."

"I won't. But she does look even better incarnate than her pics on the net," Jack replied. Telisa had surprised him with her long black hair and slim figure. She had smooth, almost perfect facial features and a good smile.

"Shall we take precautions anyway?" Thomas asked.

"Everything looks good, but let's stay in practice. Follow her and keep monitoring her link."

"You better pack your bags in case this all goes wrong."

"It won't come to that. She's one of us. I know what I'm doing."

***

Telisa spent a sleepless night in contemplation of her opportunity. She needed a job. So far she had spent her adult life as a parasite, producing nothing for herself, her family, or society. And now someone had approached her offering the very thing she sought. And in her field.

But Jack had been very straightforward about the fact that what he was doing wasn't quite on the level. How could he trust her? How could she trust him, knowing that he was into illegal trading of artifacts?

Artifacts that she desperately wanted to find and investigate for herself. What did the stupid UNSF think it was doing, anyway, trying to keep her from the legacy left by dead races for the whole universe? She hated the space force, hated her father, and didn't give a rat's ass about their oppressive laws. But she could end up in trouble, handling illegal artifacts, even helping to bring them to Earth or other developed planets.

In the end it was the Trilisk artifacts that convinced her. Or so she told herself. She wouldn't do something crazy just out of sheer boredom, would she? The lure of adventure was strong to Telisa, who had led a sheltered, purely academic life. But mostly it was the Trilisk artifacts.

The Trilisks were advanced almost beyond human understanding, and the few artifacts from that race that were in human hands were enigmas of the highest order. If Telisa could get her hands on enough Trilisk items to achieve some kind of critical mass of understanding, she could become the foremost human authority on the lost race. Understanding such an advanced race would surely have an impact on the way future humans would live.

She wanted to be a part of that discovery, bringing about those changes by unraveling the mysteries of the Trilisks, or other alien cultures for that matter. What could be more fascinating than the devices left behind by dead races, beings that didn't share anything with humans except intellect and the ability to create tools?

She contacted Jack in the morning and told him she was interested in joining his group. He seemed very pleased and told her that she could come over to his house and meet the rest of the team after lunch. When she arrived at the estate, she was greeted at the gate by a tall, dark-haired man in an old leather jacket.

"I'm Thomas. Come on in."

"Are you a part of the expedition team?"

"Yes. I'm the pilot, also a business partner of Jack's. We've been working together for several years now."

"So you've been on a lot of expeditions?"

"Smaller stuff, here and there."

Telisa thought that was a suitably elusive answer for a smuggler. For a moment she wondered if she had gotten involved in something she shouldn't have, until she thought of the Trilisk artifacts again. Telisa was so absorbed by the wonder of superior alien technology that she'd take some risks to study it.

Thomas looked better than Jack, she decided. It wasn't only his height, but his face looked smoother, thinner, and yet his dark eyes were mysterious. The classic tall, dark, and handsome. Telisa didn't generally go for older guys, but if she did then she'd pick one like this, she thought.

The two walked to a meeting room on the first floor of the large house. They were met there by another man with blond hair and a strong build. He looked handsome despite the roughness of his facial features. His physical presence was intimidating, although his hazel eyes seemed friendly. He wore some kind of armored one-piece garment in black and red.

"Telisa, this is Magnus. He handles our…" Thomas trailed off.

"I'm a military advisor to the team," Magnus explained calmly.

"A military advisor," Telisa said neutrally, trying to hide her surprise. It was as if this group was straight out of the action VRs. Magnus seemed very reserved and calm, and he regarded her openly. She felt her heart beating in her chest under his scrutiny.

"Did you see action in the Torn rebellion?" she asked suddenly, then bit her tongue for being so brash.

"Yes. The 137th. I was an ECM engineer in infantry units."

"Didn't the UNSF use the robotic units for most of the fighting there?" she asked, emboldened by the response. Magnus seemed stolid, unaffected.

"The robotic units were first in, first out. The human units were used to garrison the conquests and rebuild the areas retaken by the UNSF. But the UED was fighting a hit-and-run battle, so the garrisons got hit all the time."

"Well, if you survived all that, you must be good."

"Not really," Magnus replied. "It just means I was lucky. We were just sitting ducks. There wasn't a lot we could do about it, so skill didn't enter into the equation very often."

"Why were you sitting ducks? I take it you mean you never knew when an attack was coming, right?"

"The UED used precision laser strikes from high orbit. I served in garrisons on three moons with thin atmospheres. They could take us out a man at a time with ship-mounted weapons until one of our own ships could drive them back. They played at hit and run the whole time, since they couldn't afford a direct confrontation in space without risking losing it all."

"A spaceship weapon used against individuals? Was there any way to defend against that from the ground?"

Magnus shook his head. "Only by getting into a bunker, or staying hidden by scrambling their scans. The UNSF didn't provide our units with sufficient countermeasures. The robotics are the heavy hitters; when it comes right down to it, the infantry is cheap and expendable."

Telisa had been following along with an encyclopedia link as Magnus related his story. She was trying to brush up on the Torn conflict without looking ignorant. What Magnus had said so far was checking out. She decided to learn more and have another conversation about it later.

Thomas snorted. "Don't believe all those war stories of his. That's just stuff he uses to impress women," he said. He said it with mild scorn in his voice so that Telisa couldn't tell if he was joking or not.

"Well, Thomas, what do *you* tell women to impress them?"

"I tell them that I fly a spaceship, make a five-digit salary, and vacation in Brazil," he paused, then added, "Someone once said if you have to tell a lie, sandwich it between two truths."

Telisa chuckled. "Sounds like a good strategy to me."

The door opened and Jack arrived hurriedly. "Sorry I'm late," he said, "it couldn't be helped."

Jack joined them at the table and looked at everyone momentarily. "I trust you have all had a chance to get to know one another a little?"

"Yes, a little," Telisa said, trying to sound positive. She wanted Jack to know that there were no personality problems emerging, at least not on her end.

The meeting started. Jack ran over the government forms required to prepare a mock expedition that would cover for their real activities. Telisa would have to spend some time putting information into the company computer so Jack could get her employment squared away. Jack assigned Thomas to help Telisa outfit for the trip; he would get her in touch with their usual equipment suppliers so she could buy everything she needed quickly. He gave her an access code to a financial account to purchase her gear.

During the meeting Telisa could see that Jack and Thomas were both very involved with the business side of things, while Magnus seemed uninterested in those aspects—almost withdrawn.

"Let's get down to the real stuff," Jack said, and looked at Thomas. Thomas accessed the home computer.

"Link in, if you please," he said. Everyone at the table linked into the computer just by thinking about it. Telisa received the images to which Thomas referred. Telisa closed her eyes to make it easier to view the mental star chart.

"This is the target planet," Thomas began. "No real name, just the second major orbiting body in the Thespera Narres System. Just call it T2. The UNSF just started laying into it two weeks ago. We know there are many sites on-planet, and the ruins are definitely Trilisk in origin."

Telisa thought this information was amazing to have if the UNSF had only started two weeks ago. She wondered if the group spied on the UNSF or if they knew people on the inside. She also hoped they had friends in the government, because it was surely dangerous to eavesdrop on the space force. Anyone caught at such an activity could be put away for a long time. Once again she found herself pushing back a tinge of fear at what she was doing.

"Since operations have just started up here, and because it's on the fringe of explored space, we know there's a good chance we can get in and out undetected."

Telisa decided to be bold and ask questions at this stage. "Isn't it true that the exploration vessels have better detection equipment than most? Won't they have a good chance of noticing our ship?"

"Yes, they might notice us, if they're there at all," Magnus answered.

Thomas nodded. "There is that risk, but I believe the initial survey vessel will have already left the system. It may have left lot of probes behind, but usually those probes are highly specialized to gather different types of planetary data and we can deal with them."

Thomas changed the display to a generated image of a planet with two landing sites marked on it in blinking white letters.

"Our information is too sketchy at this point to plan a landing site ahead of time," Thomas explained. "We'll have to pick a spot, obviously avoiding these known UNSF bases, when we arrive in-system."

"We'll have plenty of time to form some goals on the way there," Jack put in, "since we'll be in transit for two weeks at least. We should come up with a plan for what to look for in a landing site and what to go after once we're there. So everyone try and put some thought into that the next few days, and we'll get back to it on the ship."

"What kind of ship are we taking?" Telisa asked.

"That's a good question. I tell you what, I'm going to have Thomas fill you in on the ship after you get your stuff." Jack looked at Thomas and said, "Why don't you go over to the *Iridar* with her tomorrow afternoon?"

"Sure thing," Thomas said. He seemed genuinely pleased to get the assignment.

"Just for a brief curiosity dampener," Jack told her, "It's an ex-UED scoutship. A little old in some ways, but we keep it updated as best we can. Magnus has some contacts that we make use of, just to make sure we have some tricks up our sleeve," he said. "So we can be hard to detect if we work at it, but of course our cargo space is very limited."

"What about robots?" Telisa asked.

"For now, we do things the old-fashioned way," Thomas said.

"Robots are nice, but they're a big overhead on this kind of mission," Jack added. "The government has tough requirements that are expensive to circumvent, both in terms of time and money. The law requires frequent inspection of any robotic units we own. Unlike the privacy we enjoy for our links, robot logs are property of the government."

Telisa thought about what that would mean to the smugglers. If they used robots, the automatic logs that recorded everything the robot sensed would have to be carefully doctored to eliminate all evidence of illegal activity.

"I guess they left our rights to bear robotics out of the constitution," Telisa grumbled. "What about the ship logs?"

"Takes a lot of work, but we're getting pretty good at it," Thomas said.

"Actually, we have an idea for using a robot that I can tell you about on the trip. But it won't be this mission," Magnus told her.

"Okay," she said. Telisa knew the government feared robots in the hands of civilians, because of their tremendous potential for misuse. Only the most fragile of household robots were commonly owned by individuals.

Jack broke up the meeting and left the room with Magnus. Telisa got up with Thomas, assuming that they would be buying equipment.

"So what kind of stuff should I purchase?"

"I can tell you the things that we all carry, but obviously I'm not qualified to advise you on any gear that you might want regarding the analysis of artifacts or their value."

"He gave me more money than I would need, I think," she said in a worried voice.

"I wouldn't sweat it if you have money left over," Thomas said. "Just make sure that you have everything you need."

Thomas presented her with a wide array of items to purchase, including an assortment of survival gear for all types of environments. They placed a large order with directions to deposit the items at the business the next day. The equipment ranged from medical supplies to climbing gear. Telisa was not an experienced climber, but Jack said that it was "just in case."

"You may want to get a stunner too," Thomas suggested.

"A stunner?" she asked, and then felt foolish. "Well, what make do you recommend?"

"I would get a good PSG stunner, with a large energy reserve," he said. "I have only had to use mine once, just to avoid being mugged in a scummy backport alley, but if you need it once in your whole life, that's enough to warrant getting one."

He was talking about a nonlethal sonic weapon. Telisa had heard of Personal Security Gear, and she knew they were top of the line.

"Okay, I'll pick one up," she said.

"Then that should do it. I'll see you tomorrow afternoon, and we'll leave the day after that."

Chapter Two

Magnus walked steadily toward the next checkpoint at Grenadin Spaceport. He noticed the looks he got from other people. He figured everyone saw the skinsuit and marked him as military or ex-military. Magnus knew a few other types who'd wear the Veer skinsuits: bounty hunters, frontier planet types, and big-time pretenders trying to pick up women.

He came to an automated counter and linked up. He watched a document fill out in his mind's eye, identifying himself and his incoming packages. After he verified the information as correct, he stood and waited while the requests were processed. He ignored the complimentary drink that had been dispensed at the counter for him. Neither did he change his preferences with the customs computer to prevent the drink from being dispensed next time—anything to spite them.

"Magnus Garrison?" a voice said.

Magnus turned and saw an old acquaintance of his. The man looked like hell, ragged and ill-dressed. The man's face held heavy lines and circles under the eyes. No attempt had been made to hide a burgeoning waistline that pushed forward under the spaceport uniform. Magnus tensed.

"Yes, that's me." Magnus picked up a secure connection through his link.

Cracker. What's up?

"I'm afraid there are a few issues I need to speak with you about, regarding your luggage," Cracker said.

Magnus felt a spike of anger. If this snake had—

Relax. I have to bring you in here with an arsenal like that, or it'd look bad, Cracker said back through the link.

"Okay," Magnus said neutrally. He remained tense. Cracker led him away from the autocounter and through a security door. They walked past two other clear glass rooms, which held other people who'd been delayed at customs. Magnus saw one of them, an old lady, being interrogated by two men in dark suits. He cursed to himself silently. He hated this part.

"Okay, come in here, please," Cracker said loudly.

Magnus walked into the glass interrogation room and found a seat. Cracker sat across from him and got a distant look as he brought up paperwork through his link.

Relax, Mag, this is just procedure I gotta do, Cracker sent him through his link.

"I see that you've requested clearance for an assault weapon," Cracker said aloud. "Wow, this thing's an antique."

"It serves me well enough," Magnus said.

"Why do you need such a device?" Cracker said, and then sent through the link:

It's gonna be hard to clear through. It's gotta link lock, but it won't log your shots. Government wants to know these things.

"It's required for my work. I'm a guide. We have several contracts for accompanying clients on very new, undeveloped worlds. Many of these places have dangerous predators."

I've put an amount in our usual place, Magnus transmitted. *You should find it adequate.*

"Your weapon is out of date. It doesn't adhere to the latest shot-logging protocol."

"I can't afford an upgrade right now. Business is tight."

"Well, I'm afraid this is the last time I'm going to allow you through with this particular piece. Keep it on board until you can afford a safer replacement. Many of the stunners are getting relatively cheap these days—I suggest you get yourself one of those and sell this thing on one of those frontier planets you work on."

"Thank you sir, I'll do that," Magnus said.

Magnus watched through his link while Cracker went through the motions, marking and logging the suspect items for rendezvous with the *Iridar*.

Cracker nodded. *Good. Real good. Now whaddaya say next time you just leave this damn thing on the ship so we don't have to do this crap again?*

I will, Magnus transmitted.

Good. Good. Cuz I don't mind gettin' rich, but I gotta be a free man to enjoy it.

"You have a good day, sir," Cracker said aloud. Magnus felt impressed. Cracker's business voice was actually starting to sound reputable.

Magnus made his way back out and past the throng at the autocounters. He came to the next checkpoint and moved into a tunnel on the right, which he knew he'd have to pass through because of his Veer skinsuit. He had to get out of the material since it would absorb or reflect most of the security scanner's energy. He knew this was one of the disadvantages of wearing the suit, but he stubbornly refused to give up the safety it provided.

He took off the suit and handed it to a skeletal robot made of a few slender tubes of silvery metal. Wearing only his undersheers, he stepped onto a conveyor belt and passed through the scanner bank. Everything looked clear to the automated system, which routed his examined and cleaned skinsuit back to him. Magnus calmly dressed and made his way out of the side tunnel.

Past the last checkpoint, Magnus stepped on a conveyor belt that whisked him over toward the merchant cargo area. Magnus came to the *Iridar* at last. The gray ship rested among many other cargo vessels on the main deck. It had a round flat shape like a pancake slightly inflated with air. Eight giant struts held it above the landing area.

Magnus let himself aboard and checked the security logs to make sure everything remained in order. He had several electronic traps waiting for any UNSF electronic attack operative who might have attempted to compromise the ship while the crew was gone.

When he'd satisfied himself that all was secure, he went to his tiny quarters and opened a communications port through his link. He stared at a blank spot on the wall, making it easier for him to see a visual display in his mind through the link.

A face resolved on the virtual screen. It showed a bearded man with a bald head and thickset neck. The man wore the uniform of a UNSF officer.

"Henman. We're getting ready to head out. Do you have the latest for us?"

The man nodded. "Sure do. I got the bases and the satellite info for ya. There's a clear continent you can try out, a good distance from any of the heavies."

Henman would know. He served as an intelligence officer in the organization that kept tabs on communications across the entire human civilization. Magnus wondered, who watched the watchers?

"Yeah, well, we'll make that choice when we get the info."

Henman guffawed. "You guys do whatever you want; you just make sure that money gets to my kid."

"We stick to our deals."

"Awright then, we got nothing to argue about. You got anythin' for me?"

"Yeah, we have a new team member. She's a xenoarchaeologist, and get this—she's Captain Relachik's kid. Not that they keep in touch anymore…still, pretty amazing."

"Wow, whatta angle! You guys are slick. Talk about an insurance policy. If the *Seeker* gets on your tail, all you gotta do is play your ace. Nice."

"Do you really think that's what we're up to? Thomas is pretty into these artifacts, and so is this girl. I don't think it's like that."

"Jesus, how can you fight through a whole friggin' war and still be so naive? You musta caught something from that femme that really made you lose your mind."

"I hardly know her. I just think if Jack was planning on using her as a shield he'd mention it to me."

"Well, shit, it's a good thing I'm here to set you straight," Henman said. "Of course that's what they have in mind. And if you know what's good for you, you'll play along. These guys didn't hire you for your picnic skills, pal. Don't get attached to this bimbo, they may be needing to cash out their policy at some point, y'know?"

"Hrm. Maybe…anyway, I just wanted you to make sure she was clean. It makes me nervous, having someone along so close to the force. Besides us, I mean."

"She's too obvious to be a spy," Henman said.

"Yeah that's what Jack says. Can you check her anyway?"

"Yeah, I'll friggin' check."

"Good. Then I'll see you next time."

"Yeah. I hope you do, Magnus. Grow up and get real, and you'll make it just fine." Henman rolled his eyes and broke the connection.

Magnus sat back for a moment, thinking about the new kid, Telisa. He knew Thomas and Jack weren't angels, and he wasn't either…but would they really blackmail the old captain with her? And if they did, would he go along with it? Magnus shook his head. He didn't really have the stomach for that kind of shit, he decided. He could convince them to drop her off somewhere quiet if it came to that. He had enough blood on his hands for a lifetime.

Chapter Three

Three days later Telisa was in deep space on an illegal mission with three mysterious men whom she had only known for a week. The enormity of her venture began to make itself felt. She worried about her decisions and wondered if she had made a terrible mistake.

But she had never felt more alive in her life.

Her quarters were small but completely private. The showers on the ship were barely larger than human-sized tubes and the kitchen was the size of a walk-in closet, but she had known it would be like that. She considered it a small price to pay for money, career, and adventure.

The quiet surprised her the most. Without the thousands and thousands of microdevices embedded in almost every manmade object talking to her link, space seemed quiet. And the *Iridar* had a few hundred such services on board, a lot of traffic compared to an undeveloped planet. Once there, she realized she would have practically no contacts on her link at all. That must have been what it was like before humans had links, she thought. The world must have been so silent and lonely in those times.

One of her tasks during the voyage was to organize packs of equipment to bring with her on various kinds of sorties from the ship. She started with one basic pack that she would need at all times. Clearly the medical supplies were a good choice, as well as her tablet device, which she would use as a reference when evaluating artifacts. Although her link might be usable for that, the handheld device contained more memory and computational power. Telisa decided to keep her stunner in the primary pack. Having it around helped to dispel her nervousness.

Magnus carried a stunner as well, strapped to his belt, but it was hardly his only weapon. Telisa considered it reasonable since security was his job, but she still found his everyday gear slightly barbaric. The man lived in his Veer Industries military skinsuit; Telisa read about them and learned that they were light and flexible but capable of absorbing a great deal of kinetic and electromagnetic damage. He had some kind of a sleek black slugthrower strapped to his back, also of the notorious Veer Industries. Telisa thought it looked large enough for two-handed operation, but she imagined that the mercenary could probably wield it with one. There was also a long knife at his belt. She wondered how he managed to get such items near the spaceport. It might be that they stayed on the ship at all times, but she wasn't sure; after all, he was a smuggler.

With Magnus in the group, she did not feel a great deal of fear about who or what they might encounter in their travels, although she had not grown to feel trust for Magnus himself. He seemed somewhat distant and she didn't think they had become friends yet, although he was always polite.

The second day of the trip, after Telisa had adapted to the feel of the ship, she met Jack in the galley.

"How are you getting along? Everything okay?"

"Yes, it's about what I expected," she said.

"I have something that may help with the tedium of the trip. Each of us has a secondary skill set that we use to back each other up on missions," Jack explained. "I'm the backup pilot, and Thomas has medical skills that may be useful in certain situations. Do you have any unusual skills we should know about?"

"Not that would help on a mission—not that I can think of, anyway," Telisa said guardedly.

"We're covered pretty well in most areas already; the only one of us I can think of that doesn't have a secondary is Magnus. He's currently the only one with significant combat skills. Perhaps we should check your aptitudes in that area?"

Telisa looked at Jack for a moment. Did he expect her to balk? She nodded serenely. "Very well. I assume Magnus will be assigned to this?"

"Of course. He can take you as an apprentice of sorts. How about you get together with him tomorrow, and he can go over some basics. We'll see how it works out."

Telisa reported to Magnus the next day in a cargo bay which had been turned into a small gym. Magnus was wearing his usual skinsuit, and Telisa had donned a tight-fitting exercise suit in anticipation of her training.

"You have strong legs," he observed. Telisa thought he sounded like he was getting ready to sell her as a slave.

"I guess it's from the slide dancing," she said. "I was a slide dance champion at my high school."

"Excellent. That may help you out with your agility and balance, which are important for many types of combat."

He doesn't mean to be so brusque, she thought. *He's just being businesslike.*

"The training takes place as pure sim, pseudo-sim, and actual practice. The idea is that you learn concepts and strategy from the VR sims. Sometimes it's necessary to hardwire certain physical responses into you, and that's where the pseudo-sim comes in. In the pseudo you wear a helmet but you use your body for real, with the computer providing your sensory feedback. That way the actions you perform result in real coordination skills. Then there's also a certain amount of the real thing. In hand-to-hand combat especially, the pseudo-sim can't simulate the forces that occur."

"You mean I need to practice getting hit?"

"Yes, but more than that. With the VR helmet on, you can shoot and punch and kick for real and battle virtual opponents, but at this facility we have no way to apply forces to your body as you work out. We can make you feel your opponents through the neural feedback, but if you get kicked it doesn't throw your real body off balance. There are certain balance and feedback aspects you must learn about striking an opponent, the feel of resistance on impacts, and the sensation of getting hit. Of course we can make it all work in full VR, but then only your brain experiences it, absent your real nervous system. No body hardening occurs as a result. You have to get used to using your real muscles for all this to work best."

That first day Magnus illustrated the use of the three methods and the strengths and weaknesses of each one. She started in a pure virtual environment, with her body completely cut off from the real world. Since her link did not have the bandwidth or neural connections necessary for a five-sense VR connection, she used a tack-on unit that could be adapted to anyone within a few hours, using temporary, noninvasive linkage with the spinal cord and visual cortex.

In the VR simulation she possessed a body that was strong, fast, and trim. The environment was set up to look like a large auditorium with mats on the floor. She wondered for a moment if it had been created as a model of a real place. She could hear Magnus's voice here, and it sounded as if he were close by, but she didn't see him anywhere in the illusory gym.

Magnus showed her how to fall backward and roll forward, and she practiced until she understood how the moves were to be done. The sim felt nearly real, including the sensation of falling onto the mat. After the initial trials, she found herself atop a low white wall that appeared in the center of the workout area. Magnus instructed her how to roll with a fall, and she practiced this. Each time she dropped, she found herself atop the wall again after a few seconds. After a while she noticed the wall was getting taller.

"It's getting harder," she said.

"Remember, it's not real," came Magnus' disembodied voice. "Just do your best."

Telisa dropped and rolled a few more times. The falls were becoming jarring. Telisa felt anxiety building inside of her, but she suppressed it. *He's testing me*, she thought.

"Just out of curiosity, what's the point of doing this to failure?" she asked levelly. "It is inevitable that eventually I'm going to get hurt…not for real, of course, but…" Telisa realized that she would be able to learn from experiencing breaking bones and getting shot in VR, without ever having to recover from real injury. But it would still hurt like hell.

"You need to know how the technique fails. And you need to be able to perform it under stress."

Telisa sat atop the wall again. She dropped, ready to collapse forward into a roll. When she hit the ground she felt a pain in her foot, then she fumbled the roll and the impact knocked the wind out of her. Her head hurt.

"Good. One more time," Magnus said.

The pain went away. She started from the wall again. This time she thought it looked quite a bit higher. She hesitated. Should she complain again, or go through breaking something? She realized her body was shaking in the virtual world. She took a deep breath and fell off the wall.

This time the snap was loud and a spike of agony came with it. Instead of rolling forward, her legs collapsed beneath her and she fell to the ground on her tailbone, shocking her entire spine. She rolled weakly to one side, crying out as the pain crested…then she found herself on level ground, whole again.

"When a person gets really hurt for the first time, often they panic. And sometimes it's traumatic mentally as well as physically. But believe me when I say that it gets better. A person can become used to getting hurt just like anything else. You learn to deal with the pain and the damage calmly, and your fear of it will subside. After a year of this you'll avoid injury, but you won't fear the injury itself. It will still hurt, but you won't shy away from it if it's something you need to do."

"So I'll be able to think clearly about it, and suppress my instincts?"

"Yes. The decision, for instance, about whether or not to fight will be a rational one, and it won't be made based on your fear of injury."

Having learned the proper form for the rolls and the falls, she left the pure VR environment and they went to the gym. There Magnus fitted her with a pseudo-VR helmet that provided her with fake sights and sounds along with an instructional program. The first time she tried the roll, it was much clumsier and more painful than she had last achieved in the VR trials; now she was rolling with her own body in the real universe. Magnus said that the pseudo helmet was extremely useful for conducting mock fights with ranged weapons, and useful to a lesser degree for practicing unarmed combat moves. Here she would train her muscles and increase the stamina of her real body while still in environments generated by the computer.

Finally the helmet was put aside, and Magnus ushered her into the center of the mat that covered the floor of the tiny gym. Without warning he pushed her backward violently, and she fell hard, slapping the mat too late.

"We can't do that with the pseudo VR," he said, "at least not at this facility. You did well enough for the first time—at least you tucked your chin to your chest."

Telisa stood back up, regarding Magnus carefully now. She was slightly intimidated by the attack, and dreaded that he might hit her next. Was this to be another lesson in pain? He looked so strong, so invincible, the cut of his muscles visible even through the heavy skinsuit.

"Let's see some forward rolls without the helmet," he said. "Your body already knows how to do this, so it shouldn't be that much different than the pseudo."

Telisa finished up the rolls and falls. Magnus didn't attack her again and he seemed satisfied, although he didn't say anything encouraging, either. She wobbled back to her quarters completely exhausted. She went to sleep that night trying to decide if she was mad at Magnus for pushing her, or grateful that he took her lessons so seriously. The next morning was an agony of sore muscles and bruises, but Telisa remained determined. She would not shirk from these lessons no matter how difficult they became. If she did that, the others would just decide she was a spoiled academic brat, someone useless for anything except writing esoteric papers about extinct alien races.

The voyage stretched out into weeks as Telisa trained for an hour in VR, an hour with the PR helmet, and an hour in real training in the gym every day. She learned falls, strikes, locks, and throws for unarmed combat. Soon she added training programs to assemble, clean, and fire various ranged weapons, and took part in mock firefights in the PR helmet.

She felt good about in her new skills, and came to realize she was lucky to have been selected as Magnus's secondary. She could not imagine medical or piloting programs to be as varied and interesting as what she was learning. Never before had she realized the almost infinite array of moves and countermoves mankind had developed for shooting, sparring, throwing, and grappling. Telisa wondered if the Talosians or the Trilisks had spent so much time figuring out how to destroy their fellows.

As time went on, no one questioned her combat studies. She wondered what, if anything, Magnus had told them about her performance. Since she was a solitary student, she had no one with whom to compare her progress. She looked forward to the physical sessions as a welcome release from the tedium of the voyage.

She also realized she was starting to become attached to Magnus. She found herself staring at his image in her mind's eye, summoned from her link memory. She had images of the entire crew and the *Iridar* ferreted away there. Out in space, she had no place to download the images, so she had to keep them tucked away in her link. It had a lot of storage capacity, but not an unlimited amount. She'd have a lot in there by the time they returned, she thought.

At first she had found the man distant and mysterious, almost rude, but through the lessons he gave her, she saw that he genuinely cared about her. His voice, which had at first sounded cold and flat, started to sound softer, almost intimate to her. Telisa wondered if it were just wishful thinking on her part. She resolved to find out—after their first expedition.

Thomas spent more and more time in the command room as they neared the planet. Telisa gave him plenty of space, as her own nervousness increased. If the space force detected them here and caught them, Telisa would find herself under arrest before their expedition even began. She tried to calm herself and put her faith in Thomas, but it didn't work.

Jack dropped in on Telisa and Magnus in the gym. He didn't usually stop by in person like this, since they could all communicate through their intracranial links. Telisa wondered if he was curious to see her training.

"We came out of FTL pretty far from the planet and took a little look-see," Jack explained. "No sign of the original exploration vessel. We're going to insert into an orbit where we shouldn't be detectable by the ground bases."

"Then we'll select our site?" Telisa asked.

"That's the plan. He should skip us in closer—"

Red lights flashed on and Telisa's computer link emitted a warning tone with a calm synthetic voice instructing her to find the nearest g-damper. There was one terrible second when panic rose in her throat and she froze, then she was scrambling for the exit. Magnus ran behind her, a protective hand on her back. Jack had run for the other side.

Telisa came to the first pod, nothing more than a port in the corridor just large enough for a person to dive into. The tiny chamber was designed to protect a human from sudden accelerations that the pilot might have to apply in a combat situation. She slammed into the dampener module and grabbed the mask to put over her face. In less than three seconds, the tiny cramped space filled with protective foam and Telisa was plunged into darkness. Her only connection with the outside world was her wireless computer link, still droning its warning.

Telisa wondered if the dampener module would be her tomb. If the ship was blown apart, would the module break open and spill her into space, or would it remain intact until she suffocated? Or would the ship tumble into the atmosphere until she cooked to death? Telisa took a long gulp of oxygen and tried to calm down, telling herself that whatever was going to happen would happen. It was out of her hands now.

The ship buffeted violently. An explosive sound of metal clunking and rockets firing echoed into the g-dampener and she screamed. But it wasn't the end. The ship was still rocking back and forth. Suddenly everything smoothed out and Telisa just breathed, wrapped up like a child in a metal womb. A distant rumbling became noticeable, but Telisa just waited.

Oh shit. Oh shit. I should have stayed at home, she thought.

"We were spotted by a space force supply ship," Thomas said over the link. "Luckily those things are slugs, and lightly armed. Just hang in there, we're going to be planetside in a few minutes."

Spotted by a UNSF ship. Telisa's terror washed away into a terrible sadness, a feeling of being cheated. If the patrol had found them, there would be no expedition, no grand adventure.

Telisa waited forever and then she waited some more. Finally Thomas's voice came again.

"You can leave the pods. We're on the ground."

Telisa brought up her pod controls with her link and actuated the release. A spray of liquid dissolved the foam and the hatch opened. Telisa discarded the breathing mask and carefully made her way out. Her workout suit was wet, but she ignored the discomfort.

The four crewmembers gathered around the galley. Everyone was wet from a foam wash. As a group, they reminded Telisa of a bunch of shipwrecked rats shivering on the shore of a deserted island.

They all linked into the computer and Thomas brought up a display of the sensor readings that the ship's systems had obtained during their stressful landing. He used a mental interface to the machine to indicate spots on the virtual map.

"You can see the ruin sites to the north and west," he pointed out, as the sites he referred to blinked in red on the display. "But what really interests me is an installation up in the high ground to the east. I picked up a power source there, and was getting some pretty weird readings from it."

"I don't know what the hell you think we're going to do," Telisa said. "You were paying attention when the space force tried to kill us, weren't you? Do you think they're just going to let us go now? They'll be here any time now!"

Magnus spoke up in Thomas's place.

"No, we actually will have some time. We may as well continue as best we can."

Telisa was perplexed. She turned her wide-eyed stare to Thomas. "What? Is that true?"

"I'm equipped to screen us from orbital detection. We fired off several electronic countermeasure modules before entering the atmosphere. I think their jamming window was wide enough to hide us. The chances are good that they don't know the location of our landing site. They might not even know that we landed for sure."

Jack stepped up beside Magnus.

"Although I admit this is one of the worst things that could have happened, we still have a fifty-fifty chance to make it out of this. I'm not going to just give myself up. We can go and check this place out, and get some artifacts. Then if the ship hasn't been found, we might be able to make our way out without being detected," Jack said.

Telisa was speechless for a moment. Then she said, "They know someone's here, though. They'll bring in more ships."

"That'll take time—probably weeks," Magnus said. "There probably aren't many security people in system. It'll mostly be scientists. There's a chance they might not even come after us."

"We'll probably have to sell the artifacts somewhere else though," Jack conceded. "The best prices are on Earth, but it'll be too risky to try and bring them in for a long time."

"If they do come for us..." Telisa started.

"None of us will ask you to do anything but defend yourself," Jack clarified. "I understand that you didn't sign up with us to kill UNSF people."

Telisa nodded weakly. "Okay…so we'll look for artifacts and hope for the best," she said. She didn't feel as confident as she tried to sound.

"How far is the anomalous site?" Magnus asked.

"About sixty-five klicks."

"We're going to be walking it too, if you're serious about avoiding detection," Telisa said, getting drawn in despite herself. Her excitement returned as she thought about the Trilisk artifacts again. "How large a power source did you detect?"

Thomas smiled as her enthusiasm returned.

"Enough to power a small city," he said. "I'm thinking it's military. Just the kind of stuff we need to get filthy rich."

"How much you wanna bet four humans aren't going to pass Trilisk security?" Telisa said.

"Yes, but we'll only have to deal with the purely automated stuff. This civilization's clearly dead; there probably won't be any Trilisks around to oppose us."

Telisa raised her eyebrow. "Probably?" she asked. Humans had never encountered a live alien of any race. The ruins of three different races had been discovered, but they were from ancient times and were no longer around.

"Well, they are aliens, after all," Thomas said. "I try not to make assumptions about things like that. For all we know, this is just the local power plant, anyway."

"Then why don't we try some of the other ruin sites?"

"Because we're after intact tech, and there's a greater chance of finding intact stuff in a place that still has power. The entire site might be sealed up completely, utterly unaffected by the elements. That would be a find that could make us, if we can get back off this planet."

Michael McCloskey

Chapter Four

Joe Hartlet barely breathed as he examined the odd creature through the scope of his NX-37 sniper rifle. It looked like a tentacled mollusk with a flat plate-like shell, hanging upside down from a branch so the shell faced the ground. It had at least three tiny eyestalks waving around, examining its next potential meal, a big green fruit dangling in front of it. The thing was about the size of a large housecat.

"Here's another one," he said. "Let me know when you—"

"The scan is complete, sir. You may take your shot," a clean, emotionless voice responded from behind.

Joe swept some of his black hair off his face and centered on the target. He gently squeezed the trigger. His beefy 110-kilogram frame easily absorbed the light recoil.

The round hurtled toward its target, too fast for the human eye. While still dozens of meters from its target, the bullet detected a wind drift from its logged destination and corrected for it with tiny bristles on its surface that could alter its drag. The projectile slammed into the unfortunate tree dweller and tumbled through its innards, dropping it from the branch.

Joe searched through his scope for a moment, looking for his target. He found it lying on the ground, leaking red fluid. The thing looked very dead.

"Looks like it's got iron-based blood, anyway," he noted happily.

To Lieutenant Hartlet, this was a dream job. Travel to strange planets, scan every type of lifeform, catalog it, and make sure that it could be killed. After all, part of his job was to identify species that were potential threats to the UNSF personnel who were working on-planet. Besides, none of the scientists ever complained if he brought in an extra corpse or two for dissection.

"That would be consistent with other life forms catalogued on this planet, sir," the robot behind him agreed flatly. It was a humanoid constructed of black plastic and metal, its head smooth and featureless other than a black plate where a human's eyes would be.

"Okay. This critter is definitely not a threat," Joe summarized. "Let's pick up some big game. It's kinda fun to plink at these things, but I doubt anything that small could hurt humans anyway."

"Size is only one of several variables involved, sir," the Series Seven commented.

"Agreed. I don't care. Now, big game," Joe insisted. He scratched at the dark stubble forming on his chin.

"I'm afraid we're needed at the base, sir."

Joe's eyebrow rose, but he didn't have time to reply. His comm link announced an incoming message with a mental flourish of musical notes. Joe connected and saw Commander Mailson waiting to speak with him in his mind's eye. He immediately joined the channel.

"Hartlet here," he announced.

"Lieutenant. We have something requiring your immediate attention."

"Yes sir. What is it, sir?"

"Looks like we have a surprise visit from some smugglers. Over on Yarnitha."

Joe considered the news for a moment. Yarnitha was the second largest continent on the planet. So far no UNSF bases had been set up on it.

"Smugglers? That sure was quick. We just got here. What's the plan of action, sir?"

"Here's the suspected landing zone," the commander said. A map appeared on the link and Joe mentally examined it. The continent of Yarnitha was displayed with a wide red swath over about a third of its surface.

"I know, it's large. They were quite resourceful in our orbital encounter. Take your copter out there and see if you can snoop them out. If you do find the landing site, try and identify the ship so we can intercept it at its destination port if they elude us here. Of course, if you run across any of them while investigating..."

Joe knew what that meant. Smuggling alien artifacts was a grave offense, posing a considerable danger to the United Nations. Grave enough, in fact, that anyone caught doing it could be shot if they didn't surrender immediately upon coming into contact with the space force.

Commander Mailson knew Joe quite well. The lieutenant's line of thinking was transparent to him.

"I thought you'd enjoy the chance to bag something other than alien varmints, for once."

"Yes sir! I appreciate that, sir."

"Be careful. They know it's a dangerous business and have already proven to be well prepared. They're more likely to start shooting at you than surrender."

"Yes, sir. What do I have at my disposal for this operation?"

"I requisitioned some hardware for you. The scientists are having a shit fit over it. I managed to get you another Series Seven, a variety of small arms, and some satellite coverage to help search for them. We'll drop a refueling station for your copter near the search zone. Since the copter travels light, we'll drop most of the other supplies you need with the fuel."

"Sounds good, sir. Anything else?"

"That's it. Keep me notified."

The commander broke the link. Joe opened his eyes and threw his rifle over his back.

"Big game it is," he said happily and marched back toward the copter.

***

The refueling platform was a huge metal spider, its gasoline-filled abdomen resting against the green earth. Joe skillfully maneuvered his one-man copter in a spiral down toward the landing zone on the spider's back.

He landed the flying machine expertly, then pried himself out of the tiny seat. He winced, coaxing sleeping muscles back to life. At least the weather had been good; it was summer here on Yarnitha.

Joe walked down into the small living center of the platform. As Commander Mailson had promised, two Series Seven robots were waiting for him. Joe

wished that he could make use of more formidable
hardware than this. These were general purpose
robotoids and could perform a wide range of
functions. The real combat robots, which looked more
like tanks than humanoids, were needed for base
protection. The Series Sevens would have to do.

He looked the robots over and checked their
programs. They were both loaded with
reconnaissance software as he had expected. He left
one alone and cleared the other one's brain, loading a
combat package instead.

The robots were too heavy to ride on the small
copter. There was a large, slow hovercar provided for
their transport. It would serve to shuttle them back
and forth but would be worse than useless in a combat
situation. Joe decided that he would have to get a
bearing on the smugglers before calling for the robots.

Joe had no choice but to sleep before getting
started. The day-and-a-half trip over from the other
continent had been long and uncomfortable. He was
completely exhausted. The copter was fast and
maneuverable, but sitting in the same position for
several hours between rest stations was less than
ideal. Still Joe spurred himself on, eager for the
opportunity to hunt some real prey for a change. He
was bored with the routine of sniping at helpless
creatures while the robots catalogued them. This time
the targets of his hunt might be able to fight back.

He cranked open the two tiny windows on
opposite sides of his cramped quarters. He thought
briefly about the dangers of allowing something in
while he slept, but decided the robots could watch for
him. He wanted to feel the warm night air and hear

the sounds of the forest outside. It reminded him of summer nights on the frontier planet where he grew up. It seemed that he had done the same sorts of things back then as he did now, wandering around through parts unknown with a rifle on his shoulder. He fell asleep quickly with old memories of his childhood adventures knocking around in his head.

It was night when he climbed back into the refueled copter and took to the air. Switching on his scanning equipment, Joe searched for lifeforms. The devices he had were for his usual job of cataloguing new species. Joe increased their helpfulness by setting the computer to screen out creature types which had already been catalogued; anything he detected would be either new species or humans.

Joe set a search pattern into the computer and then let the copter fly itself over the dense expanse of spiny trees. He realized that the search was going to be long and perhaps futile. He thought about ways to increase his chances of finding the smugglers. He remembered that the commander had allocated one of the new satellites to gather data for his search.

Joe linked into the satellite network to look over the information that had been obtained from orbit. He looked over the raw maps, searching for anything that would give him an idea. Something caught his eye— an electromagnetic anomaly on the surface. It didn't look like any kind of spaceship, but some form of power generator was functioning on the planet—a big one.

Suddenly Joe had an idea. If this power source was so prominent to him, it might be seen by the smugglers as well. Which meant they might show up there. Since the robots were wasting their time just sitting at the refueling station, perhaps he should put them to use. He could set up an ambush at the power source, tell the robots to wait there, and then continue his search. Joe liked the plan. If he couldn't find the smugglers, he might get lucky and get them to come to him.

Joe hailed the robots waiting at the refueling platform and set up a rendezvous near the odd readings. They would meet close enough to walk toward it without alerting anyone there. He broke the copter out of its current search pattern and headed out.

At the rendezvous, Joe found that finding a spot to set the little copter down in the middle of the night was difficult. In the end, he had to have the robots set the hovercar down first and clear away a few trees before he could land.

Once on the ground, Joe converted the second Series Seven to a combat program and designated them simply One and Two. They each had an assault rifle of standard UNSF issue and plenty of ammunition. Joe gave a backpack of miscellaneous gear to Two to carry.

"There are no other UNSF personnel on this continent," Joe told them. "If we encounter anyone, it's safe to assume that they're smugglers operating here illegally. Shoot to kill."

"We are to allow no surrender, sir?" asked One.

"The smugglers waived their surrender opportunity in an encounter with a UNSF ship in orbit of this planet. We are now authorized to use lethal force in apprehending them."

"Yes, sir," both robots responded simultaneously. Joe waited the last half hour until daylight, pacing about impatiently. Finally he decided that the light had increased to a level that would be safe for him to walk in.

"One of you to each flank," Joe said. He took a bearing using his satellite link and headed out through the trees, cradling his rifle. The robots moved to either side, holding their rifles in similar fashion.

Joe remained linked with the automatons, making use of their scanning information so he would know if they detected any human signatures. Joe picked his way through the spiny forest. The small battle group had made it perhaps a hundred meters into the forest when a transmission came in.

"This is Two. I am falling out of formation due to inordinate difficulties negotiating the terrain," a voice said over the link.

Joe rolled his eyes. "This wouldn't happen if I'd been assigned one of the Veer Leviathans," he complained to himself.

"Do you need assistance, Two?" Joe transmitted.

"Negative."

"You are making progress?"

"Five minutes added to ETA at logged destination."

"I'll slow down. Notify me of any further difficulties."

Joe stood for a moment, listening to the sounds of the forest. He realized that he could hear One and Two churning through the woods nearby. He debated moving ahead and scouting out the area alone.

"This is One. A native lifeform has attached itself to my leg."

"My momma Veer!" swore Joe.

"Repeat last, sir?"

"One, remove it with all due haste. Stay focused on our priority," Joe said.

"I am unable to remove it, sir."

"Can you still make progress?" Joe asked, exasperation drenching his voice.

"Five minutes added to ETA at logged destination."

Joe clenched his teeth. If some critter still clutched the leg of his Series Seven when they got to the power source, he felt inclined to shoot whatever it was.

"This is Two."

"Let me guess. Five minutes added to ETA?"

"At logged destination, sir. For a total delta of ten minutes over original estimate."

"Both of you, break inward. We'll assume a file formation; I'll take the point."

"That is not an optimum skirmish formation," Two transmitted.

"I'm aware of that."

One came limping through the undergrowth. A huge orange ball dominated the lower part of its left leg. Joe carefully knelt to examine the thing.

"What the hell is that?"

"A primitive hexapod with a thick exoskeleton," summarized One.

Joe reached out to try to pry the creature off.

"I suggest extreme caution, sir. The creature has manipulators with an extremely high mechanical advantage," said One. The robot showed Joe its hand. One of the metal fingers had been removed, leaving a small stub of twisted metal.

Joe snatched his hand back.

"We'll shoot it off once we've reached the site and made sure there's no one there already," he said. "Catalog it and warn me if we near any other ones like it."

"Yes, sir."

Two eventually stumbled through the forest and joined them. Joe took the lead, weaving back and forth through the vegetation, searching for the easiest path. He could tell by referencing the satellite data that they were almost at the location of the power anomaly.

Joe slowed the column, stopping every minute or so to listen. The group crept along until Joe could see a ruined building ahead. The structure was dark gray and covered with vines. A gaping hole beckoned in the side of the building.

"One, move in and investigate the interior," Joe ordered.

He hooked up with the Series Seven's optical receptors and got a view of the inside in his mind's eye. Dust covered a series of chest-high pieces of inexplicable equipment. The devices could have been anything. It might take a detailed examination and a year of work from a Trilisk expert to figure out their function, if they ever did figure it out. In any case, it was certain that they were ancient; Joe ignored them.

A huge cylinder opened into the room from the floor. It seemed like the only other interesting feature.

Joe and Two moved through the hole in the building's exterior.

Joe took a look at the inside for himself. At one time it might have been a high-tech facility, but it didn't look like much now. Joe realized that the fresh footprints they were leaving in the dust would warn any smugglers away.

"Two, clean up our trail. I don't want it so obvious that we came through this way."

"Acknowledged," said Two. It shifted foliage and ruined pieces of equipment to cover up the footprints. It smoothed over the remaining tracks, backing up toward Joe.

Joe watched the process until he was satisfied. Then he spoke quietly into his link.

"This is Lieutenant Hartlet. I'm investigating a local ruin site with subterranean components. I may be out of reception for a short time."

Joe linked out from the satellite network and gave some more orders.

"One, move into that tube and tell me if there's anything in there."

The Series Seven clumsily climbed into the aperture. The tube was taller than the robot. One moved deeper inside until it was no longer visible.

"The tunnel is descending and spiraling to the right," One reported. "I am continuing forward."

"Keep us posted. We're coming in behind you," Joe said. He motioned Two forward and followed it into the odd tunnel. The inside was dirty, but the tunnel walls were intact.

"I have reached the end," One reported.

"Shit. Dead end?"

"There is an anomaly."

"Did you find the power source?" Joe asked. He linked in to take a look at what the robot was seeing. The tunnel was blocked by a narrow circular rim with a dead black center.

Joe couldn't tell what it was. He jogged down to the spot with Two.

"Can you detect anything beyond that circular...thing?" Joe demanded.

Two moved slightly forward, turning its head side to side. "There is nothing there," it announced.

"Nothing beyond the opening?"

"I detect nothing, sir," the robot said.

Joe didn't feel comfortable with the entrance. He decided not to risk it. He would send the robots in first.

"One and Two, move forward and take up positions beyond the...beyond the circular frame ahead."

The robots stalked forward, their rifles cradled in cold metal hands. They moved into the blackness. Joe blinked. It was as if the robots had stepped beyond a black curtain. They were not visible.

"One and Two, are you in position?"

No answer came. Joe transmitted again, trying to reach the robots without luck. His link refused to acknowledge their mental interfaces.

"Shit. What the hell..."

He paced nervously.

One emerged from the blackness.

"One. Are you functioning? Is Two okay in there?"

"Affirmative. I returned to investigate a communications dysfunction. I did not read the presence of your link once moving beyond the barrier."

"Describe what's beyond the portal," Joe commanded.

"There is a concrete corridor with a white tile floor and standard lighting. The corridor extends—"

"Wait. You said 'standard' lighting. Explain."

"The lighting is provided by long LED filaments, commonly referred to as glow rods," One replied. "An analysis of wavelength and intensity reveals that the illumination falls very close to the Terran average for such fixtures. Hence the term standard."

Joe frowned. That couldn't be right. Humans hadn't built any installations here. The two UNSF bases were it. Unless smugglers had actually discovered it first and built a base…the thought alarmed him.

He moved up to the black area and tested it with his hand. It seemed harmless.

"Follow me through," he said.

Joe moved quickly through the blackfield and joined Two on the other side. One stepped through beside him. He stared at the walls, floor, and ceiling as he walked forward. He felt no doubt that this was a human habitation. It could have been one of a million corridors that Joe had seen in his lifetime. Everything, from the square tile floor to the height of the ceiling and the long tube lights, was familiar.

"Follow me," Joe said.

Michael McCloskey

Chapter Five

Telisa looked at her packs of equipment in the cargo bay. The four crew members had assembled to prepare for the hike to the odd power source they had detected. A small subset of the equipment would have to be selected; there was too much for them to carry it all.

"So we just have to decide what to bring," she said.

"Well, all the cold-weather gear is out. It won't be getting cold here for a long time, even at night," Thomas said.

"Okay, that makes it a little easier," Telisa said. "How much food?"

"It'll take a day to get there. I'd say a ten-day pack would be fine. What do you think, Magnus?"

Magnus nodded. "A ten-day pack should do. We can carry less water. There will be sources of water out there that we can use in a pinch."

Telisa assembled a food pack for ten days. She then considered the remaining packs.

"The terrain isn't mountainous. Climbing gear stays," she noted.

Jack nodded. "Yes. I'll take some light digging stuff. Since the space force is looking for us, we should wear the active camo suits."

"Okay, you've got digging stuff, I'll take some cutters and a little explosive, in case we have to let ourselves in," Thomas said.

Telisa put on a camo suit over her ordinary jumpsuit. Jack and Thomas did the same. The camo suits shifted color moodily, trying to emulate the drab gray of the deck and the flat black of their equipment packs. Telisa knew from reading the manual of her camo suit that they broke up the wearer's heat signature as well, directing any radiant heat straight down into the ground. The suits would make them much harder to spot in an aerial or orbital scan.

She looked at Magnus expectantly. "You're not wearing one?"

"Momma Veer already took care of that," Thomas said.

Magnus nodded. His suit slowly turned gray and black like the other camo suits. Telisa assumed he had turned it on using his link by sending a message to microprocessors in the skinsuit.

Telisa linked up with the ship's computer and looked up the phrase "Momma Veer." She had heard soldiers say that before, but she had never bothered to learn exactly what it meant. The information came through from the ship's cache, feeding a visual report back into her brain. Apparently soldiers were occasionally supplied with Veer Industries equipment when the government ran short of its own supplies. Oddly enough, the Veer equipment had often proved superior to government issue, and the soldiers used the nickname "Momma Veer" for the company that provided for them when the UNSF could not.

She looked up the price for the famous Veer military skinsuit. At around 2000 ESC, it was a very expensive piece of equipment. Her eyebrows rose.

"For that much money, it ought to, I guess," she said.

"Worth every penny," Magnus said, patting the material over his chest.

Telisa hefted her primary pack over her shoulder and had a second bag of food concentrate. The others carried similar loads. She saw that Magnus had insisted on carrying the massive slug thrower as well. Telisa had her stunner and a pair of good long knives—just in case. She smiled to herself. It wasn't long ago she had thought Magnus odd for carrying weapons; now she had three herself. Apparently being a smuggler hunted by the UNSF could change your attitude pretty fast. Or maybe it was the training. She'd used knives many times in simulated combat now, so she felt vulnerable without them.

"I don't feel like I could carry a whole lot of stuff back," Telisa said. "I guess we'll have less food and water to carry by then, though."

"If we hadn't been detected, we could have made better arrangements," Thomas explained. "As it is, we'll just have to play mule. Trilisk artifacts are so valuable on the black market that we could still carry enough to make us rich several times over if we find the right spot."

Jack looked grim. "But I'm willing to write this one off if we have to. If we make it out alive, then we can try again."

Telisa was glad to see that even Jack wasn't so greedy as to insist that they stay until they were rich no matter what. She walked with the others to the exit.

The loading ramp was extended from the belly of the ship, and everyone sauntered out onto the forest floor, absorbing the alien forest scenery. The plant life looked spiny, like species in arid areas on Earth, but they grew in a jungle-like density. They saw a wide variety of plants, but only a few animals. The creatures appeared to be crabs or snails that moved slowly through the trees. The ship had cleared a small area of the forest, felling trees and blackening a spot in the lush green wilderness.

"Wow, look at that," Thomas said and pointed.

Telisa looked into the forest where he indicated. She saw that a thickset tree with a bare trunk and a wide, spiky crown supported an identical tree on top of it. The roots of the piggybacking tree intertwined with the crown of its supporter.

"There are several of them doing that," Magnus said. "They must be getting some kind of competitive advantage."

"Maybe the crown collects water. It's very wide," Telisa said. "The tree on top sends water down to its own roots, and the extra heads down to the tree below it. They deprive water from those below."

"Or maybe the top one even helps feed the one supporting it, who knows?" Thomas said. "The supported ones probably get more sunlight."

Jack nodded. "Well, if you're this fascinated by the damn trees, I can't wait to see you guys when we find the ruins."

"They won't spot this mess from orbit?" Telisa asked, looking back at the damage their landing had caused.

"Got it covered," Thomas said. "Looks the same from down here, but I have us cloaked from above. Our equipment should fool any but the most sophisticated sensors. If they don't have a scouting vessel in orbit, we should be hidden for now. Well, unless some scientist just happens to have a specialized satellite for some experiment that can notice an anomaly."

Telisa didn't comment on that. Apparently there were risks everywhere that she hadn't realized they would have to be taking. It must be part of the routine for an interplanetary artifact smuggler. She looked around the landing site again, wondering if there were predators out there. She hoped the noise and destruction of the landing had scared any bigger creatures away.

The group moved into the forest. Telisa looked over her shoulder at the ship before the view became blocked by vegetation. The fat ovoid shape had settled just below the surrounding treetops. She wondered if it would still be there when they got back. What would happen if they became marooned on the planet? Would they be able to survive? Would it be worth living in such a desolate place? She checked her link and realized the nearby ship and her companions' link chips were the only devices broadcasting services here. The planet was truly empty wilderness.

Thomas indicated the direction and then Magnus took the lead. Telisa asked for a link from Thomas and got it. Now she could see a map of the surrounding landscape in her mind's eye, with the destination clearly marked. They fell into a line behind Magnus, with Telisa in the rear.

"Stay alert," Magnus said over his link. "The flora and fauna are largely unknown. If we get in over our heads, there won't be anyone to save us."

Telisa acknowledged the message and dug out her stunner. She attached it to the webbing on her belt.

Normally the webbing held onto the stunner firmly, but if she touched the weapon with her hand, it weakened so that she could tear the stunner away easily. Then the separated fibers would intertwine again as good as new. She scanned the surrounding vegetation, searching for anything that might be dangerous.

Looking at the native trees made Telisa itch. Their trunks were covered in so many tiny spines they almost looked hairy. The spiny leaves added to their greenish shaggy appearance. She saw now that most of the spines were soft, liquid-filled leaves, but a few of the plants did have truly sharp spikes like a cactus. She saw three more of the piggybacking trees, this time arranged with two specimens leaning together on the bottom to support another on their heads.

The spines didn't seem to inhibit the native lifeforms' ability to make their homes in the trees. Telisa saw a large variety of mollusk-like creatures climbing around. Many sported extra protection of some sort, mostly flat plates of armor or complete spherical shells. Telisa got a good look at one hanging from a nearby limb. The creature was a round ball with holes placed randomly around it, from which tiny green legs poked out and retracted as needed. Telisa committed some images of the trees and the creatures to her link memory.

The hike continued. When Telisa began to sweat, she opened the vents in her camo suit. Her every stride pumped air over her torso and sent it down to vents at her feet. Despite the added cooling, she felt the strain of walking on the uneven ground, pushing through the heavy foliage.

The hours went by quickly while Telisa occupied herself with making her way through the alien ecosphere. She saw several more odd local creatures but nothing larger than a small dog. They broke for a light lunch at midday, with the alien sun blazing down directly overhead. The trees afforded some protection, their spines blocking a great deal of the light. Still, the humid forest seemed like the inside of an oven during the middle of the day. Telisa drank a lot of water. She wondered if they should have taken the trip during the night, but the thought of trying to make their way in the darkness with all sorts of odd creatures creeping about was not pleasant either.

As soon as they had eaten and rested for half an hour, they returned to the trek with a vengeance. Telisa had time to think about how close she really was to discovering new Trilisk artifacts. At one time the Trilisks had actually lived upon this planet and created installations or even cities. A race more advanced than mankind, yet strangely absent from the current galactic stage. What had happened to them? What could have possibly caused their civilization to be destroyed? These questions and more drove her forward.

They forged on for several more hours. Telisa was glad she had been working out regularly, even if the exercise was quite different. She wondered how long Thomas and Jack could continue this level of exertion, although she figured Magnus could probably outlast them all. Her questions were answered when Jack spoke up.

"Okay, let's take another break," Jack said. "This hiking is killing me."

Telisa was exhausted. The sun was no longer visible above them, although the light level told her that it hadn't set.

"Are we there yet?" asked Telisa, smiling at her delivery of the classic question.

Thomas frowned. "Actually we're barely halfway. I underestimated the speed we could make out here. I suppose we should find a spot to hole up while it's still light."

Magnus nodded. "We could sleep in the trees."

"That would be safer on Earth," said Jack. "Here, who knows? Maybe the trees are more dangerous than the ground."

"The ground should be okay, unless this planet has some particularly nasty nocturnal predators," Magnus said. "Unfortunately, we can't use a campfire without risking detection."

"How about over there?" Telisa suggested, pointing to a slight rise in the terrain. They moved over to the area she had indicated and set their packs on the ground so they could prepare the makeshift camp.

Everyone arranged their tiny one-person sleeping tubes in a circle with the zippered entrances facing inward toward each other. Magnus and Telisa gathered a bunch of arm-length needles that had fallen from nearby trees and arranged them facing outward around the area for defense.

Telisa looked at the failing light filtering through the trees. "Only a minute or two to spare, I'd say."

"Yes, just in time," Jack agreed. "Should we have someone awake all the time? Take shifts staying awake?"

"If anything comes around, I think we'll hear it," Magnus said, looking at the camp perimeter. "I think setting watches at this point would be overly paranoid. We have the spines, the tents, and a fair amount of firepower."

They each crawled into their sleeping modules and sought sleep. Telisa opened a vent to let fresh air in and then sprawled out, resting her aching muscles. She fell asleep quickly.

At some point later, Telisa bolted instantly awake. Something was wrong. She listened for a moment and realized that something moved toward their camp, breaking branches and rustling in the leaves of the forest floor. She sat upright, reaching for her pack. She brought out her stunner and unzipped the opening of her tiny sleeping tube.

Magnus stood in the center of their little clearing, holding a flashlight pointed out into the forest. His slug thrower was level with the ground, the barrel pointed out into the darkness toward the noises. Jack and Thomas seemed content to watch from their tent flaps. Telisa scrambled to find her own flashlight. The noises outside were getting closer. She forced herself to calm and found the light.

Telisa clambered out of her tube and stood to Magnus's right, clutching her stunner. She added her light to Magnus's and saw some kind of bluish tentacle waving through the brush at the height of her chest. She took a deep breath and forced herself not to shoot.

The thing pushed aside Magnus's sleeping tube with another blue tentacle. A huge shell pushed through the spiny branches, revealing the rest of the creature. It had spiny legs and about a dozen tentacles. It moved slowly out into the clearing, its tentacles wavering as it searched for the next shrub.

Suddenly Magnus yelled maniacally and kicked the ground in front of him, sending a bit of forest floor debris flying at the creature. The thing flinched away, moving in slow motion, and then it altered its course. It pushed its way though the spines on the perimeter and crawled away.

Everyone let their tension drop. Then Thomas started to laugh. The laughter spread. Even Magnus started to chuckle.

"Well, I guess we showed it," Thomas said. "That'll teach it to disturb us."

"I don't think I can go back to sleep after that," Telisa said.

Magnus nodded. "I probably can't either, but I don't want to try and walk in the dark. Let's just try our best."

Telisa crawled back into her tent. She could still hear the giant shelled thing moving away through the brush. She tried to go back to sleep. She tossed and turned for a while. Her legs itched. Telisa scratched, then she felt a small bump on her leg. She dug out the flashlight and examined herself in the tent. Her legs were covered in welts. Some of them had tiny splinters in them.

She picked at the wounds for a short while, convincing herself that they were nothing but a minor irritation. Apparently some of the plant's spines were able to penetrate the chameleon suit. By this time Telisa had become groggy again, and so she turned off the flashlight and went back to sleep.

In the morning they repacked everything and moved out about fifteen minutes after sunrise. Telisa's legs were stiff, and walking sent shooting pains through them for the first few minutes. Her pain must have been minor compared to Jack and Thomas, who were complaining loudly.

"Oh, my legs! They're gonna fall off!" Thomas groaned.

"Mine too. And be careful, some of these spines can go through our suits," Jack said.

"Yes, my legs are full of them," Telisa agreed.

Thomas nodded. "Me too," he said.

"How bad is it? Do you feel sick?" Magnus asked.

"They just seem like splinters I got on Earth," Telisa said. "What, you didn't even get one?"

Magnus shook his head. "Momma Veer…"

"Argh! I should have known."

Not only did he seem unaffected by yesterday's hike, but he had been spared the needling as well. Telisa shook her head. Somehow none of it surprised her. In the short time since she had met him, he had given her the impression of invulnerability. It wasn't the kind of bragging, pretend-out-loud sort of toughness, but a quiet, understated acceptance of the world's problems without slowing down. Telisa found herself attracted by it, but she put those thoughts aside again. There were the artifacts and getting back alive…

They spent more hours moving through the forest as in the previous day. Telisa tried to stay alert through it all, even though the constant scanning became tedious as they moved through the forest. She challenged herself to spot as many of the local creatures as she could. Sometimes the things would ignore the intruders; other times they flashed into their shells, falling back onto a lower branch or even to the ground.

For the first time Telisa found a disastrous-looking arrangement of the trees that grew atop each other. A single strong specimen drooped under the weight of two piggybackers. It seemed that the behavior didn't always work as planned. Telisa wondered if somewhere, a chain of three or four of them stacked on each other extended high above the surrounding forest…at least until the whole arrangement came crashing down like a house of cards.

Telisa almost asked about their progress but realized that she could check for herself. She examined the map in her mind, her current position indicated by Thomas's navigation equipment. She could see that they were almost upon the site of the unusual power emanations. Magnus must have been cognizant of the same thing, as he slowed their progress, scanning the area ahead carefully.

"I can see a ruin directly ahead," he reported.

Everyone followed him closely, eager to see for themselves. Telisa made out a large gray building overgrown with the local trees and shrubs. Telisa couldn't tell what it was made of. It surface remained smooth despite its age. She guessed it could be constructed of some metal or ceramic.

They approached one seamless wall and then paralleled its course. When they turned the corner, Telisa saw that the wall had been breached. Some kind of root system or underground plant had shattered the wall long ago. The hole was large enough to climb through.

Magnus fished out his flashlight and peeked inside. He turned around and shrugged.

"Looks alien to me. Maybe Telisa should take a look."

Telisa took her own flashlight and stepped up to the opening.

The disc of light fell upon dusty pieces of equipment larger than a human. The materials and angles looked right for Trilisk origin, but the dust was too thick and she was too far away to be sure.

"I'm getting a closer look," she said, and without waiting for a reply, she switched the flashlight to her left hand, unclipped her stunner with her right, and went in.

Jack and Thomas walked up to her as she brushed the dust off the nearest device. It didn't seem to have any levers or buttons, which was a good sign right off. Trilisk artifacts never did. Most human theories on the subject indicated that they were used through mental interfaces. There were flat black plates built into the gray metal surface. That was another good sign. The plates were display ports, made to show information about the state of the device, like the front panel of a chronometer. Presumably the readouts could provide their information via a mental interface as well, but the Trilisks seemed to prefer having the panels on their equipment too. No one really knew why.

It looked dead. Perhaps all she had to do was find out how to activate it. Unfortunately, Trilisk devices never had anything as simple and primitive as a power switch.

"Amazing. We're the first humans to look at this. Real Trilisk artifacts."

"So it is Trilisk. Any idea what it does?" asked Thomas.

"I have no idea. But I need to—"

"Let's take a tour of the place first," Jack suggested. "Don't settle on anything just yet. That thing you're looking at is probably too heavy for all of us to even pick up. You see what I'm saying?"

Telisa looked up from the mysterious cluster of equipment. Magnus was across the room, looking into the end of a giant tube that descended into the floor.

"I guess you're right. I want to look at everything, of course, but our time is limited. And as you pointed out, we can't carry this thing."

Thomas nodded. "We're excited too. I'm glad you can see the bigger picture, though. A Trilisk can opener could net thousands of ESC. We don't need a big piece of factory equipment or whatever this is."

Telisa scanned the floor for something smaller. Dirt and dead vegetation lay scattered around the floor.

"This goes deeper into the installation," Magnus said, calling to the others from the mouth of the giant tube sticking up out of the floor.

"And that appears to be the only other way to go," Jack said. "So let's follow him."

Magnus extended a hand and helped the others up into the tube. Telisa took out her flashlight and shone it farther into the round tunnel. The passageway was empty. It extended as far as she could see, angling off to the right and descending deeper into the ground. It gave Telisa a rather eerie feeling. She didn't normally suffer from claustrophobia, but being in a dark, dusty underground tube made her a little nervous. She realized that their ignorance held great danger. For all she knew, they could be walking into a giant machine that could turn on and grind them up at any moment.

Magnus trudged forward and Telisa followed. The tube curved in a long circle, leading them deeper into the planet. Telisa wondered why such a thing had been built. The answer probably wouldn't come from guessing without more information. Understanding aliens could be a tough business.

They came around a last curve and the tube ended with a metal rim around its entire circumference, with a flat black hole through the center large enough to for a hippo.

They walked up to the rim. Both Magnus and Telisa shined their lights into the hole, trying to see beyond the low barrier.

"It's not just dark," Jack noted. "It's pitch black. The light's not going in there."

"Or no reflected light is coming out," Thomas said. "Our ship's stealth device uses technology a little like this to shield us from orbital scanning."

Telisa walked forward, pointing her light at the edge of the zone of blackness. The light just ended at the border, giving no reflections.

"It's wonderful!" Telisa exclaimed. "And beyond our current technology. We can't make a blackfield of this efficiency, can we?"

"That's not all," Magnus said. His eyes had a faraway look. Telisa realized he was accessing the mental interface of his military scanner. "There aren't any gravitons emerging from it either."

Thomas whistled. "I wish we had equipment that could check for neutrinos. Surely it wouldn't be that perfect…"

Telisa looked at Jack. "If we could bring whatever it is that generates this field back with us, it would be enough to pay for the whole trip," she told him. "Enough to make us all super rich."

Jack looked around the circular perimeter of the opening. "Let's try. I'm not sure we'll be able to find and carry it, but let's try. The sooner we can grab something really valuable and get off this planet, the better."

Magnus shrugged. "Stick your finger through," he suggested.

"You're nuts. What if it takes it clean off? Or instantly kills all the cells in it?"

Magnus rolled his eyes. "Then we'll grow it back when we get to Earth," he said exasperatedly. He walked past Thomas and flicked the end of his little finger through the blackfield.

"It's fine," he said, holding up the finger for all to see. Then he stuck his arm through the blackness. He pulled it back, moving the arm and testing the feel of it. "Seems harmless so far," he said.

"Wait a minute and see if it bruises," Jack suggested. But Magnus had already walked through.

Telisa moved up to the edge of the field. "Magnus? Can you hear me?"

There was no answer. She examined the edge of the opening carefully, looking for any details they might have missed. Telisa didn't like the idea of just walking through to see what happened. She valued her life a little more than that. After a few more moments, Magnus stepped back from beyond the field.

"Come in here. You're not going to believe this."

Michael McCloskey

Chapter Six

Another automatic door opened before Joe. He peeked into the room.

"More of the same," he said. So far he and the two Series Sevens had traveled perhaps a hundred meters into the complex, searching for inhabitants. He had found room after room of labs, meeting areas, supply closets, and other mundane facilities, but no people.

Joe checked the services that were broadcast to his link chip from the building. There were two general information ports and a maintenance port available. So far all of Joe's attempts to link to the installation's services had resulted in odd errors after very short interactions.

He tried again, connecting to the maintenance port. A menu came up in his mind's eye, showing local water, power, and atmospheric controls. Further access was restricted, and he didn't have valid identification codes to continue. He unlinked from the maintenance port and tried another general information one. Joe requested the route to the nearest restroom. A map came up of the local corridors, showing the path in red. He panned the map view slowly to the right. The image wavered and the link was broken.

"The information computers are hopelessly trashed," Joe complained. "Two, have you had any luck getting maps of this place?"

"I do not have sufficient access to get that information. I have multiple errors logged as well. The system is highly unstable."

Joe was frustrated, but he came to a decision.

"Let's get back to the entrance. This is an amazing place—we should report it. Its presence here proves that someone beat the UNSF to the punch. In fact, now that I think about it, that explains the ship we encountered. I wondered how they got here so fast. But the truth is, they may have been here all along."

Joe knew that people resisted the world government, formed secret societies and rebel groups, but he had no idea that they had these kinds of resources. To scout out a Trilisk planet before the UNSF and to create a base here…they were stronger than he'd realized. Then another thought occurred to him.

"Hrm…I may be making some bad assumptions here. Maybe this is a UNSF base that I don't have clearance to know about. But that means Mailson must not know about it either, or he wouldn't have sent me."

The robots listened to Joe's suppositions without comment. Joe turned back and retraced their route through the underground complex. He led them through a series of rooms and walked down a flight of stairs. They exited the stairwell and walked down a long corridor. Joe slowed, looking back over his shoulder.

"One, I've become disoriented. Where's the entrance?"

"We are at the entrance location. The door has been obscured by a new wall," the robot said.

"A new wall? Two, do you agree with this analysis? Someone built a new wall here?"

"This is the entrance location. However, there is no evidence to support the theory that this is a freshly constructed wall. It may be that a wall constructed at an earlier time has been moved to obstruct the exit."

"Wonderful. But how do we get out? Maybe we've been fooled into thinking this is the same spot," Joe said. He reached his hand out and felt the wall. It seemed solid.

"Something could be interfering with our inertial sensors," Two said.

Joe nodded. "Let's test that idea. Two, return to our deepest point in the complex and then walk back here. See if there's any discrepancy in the inertial navigator readings."

Two tramped away dutifully. Joe stood thinking as he waited for it to return. After a minute there was a scraping noise, and Joe saw that the orange creature on One's leg was beginning to move downward on the metal column.

"One, don't move. Let that stupid thing run off to wherever."

"Acknowledged."

The crablike thing crawled down to the metal foot below it and hesitated. Eventually it abandoned its post on the leg and crawled away down the corridor, bumping into the wall periodically. Two returned, walking carefully around the orange creature.

"The test is complete. The inertial locating system is showing no errors," Two said.

"Okay. First thing, help me smash through this wall. I want to see if the entrance is behind it."

The robots worked with Joe to break through the wall. Its surface was made of fairly flimsy materials with a reinforcing honeycomb structure behind. Joe had a hard time with this support material, but the robots ripped it methodically to pieces, revealing the space beyond. Joe looked through the hole.

"It's just another room. The entrance really isn't here," Joe said.

"The entrance has moved," Two agreed.

Joe shook his head. "We're missing something. The inertial systems seem to be working, but the entrance has been moved. Or closed, or hidden, or something. Let's move out in a right-handed maze search of the entire place. I want to find the exit as fast as possible."

Joe indicated for One to lead. The Series Seven moved out, keeping the wall at its right side. They moved into a room with long tables and chairs in the middle with numerous metal cabinets lining the walls. Joe resisted the urge to search through the cabinets. He wanted to find the way out quickly. He felt trapped in this strange place. He would come back and search more once he had returned to the surface and made his report.

They moved through another series of rooms typical of what they had already seen. The rooms reminded Joe of an emptied university or research center. The trio had just walked up a stairwell when One came to a halt in front of him.

"Sir, there is an anomaly ahead."

Joe stepped forward and looked over the robot's shoulder.

"Whoa," Joe said. Just ahead, the smooth concrete floor ended in an irregular hole. The room at the top of the stairwell emptied into a large cavern. Clusters of odd red and beige blocks the size of his fist grew out of the wall in random patches. The groups of cubes had greenish sticks or spines poking out of them at all angles. He stared at the odd cavern for a long moment.

"One, do you have any record of this sort of…cave?"

"These structures are unknown," One reported.

Joe walked up to the edge of the cave. He kneeled down to examine the border where the floor ended. The concrete was sheared off smoothly. There were no chunks or debris of the room on the floor of the cavern beyond. The walls and ceiling had been cut off in the same way.

"This cave or whatever it is was somehow created after this place was built. The floor wasn't built this way; it was cut off."

One and Two didn't say anything. Joe shook his head and paced.

"None of this is making any sense," he complained. "This whole place…I just don't understand what's going on. Something is happening that I'm missing here. These funny blocks look like kid's toys."

Two leveled its rifle and stepped forward.

"There is a possible lifeform reading up ahead."

"The orange crab-thing?"

"No. The reading is much larger. A high-metabolism creature with metallic accoutrements. Possible electronics signature detected."

"Shit!" After years in the service, Joe had never heard these words except in training VRs. He unslung his rifle, then considered his sidearm for a moment.

The sidearm would be more useful in close quarters, but it was a lot less sophisticated than the rifle. Its slugs were undiscriminating. Joe decided to stick with the rifle.

"Send the profile over to my rifle," Joe ordered. He could set the seeker slugs to match the reading they were getting. "How close is this damn thing?"

The end of his question was lost in the painfully loud stutter of automatic weapons fire. One moved quickly, darting into the tunnel while Two moved up to the edge and added its own fire.

"Hold your fire!" yelled Joe. He almost followed the demand with the question, *Why are you shooting?* But two things changed his mind. First, Joe realized that the robots had been told to assume anyone they met were artifact poachers and should be shot at, and second, Two's head exploded.

The Series Seven's torso leaned to one side. Fragments of metal shot out in all directions and the robot's legs froze in place, sending it hurtling to the ground. It fell and twitched, more lifelike in death than it had been while operational. Then it stopped moving.

Joe hit the ground and crawled back, retreating from the mysterious smooth cavern. He heard the boom of One's rifle. There was another hissing sound and a metallic crackling. Any second he expected to feel the impact of a projectile.

"Shit! I think we've found something capable of harming humans," Joe commented dryly. He accessed his rifle's interface and logged a target around the corner, then started shooting as he backed up further, taking a few steps back down the stairs. He didn't know if he was hitting anything, but he hoped that the rounds flinging around the bend in the cave would be enough to keep the thing from pursuing him.

"What have I done?" Joe asked himself in dismay. He should have told the robots to hold their fire as soon as he realized the lifeform was possibly an intelligent alien. As it was, he actually hoped that it was just a trick of the smugglers. At least that way, he wouldn't have just started a war with an alien race.

Joe turned around and ran back down the stairs. He couldn't hear any more sounds of fighting behind. He kept running down, past the level from which they had arrived, until he hit the bottom of the stairwell three floors down.

Joe linked to the nearest information service and asked about the floor. A list came up. Joe read "archives" and then the link scrambled and dropped out. He tried again and read "fire control station" before the link disconnected.

He pushed through the stairway door. A gray corridor stretched to his left and right. He went to the left until he saw a doorway and pushed through it. Joe found himself in a restroom. The wall before him was lined with mirrors and sinks.

Joe looked at his reflection in the nearest mirror. He saw a wild-eyed man with the beginnings of a beard from his long flight to Yarnitha. He held his rifle in a death grip. What chance did he have without any real assault robots on his side? Just one man?

He had only felt this much fear one other time in his life. Years ago he had been a cadet in training at New Kellur, a student of military science at the finest academy the space force had.

Joe thought he had found a way of communication outside the censored loop at the academy and shared certain classified facts with his brother, an engineer outside the service. When they discovered his transgression despite his precautions, he had been gripped with a terror that his entire life had been destroyed. That had felt like he felt now, helpless and ruined. Joe believed that there were worse things than death, and living as a prisoner of the world government was one of those things.

As it turned out, he had been thrown out of New Kellur and assigned to another, less prestigious officer school on a faraway planet. He heard years later that his brother had been interrogated and placed under increased surveillance for a time. Joe's career had been downgraded, but despite the bitterness, he cleaned up his act after that. A life in the space force was the only thing Joe had ever wanted.

Joe thought about that close call so long ago. He told himself that if he died now, it would not have been such a bad life. Not as bad as if he had been thrown into a mining colony to rot and had never joined the space force at all.

"I'm gonna die in this shithole," Joe mumbled to himself. He checked the load on his rifle and walked back out into the corridor.

Chapter Seven

Telisa examined the brightly lit hallway. The light came from glow rods affixed in the corners of the ceiling. Thin, dull-colored carpet covered the floor. The walls were colored a deep green.

"It's amazing. We could be on Earth," she said.

"This has to be a UNSF facility. The power source—it must be some kind of secret research facility," said Thomas.

"But why hide the entrance in a tube in the middle of a Trilisk ruin?" asked Telisa.

"And where are the guards, the security robots, the automated checkpoints?" added Magnus.

Thomas shook his head. Jack shrugged.

"Something weird is going on, that's for sure. Should we bolt?" asked Jack.

"There should be Trilisk artifacts here. Let's find some and then leave as soon as possible," said Telisa. She had come so far and didn't want to give it all up now.

"Maybe the place is still under construction," said Magnus. "But I can't explain the field at the entrance. Unless it's Trilisk technology the UNSF has mastered."

The suggestion was amazing. If the UNSF had already gleaned some of the secrets of Trilisk technology, then they were ahead of what she had expected. What powers had the government scientists gained in secret from the civilian world? Could they be trusted to use the technology wisely? Telisa didn't think so. The government didn't have the best interest of the masses in mind anymore. It had grown into a beast of its own that lived for its own growth and satisfaction.

"I see some services, but don't link up," Thomas warned. "Security is really lax here, but maybe the main computer is farther along. It might report us if we link up and it finds out we're not UNSF."

Telisa automatically checked the services available at the mention of them. There were general ports for information, and a main library port. She took Thomas's warning seriously and didn't link up. It took a surprising effort of will. She'd been accustomed her entire life to querying services without a second thought.

"Which direction?" asked Jack. He looked at Telisa. "Take your pick."

Telisa shrugged and pointed to her left. A corridor extended past a set of doorways in that direction. Magnus took the lead and headed for the first door. He carefully opened it and peeked inside.

"Some kind of storage room. Let's find something a little more interesting."

No one disagreed. They moved along the corridor and started cautiously looking into each room. They found a meeting room and several more storage areas with boxes in the corners and lockers along the walls. Then they got to a series of deserted living quarters, with two beds bunked together in each one.

Telisa stood in the corridor and sighed in frustration.

"Hrm...either it's just now finished and not occupied yet, or it's been abandoned," Telisa said. "If it's been abandoned, then we're wasting our time here. The UNSF, or whoever built this place, wouldn't leave if there were still artifacts to be found."

"Something's odd around the corner," Magnus said. He was at the end of the hallway, unslinging his slug thrower. Telisa and the others walked forward to the turn in the corridor, curious to see for themselves.

After the corridor turned, it continued another thirty feet and then ended in an irregular gaping cave. There was another ordinary-looking doorway on the left wall. Everyone advanced closer to the cave, trying to see inside.

The lights of the corridor showed a natural-looking space with patches of cube-shaped blocks clinging to the walls and ceiling. The floor of the cavern was about a meter lower than the hallway flooring. The edge of the overhang looked like it had been cut, fitting perfectly into the side of the cave.

"Looks like there's some damage to the installation here," commented Thomas. "I don't understand. Could some kind of earthquake have caused this?"

"Who knows? This planet's seismicity is an unknown at this point," Jack said. "Those blocks are weird. They remind me of something. I wonder if they're worth anything?"

"Project blox," Telisa said. "They look like those kid's toys...for building all sorts of stuff." She added bitterly, "Well, at this point we have nothing to lose by taking some. We don't have any Trilisk artifacts to weigh us down." Somehow the artifacts that she had been dreaming of had not materialized other than the inoperative hulks in the building above. There had been no clue as to the source of the blackfield. Telisa wondered if they should go back to the entrance and try to break through the walls around it to find the mechanism.

Jack hopped down and approached one of the clusters. Telisa examined the edge of the floor where it met the cavern. Magnus stood next to her while Thomas milled around behind them.

"It doesn't make any sense," Telisa pointed out. "The floor meets the cavern perfectly—so do the walls and ceiling. Where is the rubble from whatever caused this?"

Thomas pulled aside a ceiling panel.

"You think that's weird, look at this," he said. He pointed to a lighting rod above. The LED filament stopped halfway along its length where it met the cavern, as if it had been sheared in half by a laser.

Magnus nodded. "Something is wrong. I don't have an explanation."

Telisa stared at the ceiling. She couldn't think what could have caused the strange transition from hallway to cavern.

"Well, I have some of these things, whatever they are," Jack announced. He had pried some from the wall with pliers and placed them into a container from his pack.

Thomas hopped down and reached for one.

"Don't do that," Jack said. "Who knows? It might be poisonous."

"I agree—you shouldn't touch that stuff until we figure out what it is," Magnus said.

"Don't touch them? This coming from the guy who just walked through the black doorway? They could be valuable. Take a few more, and we'll keep looking," said Thomas. "Nobody said this was safe. We could be hurt just by walking by an artifact."

Jack was turning back toward the wall when he exploded. Flesh and blood gouted out of his chest like a bad horror sim, accompanied by a loud popping sound.

Telisa froze for a moment, watching as Thomas absorbed in utter shock what had happened. He was literally covered in blood and body debris.

"Fall back! Run!" Magnus ordered.

Thomas scrambled for the lip of the cave and Magnus held out a hand to help him up. Telisa took out her stunner and backed away, not seeing any target.

Magnus grabbed Thomas's hand and started to pull him up. There was another awful popping noise and Thomas disintegrated over Magnus. Blood sprayed onto Telisa. She crouched, unable to believe what was happening. Time seemed to slow, and she found herself thinking that she had come too far to die here. Tears were welling in her eyes.

Magnus fell slightly backward, off balance, and released a burst from his slug thrower. The sound was louder than anything Telisa had ever heard, even with the weapon pointed away from her. She couldn't see what he was shooting at, if anything. Magnus turned and sprinted toward her. Telisa's muscles released, and she turned to run with him.

Telisa ran around the corner with Magnus close behind her. She stopped short just around the turn. Instead of the long corridor of doors they had just explored, there was a smooth empty wall on her left with another cave entrance straight ahead. An open corridor branched away on her right. None of it was the same as she remembered.

"Shit! How'd we get turned around?" Telisa asked. Her voice sounded rapid and squeaky in her own ears.

"Cover the corner," Magnus said, pointing back where they had come from. He aimed his own slug thrower in the opposite direction toward the other cavern. He moved up to the edge.

Telisa set herself a meter from the corner, holding her stunner out ready to fire. She realized she was panting and shaking. Would something come around the corner? Telisa heard Magnus behind her. She wondered if he planned on going into the other cavern.

"Let's go this way, try and find our way back," Magnus called. Telisa turned to join him, stepping closer.

The wall on the left exploded next to Magnus. He tumbled forward, enveloped in flames and chunks of building material. Telisa curled away, cringing from the smoke and debris in the air.

"Magnus!"

A second or two later she staggered back to her feet. Magnus appeared as a shadow through the haze, crawling forward. Telisa ran to his side and pulled him up. Magnus stood uncertainly.

"Somehow the thing knew where we were through the wall," he said hollowly.

Then he seemed to recover and started retreating further back, dragging Telisa along with an iron grip on her arm. They took the corridor to the right that formed the T intersection.

"What the hell is it?" Telisa demanded, on the edge of hysteria.

"Quiet," Magnus said. "I don't know."

They came to an intersection, and Magnus turned left without hesitating. She was sure they hadn't been in this section before, but she was glad to be running away from the site of the carnage.

Magnus refused to stop until they had run down another long corridor. He checked one door and saw that it was a janitorial closet. A motionless robot—some kind of cleaning machine—stood inside. They checked another door, still looking anxiously back the way they had come.

The room beyond the second door was a kitchen. They ran inside and fell to their knees behind three massive ovens.

"Have you been hit? Are you bleeding anywhere?" asked Magnus, looking her over.

Telisa didn't answer but simply stared at Magnus, trying to believe what had happened. One moment Thomas and Jack had been standing next to them, talking and alive; the next, they were gone.

Then she saw that his skinsuit had been damaged. A large patch on his left shoulder had changed color, and a small spot looked as if it had begun to blister and melt. The hair on the left side of Magnus's head was shorter, seared away. The skin on his neck was red and weeping.

"You should have been killed," she whispered, running her hands over Magnus's shoulders. The skinsuit felt rough under her hands in patches, the rest smooth.

"Thank Momma Veer," Magnus said.

"I knew those Veer suits were tough, but I had no idea," Telisa said. "If I survive to see Earth again, the first thing I'm going to do is buy one of those."

"What's the second thing?" Magnus asked.

"Take you to a hotel and get you out of yours," she said. As soon as she said it, Telisa regretted it. "I'm sorry," she said. "I don't know what's wrong with me. Our friends just died and here I am…" She shook her head.

"Don't worry, it's just a reaction to the stress. It gets harder to control your emotions. I've seen it in soldiers after combat." He seemed to consider his words. "Besides, nothing wrong with the sentiment. Of course, we should probably be concerned with survival right now."

"Of course, I agree. Let's just find our way back to the exit and leave. Whatever that was that tried to kill us, we don't have a chance against it."

"Somehow I got turned around. I thought we went back the way we came, but we haven't seen these corridors."

"We could link up and get a map," Telisa said. "I know the plan was not to do that, but things could hardly get much worse. If the UNSF finds us, it'd be better than whatever that was."

"Unless that was the UNSF."

Telisa grunted. "How could that be?"

"Maybe this installation is so secret they're willing to kill to keep it under wraps. They're allowed to shoot at smugglers, you know."

Telisa considered this possibility in horror. "Okay. Maybe it was a UNSF security robot or something. But what harm can linking up for a map do if they already know we're here?"

"No harm, unless there's a security flaw in our chips," Magnus said cynically. "Go ahead."

Telisa called up a floor map from the information port. In her mind she saw the room they were in and a diagram of the surrounding area. Telisa asked for a highlight of the quickest route to the exit. The map disappeared, and her link was broken. Her link chip reported a transport error.

"Argh! It's not working!"

"Your chip?"

"The information computer," Telisa said. She tried again while Magnus waited. Once again she got an error. When she looked at Magnus, she saw that he had a far-off look indicating he was trying too.

"No good. It's not going to work," he confirmed. "And there aren't any exit signs on the ceiling. That doesn't make any sense, unless this place is under construction. Or…maybe it's designed to simulate malfunctions caused by an attack? Some kind of a training area, maybe."

"Let's just find a stairwell and go up," Telisa said. Magnus nodded and led the way, holding his weapon level and ready.

Magnus led them through the halls, checking doors at the ends that could be stairwells. They checked two halls and then moved past a bank of elevators.

"Look. The numbers say one through six. This is four. The stairs have to be nearby."

Telisa took great encouragement from the information. "That's odd. I guess there's another entrance than the strange tube we come in from."

A heavy door nearby proved to be the stairwell entrance. They clambered up the stairs to the top.

"Something's wrong," Magnus said.

"What? We're at the top, let's get out of here."

"There were four flights of stairs. We were on level four. There should only be three."

"Maybe the elevator doesn't go to the ground floor," Telisa said, not believing it.

The two smugglers emerged cautiously from the stairwell. They were in a corridor like the others below, although there were no elevator doors visible here. The corridors were clean and bare, with no decorations. Straight across from the door there was a fire extinguisher station in the wall.

"That's the first one I've seen," Telisa said.

Magnus thought for a moment. "I agree."

They made their way to the end of the hall and tried the door. It opened into a larger room filled with boxes and heavy shelving on the walls.

"Looks like spare parts," Magnus said. "Or raw materials for fabricating spare parts," he corrected, looking over the rows of metal rods and strips. The room smelled like metal and oil.

They moved through a storage room and some kind of machine shop next door. Then they emerged back into a hallway on the far side.

As their search of the level continued, Telisa became more agitated.

"This is the top level, but where's the exit?" Telisa demanded.

"It should be the top level. We don't know for sure unless the computer starts working or we've searched it all ourselves."

Telisa tried the computer again, but it malfunctioned as before. The glimpse of the map she did get showed that they were at the edge of the complex.

"The map says this is a dead end, but let's check it," she said.

They found a tiny bar at the end of the hallway, a highly decorated and well-stocked area. Telisa looked it over and sighed. What was this place? What guests came here and needed to be impressed? She didn't recognize any of the labels on the liquor.

Magnus looked it over with her. "This area is defensible. There's only one way in, and the bar faces it. We could rest here."

"If that thing comes back—"

"We have to sleep sometime," Magnus said.

Telisa didn't have the strength to argue. She walked around into the cul-de-sac of the bar. She slipped her pack off and dropped to the floor.

Magnus followed her lead and took up a spot next to her at the opening of the bar. Even though Telisa knew that they were both outmatched by whatever it was out there, she felt safer with him nearby. She thought that it would be hard to find sleep after such a traumatic day, but somehow she dropped into unconsciousness as soon as she closed her eyes.

Michael McCloskey

Chapter Eight

Joe stared at the anomalous section of the glossy white wall. A meter-wide sphere had been carved out of it, and native plants and rocks filled it like a terrarium. He approached the niche carefully. Something moved in the foliage.

He leveled his pistol and watched. A small orange creature crawled slowly along the edge of the area. It hesitated to leave the small space, circling around and then finally coming to a halt.

"What in the hell is going on here?"

Joe squatted and contemplated the chitinous creature. It had a round shell, with short spines that stuck out at intervals to move it along. Three thick pincer arms came out of the front. In all likelihood it was the same creature that had tagged along on his robot's leg. Joe could smell the musty plant odors, reminding him of what it smelled like on the surface.

"I recognize you," Joe said to the small creature. "Finally found a spot that reminds you of home, huh?"

The edge of the floor ended abruptly at the perimeter of the sphere. It reminded Joe of the edge where the corridor became a cave. The floor smoothly ended, unscarred, as if it had been constructed to hold the soil and plants. The wall had a depression in it, continuing the shape of a sphere from the depression in the floor, and Joe could see the layers of building material. Each layer had been smoothly cut at an angle, giving way to the next deeper layer. The groove had not been built into the wall, it had been cut or melted in.

Joe rose and walked around the unusual sphere of vegetation. He realized as the odors became imperceptible again that the air in the complex smelled clean like it did in spaceships, rather than like the pollens and molds that laced the air of the surface. He surmised that the complex had an efficient air filtering system. He continued down the corridor. He moved into another hallway, holding his pistol ready. He had decided to sling his rifle over his shoulder, since it would be harder to wield in a surprise situation than the sidearm.

He came across the fire control station that the directory had hinted at, a large room with manual and automated firefighting equipment. Two large red robots sat in maintenance bays in the center of the room. They looked vaguely humanoid in the torso, but the bottom halves of their bodies were treaded like tanks. Wires and hoses were attached to the machines as if they were people on heavy life support. Like every place he had encountered in the installation thus far, the walls were immaculate—free of both dirt and scuff marks. Joe suppressed an urge to mar them in some way. Moving onward, he glanced briefly at storage rooms and a media lounge before moving on. When he didn't find any exit in that section of the complex, he turned around and started backtracking.

Joe realized something was wrong. He entered a room that he had thought was the fire control station, but somehow he must have gotten turned around; instead he found himself in a complex room filled with twisting pipes and air ducts. He turned back to figure out where he had made a wrong turn. He searched for several more minutes until he was sure he had rechecked every door in the area, but he still could not relocate the fire control station.

Joe stopped in a corridor and kicked the wall in frustration. "This is bullshit! Where the hell am I?"

Somehow the walls around him kept shifting, changing. Whenever he left an area, things moved, including walls and doorways. Most importantly, the exit had moved. Was it waiting for him someplace else, or had it disappeared altogether?

Joe knew that a virtual environment could feel almost exactly like the real thing. But he hadn't connected to any equipment that could be feeding his senses a fake complex like this. He wondered if the UNSF scientists had completed a remote projector that could seamlessly put someone into a virtual environment without their consent or knowledge.

"That stupid black disc, maybe…"

What if the black portal had rendered him unconscious? Then he could have been hooked up to a virtual reality system before he awakened. Except that the robot had returned through the portal and reported the corridor beyond.

"Okay, is this some kind of experiment?" he asked loudly. "I'm supposed to figure my way out of here?"

He'd heard rumors of experiments conducted on space force grunts, unscrupulous biological and sociological trials that had sounded creepy and brutal. But he'd always discounted them as bullshit stories, crap that soldiers told each other over poker games to see if they could get anyone to believe them. Now he wasn't so sure. The idea that he had somehow been put into a virtual environment could explain a lot of what he'd seen.

He checked his link's VR timer. The timer had been designed to track people's time in virtual environments and notify the authorities if the user spent too much time there. It was meant to be a control to keep cyber junkies from dropping out of society, spending all their time in fantasy worlds. Joe's timer said he hadn't spent even a minute in a VR today.

The link interface was supposed to be too closely interlaced with the human brain to be replaced by a virtual impostor, but Joe supposed that the UNSF probably had ways around that. For that matter, even a rich civilian could probably get around the timers. Most people of meager means like Joe believed the VR time limits didn't apply to the super rich and powerful.

Joe took a deep breath and decided to keep trying to find the exit, real or not. Even if the exit moved around, he couldn't find it by just remaining stationary. As best as he could tell, he never saw anything changing while he watched.

Up ahead, Joe saw another sphere of plants. He walked up slowly. This time the anomaly dominated the center of the corridor. It was the same size as the previous one. He approached slowly. An orange creature crawled amid the foliage.

"What the hell?" Joe asked himself.

He looked at the creature. Was it the same one?

"Time for a little experiment," he announced to himself.

Joe opened his pack and searched through it. He brought out a tin of food and opened it up. Working carefully, he held the tin over the orange creature as it crawled about. He dumped some of the soup out onto the shell of the small thing. Part of the back of its carapace was dark with the liquid, and a few chunks of vegetables stuck onto its back. Then Joe walked around to the far side of the sphere and set the tin onto the floor.

"If I see you again, I'll recognize you," Joe said to the creature. It continued to crawl around the edge of the vegetation, looking for shelter. Joe turned back the way he had come, leaving the crab-thing and his tin of soup behind.

He made a point of keeping the wall on his right and followed the corridors carefully, without opening any doors. After moving through three or four connecting hallways, he turned back and retraced his steps. The hallways had remained stable, although he swore that some of the doors had already disappeared.

When he came back to the corridor where the sphere had been, he saw that the room had changed. The little section of plants was gone. He started opening doors and searching around. He didn't have any luck at first, but he kept trying, swinging back and forth and rapidly checking hallways and rooms.

At last Joe came across a small area of plants again. They were growing out from under a table in the center of what looked like a mess hall adjoining a large kitchen. Joe ran up and moved the table aside to get a better view. Once again he saw a brightly colored creature crawling around in the plants.

Joe kneeled closer and examined the creature. A dark stain and a smashed carrot chunk marked the side of its armor.

"Aha! You *are* the same one. And somehow your environment follows you around!"

The creature crawled out of the plants and moved toward the wall along the smooth floor. It headed into a corner, turned around, and headed back the other direction.

"It follows you around when I'm not here," Joe corrected himself.

Joe stood up and looked around the dining room. He felt like a bug under a magnifying glass.

"Shit. And mine follows me around too."

Chapter Nine

Telisa opened her eyes. The bar no longer surrounded her. Fear rose in her chest and stirred her heart to a rapid beat. She was lying on a flat spot in an irregular cave with light brown clusters sticking out of the walls. She saw that the clusters were made of reddish blocks with green sticks protruding from them. Some of the blocks glowed as if they were hot, casting weak light on the scene.

Magnus lay just a few feet from her, unmoving. Suddenly an irrational fear, born of a memory from years ago, gripped her.

"Magnus, wake up!" Telisa demanded. "Please, please be alive!"

Magnus started awake. Like her, he stared in surprise at the surroundings.

"How did we...?"

Telisa almost sobbed in relief. He wasn't dead.

"I don't know. I just woke up and we were here, and I thought...I thought it was happening again."

"Then we're back in the lair of whatever killed Jack and Thomas." Magnus cautiously stood up and swung his slug thrower in a slow arc, ready for anything. "What is that shit? It reminds me of something."

"Project blox," Telisa said. "More project blox caves."

"Yeah, it's those green spikes. They remind me of the sticks that hold the project blox together."

Telisa looked at the floor. "Oh my god. Look at the floor, where we were sleeping!"

The floor beneath each of them was perfectly flat. Smooth turquoise tiles were intact in the shape of their prone bodies. Telisa remembered the color and pattern as identical to what had been behind the bar.

"Uh, whatever's going on here is even weirder than I suspected," Magnus said. "Either we got moved here with the tile by some sort of transport mechanism that we didn't feel, or the whole rest of the room melted away."

"I remember that ledge we were on before, and the light in the ceiling was sheared in the middle, like it just melted away."

Magnus nodded. "I bet that's why there aren't any UNSF people here. Their complex is slowly changing into this…whatever it is."

"And the computer network is probably damaged in the same way," Telisa said. "But we didn't get melted or changed or whatever it is."

"What did you mean just now, about it happening again? You mean someone dying?"

Telisa looked away for a moment. "It's…it's dumb, I know, but one time, years ago, a boyfriend and I snuck into some maintenance tunnels to steal some extra VR time. We were at our quotas, but we thought the rules were stupid and he knew a way to hook us in without being charged. We had a good time too, until I jacked out and found that he'd been killed right there next to me in the tunnel, run over by an automated maintenance vehicle."

Magnus absorbed her story for a moment. "I'm sorry to hear that. So it reminded you of that time, waking up next to me just now, and you thought I was dead."

Telisa nodded. "At first, I blamed myself for his death. We had been reckless for sneaking in there and cutting off all our senses to the real world. But a part of me blamed the government and their laws. I couldn't help it. I just thought we would never have had to go there in secret if people were in control of their own lives. I don't think I still hold that grudge, but it was the start of my resistance to the ideology of the world government. And of the rift between me and my father."

Magnus stood up and held out a hand for her. She accepted his boost up to her feet.

"Well, we're both still alive, and I intend to keep us that way. Let's see if we can find any of the regular unmelted place."

Telisa liked the sound of that. Being back in the alien cavern reminded her of what had happened to the others. It had occurred so quickly, with no warning. Telisa feared one of them would explode and die at any second. She had never imagined such an awful feeling before. She took a deep breath and tried to quit shaking.

"Magnus, I just realized. This must be what you went through for months, in the war. Knowing that you could die from an orbital strike at any second, and you wouldn't even know what hit you."

Magnus nodded. "Yes, it's a sinister feeling. But we got used to it. You'd be amazed what people can live with, given time." Magnus took a deep breath. "Although I'd forgotten a little, what it was like."

Telisa realized that his hands were shaking too. "My god, Magnus. Are you having some kind of…you're shaking as much as I am."

Magnus sighed. "It's my neck. I'm really feeling the burns."

"Oh no. We don't have the real medical pack. It was with the others. I have some minor stuff, though." Telisa felt foolish for not offering the first aid earlier. Somehow she had just fallen asleep without thinking to help him.

"There's nothing that can be done," he said.

Telisa broke out a can of artificial skin. Without thinking, she tried her link to read the instructions from the manufacturer, but they didn't come through.

"Damn, I forgot our links are hosed here. I guess I'll have to do this the old-fashioned way." Telisa brought out the plastic packaging and searched for written instructions.

"Says here there's an embedded analgesic," she said.

"Sounds good. Just spray some on and let's get going," Magnus suggested.

Telisa applied the spray over Magnus' angry red skin. The weeping burns had bled in spots, forming scabs. The artificial skin covered it with a smooth protective layer.

Magnus sighed. "Thanks."

"I'd say we should go back and get the pack...if I knew where that was," Telisa said.

"Yeah. Let's just keep looking for the exit."

Magnus led the way into an adjoining cavern. It seemed like just another gloomy cave until Telisa noticed brighter light coming from another tunnel. She saw what looked like a human-built set of metal cabinets in the distance.

"Look, there's a part of the human complex," Telisa said. They moved over into the next cavern. One side of the area was a normal-looking locker room, with about a dozen lockers against the far wall, and a door. Half the floor was natural stone and the other half was bathroom tile.

"Just like before," Telisa said.

"And the other side is safer, unless it was coincidence that we were attacked when we came upon the caverns before," Magnus said.

"Well, safer or not, I'd rather wander through the old installation part. These caves are too dark."

"The spot we came in from is in that part too."

"Unless it melted away to become a cave."

"If we search the whole complex and don't find a way out, then we can check the caves."

"Okay. This is just another storage room or maybe the gym lockers," Telisa said. "I hope we're about to stumble across the exit."

Magnus shrugged. "The place must be enormous. I tried the computer again, but it's still almost useless."

Telisa came to the other door and opened it slowly, holding her stunner out before her.

"It's another corridor," she said quietly. "Doesn't look familiar."

Telisa went out into the hallway. Magnus came out and closed the door. The corridor was lit from above like the others they had seen. There were three doors within sight, so they advanced to the next door on their left. Magnus opened the door, sticking the end of his slug thrower through first.

"It's an office," he said.

They moved into the room. A hardcopy machine sat next to a data-store system, the standard arrangement for creating a permanent store for sensitive information. Most people worked from home, manipulated electronically stored files, and attended virtual meetings, but there was still an occasional need to create and store real paper documents.

"Let's take a look at some of the files," suggested Telisa. "I want to know what they did here, and where they all went."

"Good idea," Magnus said. He moved up to the file store and tried to open one of the containers. It resisted him at first, but he overcame the latch with a few well-placed strikes from the butt of his slug thrower.

They slipped out several files and examined them. They each read in silence for a few moments, shuffling through several pages.

"This is bullshit. This whole report is nonsense," Telisa said. "Listen to this." Telisa read aloud:

"The elevated levels of nitrite are contributing to the advanced age of all three samples. If Algeria is unable to comply by the end of the second time span, then countermeasure two will be adopted. We predict that all the aforementioned hurricanes will reach class three within five weeks of their inception. Please take all necessary vitamins."

Magnus frowned and kept leafing through the folder he held.

"They're all like that," Magnus said. He threw down some letters. "This is all just a bunch of fakes. This whole office is an elaborate fake."

Telisa sat down in a plush chair. In a cursory examination this looked like an ordinary hardcopy storage office. But it wasn't. Someone had gone to a lot of trouble to create this illusion that simply didn't hold up under close examination.

"So the next question is, is the whole complex a fake, or just this office?" Telisa asked.

"That's a great question," Magnus said. "We've been so busy just trying to find artifacts or survive attacks that we haven't really been looking at things all that closely. I passed dozens of lockers, shelves, boxes, all kinds of stuff, but I didn't stop to look inside because I assumed anything valuable would be in a lab or a vault."

Telisa stood back up. "Well, let's go find out."

"Okay." Magnus turned toward the door. "You know what? The computer system is either broken or a sham too. It sort of works, just a little bit, but it starts to fail if you really try to make use of it."

"Like to find the exit, for instance."

"Yes. Exactly."

"Well, we passed some lockers just a couple of rooms back; let's go look in those."

Magnus readied his weapon and opened the door. He looked out into the hallway and slowly stepped out. Telisa followed him, feeling exposed again. She had briefly forgotten their extreme danger while they had been in the office.

Magnus strode back the way they had come and opened the door through which they had entered. He stepped into the room and Telisa moved in with him.

"Something's screwed up," Magnus said. "I've really been paying attention because I didn't want to get turned around again like when we were attacked. But this room is different."

Telisa looked around. The room was bigger than before, and instead of a wall of lockers, there were squat shelves against the wall.

"I don't get it. We just walked out that door and took the next door on the left to get to the office. This has to be the way back."

Magnus sighed. "I'm beginning to think that this place changes. This is the third time something weird has happened. The first time I thought we just got turned around because of the attack. Then the bar was gone, but it looked like it just…melted or something, like the caves were eating away at the installation. But now, the installation isn't melting or turning into a cave, but the room has changed."

Telisa snapped her fingers.

"This reminds me of a VR," Telisa said. "Maybe this isn't real. Magnus, tell me now if we're on the ship, and this is some kind of test you guys are putting me through." Telisa watched Magnus carefully. The idea made sense. They wanted to see how she would act, and it was all just a test.

"I promise this is no VR, unless I don't know about it either. We haven't linked into anything. There's no way we could have been linked into a VR without our knowledge. At least not without…well, without technology way beyond anything we know about."

"We could have been hooked into a VR when we entered. The black field we passed might have knocked us out, allowed someone else to hook us up to a VR system."

"No, I came back to get the rest of you, remember? It didn't knock me out."

"So we might be in a Trilisk virtual environment," Telisa said.

"That's a good starting theory, but there are problems with that too," Magnus said. "Why would it work on non-Trilisks? You couldn't build a VR that would work on alien brains, without their linking in through an established interface, without any knowledge of their physiology."

Telisa considered that. Magnus was right. The theory sounded perfect at first, but it didn't hold up.

"We've got to keep thinking. We'll hit on it," she said. "The Trilisks were amazingly advanced. Maybe they did build a VR that could accept alien minds, just link them in without them even noticing it."

"Possible. Hard to believe but possible, I guess. But that's not the only problem we need to solve fast," he replied. "If we run into whatever-it-was again, we could be dead before we have a chance."

"Assuming dead is really dead, not just virtually dead," Telisa said.

Magnus shrugged. "I'm going to assume that dead is dead, until we prove that this isn't real. It'd be a major bummer to make that assumption and find out that we were wrong."

"Yeah, a major bummer," Telisa agreed.

Michael McCloskey

Chapter Ten

Kirizzo flashed through room after room at high speed. His attention played across the caverns briefly, always returning to a small cube cluster he carried with him. The cluster relayed the image of a room directly into one of his brains. It was the only thing that protected his hoard of collected parts.

There. Kirizzo detected just the piece he sought. The complex had finally provided it for him as it generated the faux environment. He approached the bank of cubes embedded in the wall and removed what he needed. With this piece, he would be able to complete another sensor station.

The golden, many-legged alien twitched slightly as he worked over his prize. The spasm originated from his ordeal with the Bel Klaven war machines that had chased him into the complex. Many cycles had passed since that memory had been imprinted.

Kirizzo had gone through the dark entrance and fled through familiar caverns. The machines had followed after him, relentless. A deadly game of cat and mouse had ensued. Hunters and hunted had several short, brutal encounters. Each time Kirizzo narrowly escaped with his life. One of the particularly nasty episodes had resulted in a bit of nerve damage on his right rear side.

The Bel Klaven constructs created symmetrical empty spaces in the complex of staggering geometrical complexity. Kirizzo supposed that the pseudo-intelligent machines didn't have thoughts and memories that translated well to the mechanism that created environments inside the Trilisk installation.

Slowly Kirizzo had obtained clues as to how the place worked and started to adapt himself. But the Bel Klaven machines wouldn't significantly alter their behavior. They remained inflexible. Kirizzo had been able to trick and defeat the enemies by using the properties of the complex against them. He lured the machines into areas where he had a defensive advantage, collected supplies from the environments produced by the complex, and even made clever traps that would confuse the enemy and render them vulnerable.

One by one the machines died, until finally one day Kirizzo found himself alone. Only then had he had time to select another primary goal: escape.

Ever practical, Kirizzo did not dwell on his injury but instead channeled his irritation at the twitch to increase his motivation. Once home, the nerve damage could be repaired. He would stick to the plan, a plan which included escape and eventual rejuvenation. Lamenting the damage would not help to correct it.

Once Kirizzo retrieved the valuable component, he headed back to his cache, the room he monitored through his remote sensor cluster. He reached the room after a minute or two, encountering tunnels and caves that looked different than the ones he had taken on the way out. It was a cavern that Kirizzo had hollowed out to be much larger than the ones the complex typically generated.

A mound of sophisticated cube clusters sat in the center, stacked together in an intricate pattern. They held the possibility of escape from the trap of the installation. Each cluster of cubes could encode its surroundings into a data stream and transmit the data back to one of Kirizzo's brains where he could monitor it. Those clusters were Kirizzo's only way of expanding his sphere of control and stabilizing the environment well beyond the range of his natural senses.

Kirizzo pondered the visitors, aliens who shared his little prison with him. They unknowingly helped his cause by pinning down extra sections of the facility, but at the same time they threatened all his work. If they continued to be hostile, they might destroy the stations if they discovered them. They had no reason to, but they might destroy them out of ignorance, fueled by raw aggression. Kirizzo knew very little about their behavioral range. He considered strategies for protecting his investment.

He could continue to guard the devices for the time being, although when he tried to deploy them they would be dispersed too widely for him to protect. Besides, most of his attention would be needed to watch the data and keep the stations from being subsumed by the installation. He could detach some of his personal defense modules and assign them to individual stations, but each one of the precious spheres that he went without increased his own chances of being killed by the next projectile that came his way.

Kirizzo embarked on a calculated risk. He set one of the monitors aside and activated it. The data flowed into his mind, allowing him to see himself and the clusters in the superfluous sensory channel. He gathered up the other devices in his many limbs and proceeded through the caverns ahead. He moved slowly, keeping the view from his device under intense scrutiny. As long as Kirizzo monitored it, the room he left behind would be stable.

Kirizzo picked his way painstakingly along, always watching the streams from his observer modules and slowly moving forward to place another. Kirizzo was placing his fourth module when he noticed that an alien had wandered into one of the rooms monitored by a sensor station. He watched it through the sensor cluster, concerned that they might recognize the equipment and damage it.

As the Gorgala monitored the intrusion, he considered exterminating the aliens. This sounded promising on the surface, but might be shortsighted. If Kirizzo couldn't overcome the base on his own, they might be needed. Like any living creature, they stabilized areas of the installation, drawing on the facility's power supply. In essence, they made Kirizzo's task easier. He decided to risk leaving them alive. He hoped that they would stay away now that he had shown his ability to defend himself with lethal force if necessary on two separate occasions. If the things were truly intelligent, surely they would now give him a wide berth.

After a few moments the aliens moved on, apparently oblivious to his devices. To the slow, sparsely limbed creatures, his modules were probably almost indistinguishable from the other items in the caverns. Kirizzo returned to his task of placing and monitoring the sensors.

As Kirizzo placed the seventh module, he began to feel the mental strain of monitoring so many different places at once. He placed an eighth and hesitated, seeing that the cavern wall around his fourth had wavered and changed shape when he neglected to watch it for a few seconds. His consciousness arose as an amalgam of all the processes of the nerve clusters along his central nervous cord. As they became loaded with other work, his concentration suffered, which caused the sub-tasks to become forgotten as his primitive mind took over, seizing control of the nerve bundles to re-establish itself.

He crawled away. If he could distance himself from the eighth module, then the volume of stable space would increase further. This would in turn draw more power from the installation's power supply, hopefully overloading it.

By the time Kirizzo had made his way beyond the range of the eighth module, he realized he had lost the third module altogether. It had gone unobserved for too long, and the room had been reclaimed. His third observation module was gone.

The plan of escape was not going to work.

Kirizzo guessed that he could not watch enough different locations simultaneously to overload the generators. This was not too surprising considering the immense power source that he had detected here. Nevertheless he stood still for the next couple of hours, watching the data. He might be draining a reserve even now. He could be seconds away from seeing a failure, he kept telling himself.

Or this could be futile.

He turned and retrieved the modules one by one, still watching them constantly so he wouldn't lose another. The operation was as slow and tedious as the deployment had been. Kirizzo did not falter, and he succeeded in retrieving all the remaining cubic monitor modules.

He had worked so long on this plan of escape. Kirizzo's kind did not know depression, but an analog of impatience was building to almost painful levels in him. How best to escape the complex?

Kirizzo's thoughts returned to the others that he had detected in the mazelike installation. Presumably they were adding some load to the system. Their senses seemed inferior to his own, but stable bubbles continued to follow them through the maze. Unfortunately they tended to group together, keeping their area of influence overlapped. If they would spread out, that would also help to consume the installation's energy. He wondered if the aliens had deduced the workings of their surroundings yet. Might they also pursue a plan of escape as he had? Would their plan be compatible with his own?

How could he get the others to split up? Kirizzo saw that despite his superior standing, he would need to seek the aid of the other entities trapped with him. If he could ally with them, they might not destroy the painstakingly crafted observation stations, and they could spread out to increase the load. Kirizzo didn't know about their sensory capacity, but each of them might also be able to stabilize several other locations remotely as he had.

However, given the alien's reactions to him thus far, it might be difficult to come to an understanding. Still, it had to be tried. Kirizzo was running out of ideas.

His planning stage ended abruptly, and he bolted into action. Activating one of the modules and leaving it on next to the others, he detached a single defense orb and ordered it to guard the cache. Then he moved away, observing his valuable modules through the single activated one to make sure the installation did not reclaim it. Kirizzo's many legs whirred rapidly, moving him down a twisting rock passage.

It shouldn't take long to find some of the others, he decided.

Michael McCloskey

Chapter Eleven

Magnus and Telisa finished up a snack while sitting in luxurious overstuffed chairs that they had found in a lounge or waiting room. They ate from their packs, since they trusted their own food more than anything they might find in the complex. Some weird form of elevator music played in the background. Telisa found the notes vaguely familiar but could not associate them with any particular song.

"Let's keep going," Magnus said, standing up. "Even if the surroundings change, we might be able to find an exit that just randomly appears somewhere."

"Okay."

Telisa organized her pack and rose to join him. Magnus prepared his slug thrower and opened the door. It opened into a cave.

"Shit," he said. He closed the door and exchanged looks with Telisa.

"The cave? We've been surrounded by a cave while we ate?" Telisa's voice conveyed deep dismay. The caves with those funny blocks made her nervous, as they forced her to think about the death of Jack and Thomas.

"Sometimes I think the cave part is taking over. But we always find more of the regular human complex," she said.

"It makes me think it's a trap," Magnus said. "But there's no choice. Let's go."

They each held weapons ready when Magnus opened the door again. He hesitated, looking out into the caves beyond and letting his eyes get used to the light.

"There's something there," he said.

Telisa moved slowly, stepping to one side and peering over Magnus's shoulder. Some kind of shiny thing stood in the center of the large cave beyond the door. She thought it was some kind of complicated structure made of metal.

"Is it a machine?"

Magnus stood staring straight at it for a few more seconds. "I think it moved just a little," he said. He slowly opened the door all the way so that light from the lounge came out into the redly luminous cave. Telisa gasped when she saw that the thing was golden, a complex creature with many legs that stood as tall as her chest but at least twice as long.

"Amazing," she breathed, almost afraid to make noise. "It's…amazing." She committed the image to her link memory.

Magnus was taut and stiff. He slowly took a step forward, bending low on his knees and keeping his slug thrower pointed at the thing.

"It has some kind of machinery on its back," he said. "There are…things floating around it, hanging in the air."

Telisa struggled to catch sight of what Magnus was talking about. After a moment she noticed something: a small dark sphere, moving lazily near the front of the creature. As far as Telisa could see, there was nothing attaching it to the thing's body.

"I hope it isn't dangerous," Telisa said, keeping her voice low.

"If it's what killed Jack and Thomas, it could have killed us by now. It's just sitting there, though."

As Telisa's eyes adapted further to the low red light, she could see more details of the thing before them.

"Uhhh. It's so…well, alien."

The creature shone as if covered in gold plating. It had many long thin legs, at least a dozen on each side of its body. The thin central trunk tapered to a sharp point that arced down toward the ground on the far side. It reminded Telisa of a sharp beak, and she wondered if it could be used as a weapon. The other end of the flexible body came up into a round knob a little smaller than a human head. The protrusion was mostly featureless except for what looked like hundreds of bean sprouts gathered underneath it. The top knobby part moved back and forth slowly. One of the many legs in the back twitched a little.

Telisa saw that the top of the long trunk had small silver knobs and rods across it, and a silver coating covered the predominant gold color across parts of the trunk with holes for the legs to protrude. She suspected the silver parts might be its clothes or equipment, because their knobs and rods looked more regular than the smooth curves of its golden parts. When the body flexed, the rods stayed straight. She stored another two images of the creature away in her link in case she needed them later.

"I can't tell anything about it. Are there eyes, ears, anything? I don't even see a mouth," Telisa said.

"You got me there," Magnus said. "Another important question is: is this a Trilisk? Is it native to this planet? Does it have anything to do with whoever or whatever killed Jack and Thomas?"

Telisa took a deep breath and tried to relax. "Okay, maybe you keep covering it and I'll try to communicate."

"Okay. Good luck," Magnus said neutrally.

Telisa lowered her stunner and took a slow step forward. The thing was shifting quite often, as if excited or impatient. Telisa had no way of knowing if she could make any assumptions about that or not. Instead she just attached her stunner to her belt and held out her hand.

"Hello. I am Telisa," she said loudly. Telisa felt immensely silly, but the enormity of facing a living alien kept her focused.

The alien kept its feet planted but it fidgeted again. Telisa watched it carefully. The knob where its head should be was bobbing back and forth in a smooth and repetitive fashion, but there didn't seem to be a reaction to her greeting.

Telisa pointed at herself. "Telisa," she said.

Suddenly the creature began rhythmically lifting and dropping its legs in a complex pattern. Telisa whimpered in fear but quickly regained her composure. She glanced at Magnus. He lifted his eyebrows and shook his head.

"Is that how you talk?" she said. The alien gave no visible reaction.

She stamped her foot. The creature stamped its front foot on the opposite side, mimicking her.

"We're doomed. I don't even know if it can hear me," Telisa said.

"Maybe it isn't intelligent," Magnus said. He was still keeping his slug thrower aimed at the creature, although he was standing straighter now.

"It almost has to be. It was waiting here for us, and there's that machinery on its back."

"Dogs can be told to guard doors. And they can wear collars with electronics or have links in their brains."

Telisa looked back at the alien thing again. "Well, it's possible. But I get the feeling it's smart. It responded to me, a little bit. You know, with no eyes or ears…it probably can't hear us."

"It senses us somehow," Magnus said, strolling to one side. The knob on the front end of the creature kept waving side to side, although it seemed to center more on Magnus as he moved. After a moment it pointed back toward Telisa.

"So assuming it is intelligent, should we try and get it to follow us?"

"You want to go look for human corridors again?"

"Well, this place is dark, and these glowing blocks are creepy."

"To us they are. This thing might live here, in this part of the tunnels. Still, it's worth a try. Let's move away slightly and see if it follows us."

Telisa faced the thing again. She waved her hand through the air, motioning for the alien to follow. "Come this way," she said slowly.

They took a few tentative steps to their right, toward an opening in the stone wall.

The creature waved its front right arm, the thin appendage mimicking Telisa's arm wave. Then it advanced slowly.

"Its arms each have three stubby fingers or pinchers," Telisa said.

"We can examine it more closely when we find the human corridors again," Magnus said.

"Yes, you're right," Telisa said. She followed Magnus into an adjoining cavern, looking back frequently to make sure the thing was following them. It kept a distance of two or three meters but seemed to be content to let them lead through the caverns.

They moved through several more caverns, but no human constructs were apparent.

"Let's try another direction. We must be deeper into the caves than last time."

"Remember it all shifts around," Telisa said. "The human part could be gone."

Magnus shook his head as if he didn't want to consider that possibility. They shifted directions and traveled for several more minutes, but failed to find any human-friendly areas.

"We're really lost this time," Magnus said. "I don't sense any links in range except yours."

Telisa realized that the thing was waving its arm at her. It made the motion twice and then took several intricate steps away, its many legs working rapidly.

"Looks like it's our turn to follow," Telisa said. "If we can't find the human complex anyway, I suppose we have nothing to lose."

Magnus nodded. "Okay. Maybe it knows the way to someplace interesting." His face brightened. "Actually, maybe it knows the way out of this place!"

"I hope you're right!" Telisa said.

Magnus and Telisa followed the alien. They had begun to relax in its presence, gaining confidence that it meant them no harm.

The creature moved slowly at first and then darted forward. It stopped to wait but didn't turn around.

"It knows we're back here, and it isn't pointing that thing that looks like its head back toward us," Telisa said.

Magnus nodded. "It can sense us, I don't know how. I think maybe it wants us to move faster. Should we try and run?"

"It might be dangerous...let's try moving a little faster since it seems to be urging us on."

Telisa and Magnus broke into a light jog, following the alien. It picked up its pace accordingly, its legs moving at blinding speed. It still easily outdistanced them but always waited at intersections in the caverns to guide them. Finally they jogged into a particularly large cavern, and the thing was waiting for them in the center next to a tremendous stack of the beige blocks. Some of them glowed steadily. Most of them had one or more of the protruding green spikes.

"This is the largest cavern by far," Magnus said.

Telisa stared at the objects in the center. Stacked on the floor, they rose as high as her head. For the first time, Telisa noticed some warmth emanating from the glowing ones.

Magnus was also examining the clusters in the center. "There's some other metal in here too. See the silver parts?"

Telisa nodded. She examined the pile closely and realized that many of the clusters were arranged in repeating patterns. "Look, there are several identical clusters here. Actually, it looks like most of this stack is the same thing replicated over and over."

"That warmth…we may be in trouble," Magnus said. "If there is radiant heat, there might be radiation in other wavelengths too. It could be dangerous. Friggin' radioactive alien project blox."

Telisa looked at the pile and stepped back. The alien was waiting nearby.

"I guess that might be true. If this creature is more resistant to radiation than we are, it could be dangerous here."

Magnus and Telisa backed off to the outer wall of the cavern. The golden creature didn't move after them, but after a moment it moved up to the stack and manipulated one of the clusters.

"What could it be doing?" Telisa asked.

"Look at the cluster it's holding," Magnus said. "It's glowing brighter than the others."

Telisa saw that the object did get brighter, but then it dimmed to the level of the rest of the cube clusters. Then the alien set it back down with the others.

"This is gonna drive me nuts if we don't figure out how to communicate," Telisa said. "Whatever those things are, they aren't Trilisk artifacts. The fact that this thing—Shiny or whatever we should call it— is using them makes me suspect that they are devices of its race. So this probably isn't a Trilisk."

Magnus shrugged. "It's too hard to say. It could be using these things just like we use some alien artifacts. Maybe it has figured out how to use them."

The creature came back toward them and stopped about two meters away. It moved its legs rapidly in place in complex patterns.

"We're in deep trouble on the speech part all right," Magnus said. "It's looking more and more like you said at first, that's how Shiny talks. He stomps his feet. And he's using complicated patterns of all those legs…so many combinations that we'll never follow."

"Yes, that's gonna be hard to learn, considering that we have two feet and he has…forty! Forty exactly."

"I wonder if it's the vibration of his feet hitting the ground that he senses. It would be either that or sight, and I don't see any eyes."

Telisa shook her head. "He could see through his skin for all we know. Let's do some tests and see if we can find out."

Telisa took her arm and slowly waved it over her head. Shiny copied her move, his body flexing beneath the silvery coating.

"How can we tell how he senses it?" Magnus asked.

"Keep watching him, we'll learn what we can," Telisa told him. She walked around to the other side of Shiny. The alien didn't move much, shifting its legs a little. Telisa waved her arm again. Once again, Shiny waved its arm.

"Well, it still notices, even though you're behind it," Magnus said.

Telisa walked about twenty paces farther back, still on the other side of Shiny. She waved her arm again, and Shiny matched it.

Telisa thought for a moment. "Wait here. Tell me if he does anything," Telisa said. She walked around to the far side of the large cluster of cubes and waved her arm.

"He's waving his arm," Magnus said, his voice distant. Telisa walked back around.

"He can tell I'm waving my arm on the other side of that," she said.

Magnus shook his head. "Maybe he can hear, I mean maybe he can hear so well that he can hear us move limbs through the air."

"Or maybe he can see through stuff we can't," said Telisa.

Telisa noticed Magnus had started pointing his rifle back at Shiny again. He had a frown on his face.

"Magnus, what's wrong?"

Magnus shifted uncomfortably. "This reminds me, Telisa. After Jack and Thomas were killed. Remember, we were in that corridor and the wall exploded right next to me from some kind of projectile hitting the other side. I'm pretty sure whoever killed Jack and Thomas could sense through rock too."

Chapter Twelve

Magnus and Telisa sat down against the rock wall of the large chamber while the alien worked with the cube devices piled in the center of the cave. The creature worked rapidly, its limbs moving almost faster than Telisa could follow. She saw that each of its legs ended in three stiff, pointy toes that were equidistant from each other around the perimeter of each foot. Each foot reminded her of a three-way crab pincher.

"Do you think he's trapped here just like us?" Telisa pondered aloud.

Magnus grunted. "Maybe. Probably."

"He must have brought a lot of equipment with him."

"Or he collected it. We should probably start doing that ourselves. If everything shifts all the time, we should search every room for food and supplies and take it with us."

"So maybe this is his hoard of stuff that he's collected," Telisa thought out loud. "But how does he keep it from going away when he's gone?"

Magnus blinked. "I never thought of that. That's a great question. Maybe the corridors change but the caves don't...or maybe he is a Trilisk after all."

"Or he may have learned how to tell what's going to change when."

Shiny abruptly stopped and waved the head-like bulb on the front of his body.

"He seems to be acting differently," Telisa said.

"I wish I knew if that was its head," Magnus said. "I mean, I wonder if its brain is in there."

Suddenly Telisa caught a glimpse of movement at the nearest adjoining tunnel mouth. She gasped as she realized a human stood at the entrance looking at them.

The person stepped closer, coming into a patch of reddish light so that Telisa could see a man dressed in a UNSF officer's uniform.

"Shit," Telisa whispered. She realized that the newcomer held a deadly-looking pistol in his hand, pointing it right at them. She glanced at Magnus and saw that he was covering the man in turn with his own weapon, his finger resting on the trigger.

The UNSF man spoke.

"No one move. Tell me what's going on here. What is that thing?"

"We don't really know what it is," Magnus said. "It's intelligent, though."

"We call it Shiny," Telisa added. "There's no need for the weapon." Telisa's heart thumped against her ribcage. She feared that a gunfight would break out, and more people would end up dead.

"Put the weapon down," the man commanded.

"No," Magnus said.

"There's no point in us shooting each other," Telisa said.

The officer stared back at Telisa and Magnus. Then he took a long look at the alien. Shiny seemed content to stand idle while the humans talked.

"I'll make you a deal. Tell me how to get out of this place, and I'll forget that you were ever here," he said.

"We don't have any idea," Telisa said. "Everything changes around here."

"What about him? Shiny?"

"We're just trying to communicate with him…or it, I mean," Telisa said. "Look, let's cooperate. I don't know who you are, or how you got here, but I bet we all have the same problem."

"Eminently reasonable," the officer said. "But I don't trust you. How did you get here?"

Magnus and Telisa exchanged looks. "We're here illegally," he said. "I'm Mark and this is Tam."

"I'm Lieutenant Joe Hartlet, UNSF," he announced. "As you've probably guessed, my job is to arrest you. But I meant what I said before. If you know how to get me out, I'm willing to forget about you. I need to tell the UNSF that this complex and this alien are here. It's possibly one of the greatest discoveries we've ever made. That's all I care about now."

"The alien may not be real," Telisa said. "None of it may be real. Hell, you may not be real."

Joe nodded. "This place may be virtual. I don't know how, but it might be possible. But it's a weird kind of virtual. Different things bring their environment with them and interact here."

"What do you mean?" Magnus asked.

"Well, this place doesn't just happen to look like a human-built complex. It looks that way because we're here. I accidentally brought in an orange crab-thing from the surface, and when I encountered it again later, it was surrounded by a little sphere of dirt and native plants, just as if it were up above. Then there's these caves. I figure that they must be this guy's usual habitat."

"Caves? I'm not sure," Telisa said, looking at the alien. "I think it's an advanced creature, capable of using technology and communicating. Wouldn't it live in a constructed environment like we do?"

Joe shrugged. "Who knows?"

"The cubes aren't natural though," Magnus pointed out. "It uses them to create devices of some kind. So maybe this is the kind of surroundings it's used to."

"So what you're saying is that this isn't a UNSF installation?" Telisa asked. "This place just made all the human areas up?"

"If it's UNSF, then it's a secret I wasn't let in on," Joe said. "It probably isn't UNSF since the technology required is beyond our current capability, unless it is virtual and we're being used as guinea pigs…" Joe stopped for a moment, as if considering the possibility. "My theory is it's Trilisk, and as I said, any creature that enters this area is surrounded by an environment that it's used to. Like a holding pen for aliens, or for all I know, some kind of Trilisk hotel for varied lifeforms."

"We aren't used to this," Telisa said, indicating the surrounding cave.

"I was wondering about that too," Joe said. "Sometimes you get something like your own environment. In our case corridors and rooms of all sorts. Sometimes you don't. The crab I saw was in its own habitat when I spotted it, but then it crawled out onto the tile floor as I watched. The area didn't follow it when I was there."

Magnus had been listening, but now he spoke up. "So it makes sense to suppose that the caves, with these red cubes, are what Shiny is used to. I'd like to find some corridors and try and lure Shiny into them, just to prove that he can end up out of his environment. We went looking earlier for the human part of the area but couldn't find it."

"I came from an area that looked like a university or something, made by humans, straight back about forty meters," Joe said.

"Well, we couldn't find it. It's probably gone by now," Magnus said.

"I think I figured this out," Telisa said. "This place is like first come, first served."

"How's that?" asked Joe.

"If we're someplace, it becomes like a human complex, like when we entered. But if we come across an area Shiny is in, then it stays like he likes it. That's why one human corridor seemed to join the caves so abruptly. But once the area moves out of sensory range again, it can be anything."

"And the crab was surrounded by its own environment until I came along and trapped it in a human area?" Joe asked.

"Yes. Your senses can go farther than the crab's. You surrounded it with your own type of environment."

Magnus shrugged. "It's as good a theory as any, I suppose."

Telisa wasn't done. She continued excitedly.

"It gets better. This theory explains why we can't find any corridors now. Shiny is the problem. He's trapped us. Joe, Shiny can see through walls."

Joe blinked. "He can?"

"Yes. We proved it to ourselves earlier. Somehow he can sense through dense matter or around it. So he forms caves as we move around, beyond our range of sight and sound. He traps us in the caves just like you walked up and trapped the crab in a human corridor."

Magnus nodded. "That does sound like it all fits."

Joe scratched his head, allowing himself to lower his rifle. "Very well. I like that theory too. It should be simple to test. You two stay here with Shiny, and I'll walk away through the caves. If it works, I'll eventually move beyond his range and run into some human rooms or corridors."

Telisa shrugged. "Sounds okay to me. I hope his 'range' isn't too far."

"It's worth a try, but that doesn't explain what you mentioned earlier about how Shiny keeps his hoard here from disappearing whenever he goes for a walk," Magnus said.

Telisa nodded. "Let's try this experiment first, then we'll try and tackle that mystery."

Joe looked at the other two humans for a second. "Well, since I'm already used to making my way around on my own, I guess I'll go look for the corridors. I realize that you two may run away while I'm gone, but I really do just need to escape, so I give you my word you're in no danger from me. We'll have a better chance of escaping if we keep sharing information and work together."

Telisa nodded, trying to encourage Joe. Magnus gave no reaction.

"Okay, be back in a while," Joe said and walked back out the way he came.

"Well, what do you think? Is he our friend or our enemy?" Telisa asked.

"I think it's more complicated than that. Should we trust him? Almost certainly no. But still, we may have to work with him to get out of here. I think we should just stay calm and cooperate with him, but if we get out of here, the situation may degenerate back into a fight between us."

"The most important thing is communicating with Shiny, I think. We can still try and learn more about the complex, of course, but it seems that Shiny understands it better than we do."

"I agree. But I'm also tired. I don't know how long we slept before, but I feel like I've been up forever."

Telisa realized that fatigue gripped her as well. "I guess it's just hard to think about sleep with so much going on. I do feel tired."

"Sleep may be a problem with Joe around. Should we rotate our sleep so one of us is always awake?"

"No. I'll hide my stunner somewhere he can't snatch it while I'm asleep. If he takes your weapon, then I'll get him later. Besides, you have a lot more weapons than that thing on you."

Magnus smiled. "So true. And this strap will make the slugthrower hard to snatch quickly. I can also disable it with my link."

"Oh yeah. My stunner has that feature too. I forgot about it."

Joe returned from the same entrance as before, walking slowly.

"I found Terran-style rooms about fifty meters in that direction," Joe said, indicating his exit point. "Of course, they looked different than anything I've seen so far. Things are still changing around behind our backs, I suspect."

"So it probably was Shiny, since he was walking with us," Telisa said.

"Have you talked with it?" Joe asked.

"The only thing we've really managed is wave your arm for 'follow me,'" Telisa said, demonstrating with her arm.

"Look. We have to sleep. We've been up for a long time now," Magnus said.

"Go ahead. I slept just a few hours ago. I'll stay up and watch him."

"Don't come over near us. I'm sleeping with my weapon, and I intend to keep it," Magnus said. "I don't harbor any ill will toward you. I just want to escape."

Joe nodded. "You do the same when I go to take a nap," Joe said. "I give you my word I won't disturb you."

Telisa and Magnus curled up against a wall and prepared to sleep. Joe walked over closer to Shiny and watched the alien attentively. Shiny had quit watching the humans and was working with the cubes again. Telisa wondered what he was doing with the complex items and thought that she should examine them, since they must be artifacts like she had come to find. That was her last thought before sleep claimed her.

Magnus awakened hours later, uncertainly rising and checking his equipment. It didn't seem that anyone had interfered with his things. He checked his clip just to be sure. Everything seemed to be in order.

"Time to get up?" Telisa asked sleepily. Magnus's fiddling had brought her to consciousness.

Joe saw that the two were starting to rise and walked over a little closer to their sleeping area.

"Anything happen while we were asleep?" Telisa asked.

"Not much. I've been trying to communicate," Joe replied. "I've figured out that he says 'yes' by lifting his first right arm and 'no' by lifting his front left arm. Past that part, it starts to bog down."

"Progress is progress," she said. "But we don't have many days of food left."

"Food is no problem," Joe said. "I've found food and water here. There was a vending kiosk with phony product names, but I broke into it and the food was real enough. Also, there were water spigots in a chemistry lab I went through."

"That might do if we have no other choice," Magnus said. "But if the food is as phony as the reports in the office, we're in deep trouble."

Joe grunted. "I didn't get that far. The reports are phony how?"

"They're full of gibberish. Well, each sentence has good syntax, but there's no real meaning to any of it," Telisa said.

"Well, let's hope it's hard to screw up water," Joe said.

***

Kirizzo considered the situation. He had managed to round up three of the aliens. In each case, it seemed that violence had been narrowly avoided.

At first he thought they were going to fight amongst themselves. He wasn't sure what the contested resource was, but they were clearly preparing their primitive weapons for some kind of exchange of force. Just as quickly as the competition escalated, they then backed down from it. The species seemed to have mastered the ability to select the optimal path when faced with decisions between eliminating competition and cooperative alliance. For the time being, it seemed they had decided upon alliance. This suited Kirizzo just fine, since he had also decided to pursue an alliance, at least until he managed to escape.

Communication was proving to be problematic. The poor creatures only had four limbs, and their range of expression was sadly limited. So much so, in fact, that it seemed they were forced to use their mandibles as additional encoding sources for informative exchange. Kirizzo had to watch very carefully to even detect the waving mandibles as they were so much shorter and stubbier than his own race's limbs.

Kirizzo considered launching an all-out effort to form some basis for sophisticated information exchange between himself and the aliens. It would be a time-consuming process. He had no doubt that this would eventually result in improved communications, but this layout of time and resources might not prove necessary. He needed only the most basic cooperation from them in order to have another chance at escape. He might be able to show them what was required by simple demonstration. If he could further secure the cooperation of the aliens, then he could stabilize a larger portion of the base than ever before.

Kirizzo contemplated the aliens and their mysterious motives. He wanted to ensure that they had reason to continue to cooperate with him. Perhaps he should somehow make it clear that he was willing to recompense them for their assistance.

On the other hand, if he showed that he was capable of providing things of value to them, he might become more valuable in their eyes, which might re-spark a violent competition amongst them for a monopoly on his offerings. Kirizzo considered this a very valid possibility.

At last he decided that it was worth the risk. He needed their assistance, so he would demonstrate the value of working with him. Then he would communicate what he wanted by establishing a simple spatial demonstration of what was required.

Kirizzo flew into motion, setting things up to create gifts for the aliens.

Michael McCloskey

Chapter Thirteen

The group of humans looked up as Shiny abruptly quit working and approached them. Telisa saw that the creature held many new cubes in the tiny fingers at the ends of many of its legs. The alien sported so many legs that it was able to move fluidly even though it carried the items.

"Look, he's carrying lots of..." Telisa's voice dropped off as Shiny walked up to her and held out one of the devices. It was a long stack of reddish cubes held together with strands of a silvery metal. One end of the thing curved away at an angle and had a hole in it.

"Uh, should I take that?" Telisa asked.

Shiny saw her hesitation and held up another leg toward Joe. The alien held an identical item in its grasp.

"I suppose we should...do we have any reason to refuse?" Joe said. He accepted the device from Shiny and stepped back to examine it.

Telisa took hers next, making sure to point the hole away from her. It reminded her of Magnus's slug thrower and she didn't feel like taking chances.

The alien offered Magnus a device that looked the same as the others. Magnus took the item and examined it.

"Any guesses?" he asked.

"I haven't the faintest clue," Joe answered, turning the collection of cubes over in his hands. "No mechanism, as near as I can see."

Shiny walked over toward the wall. Telisa noticed first.

"Wait, guys. I think a demonstration is coming up!" She darted over beside Shiny, eager to see what he would do next.

"Yup, he's still got one," she said.

Magnus and Joe walked over to join them. Telisa noticed that the two were starting to relax in each other's presence, content to cooperate for the time being.

When everyone assembled nearby, Shiny went back into motion. He placed the flat end of his device against the wall. A slight wind rose, startling Telisa. She heard a whirring sound and saw gray jelly flowing from the hole in the device. Shiny had turned it so the curved end pointed toward the ground to drop the goo onto the cavern floor. The alien waved the device along the wall several times and then ceased, stepping back.

"It put a hole into the wall," Joe pointed out.

Telisa looked from the gray pool on the floor back to the wall. A small hollow about the size of a bowling ball had been excavated from the rock wall.

"They break up rock? What does he want to do, make us into miners?" Magnus asked.

"I dunno," Telisa said.

Joe stepped toward the wall. He selected a spot to the right of Shiny's hole and tried to duplicate the feat. When he placed the thing on the wall, the breeze came up and the soft murmur returned. Joe pulled his device back and Telisa saw a fresh hole in the wall.

"Easy to use," he said.

Meanwhile Shiny had moved back to the center of the room and stood facing them. When Telisa looked, he made the motion they had used earlier for "follow me."

"You guys, he's motioning for us," Telisa said. The humans walked back to the center of the room and collected in a semicircle facing the alien. Shiny reached into the silvery metal machinery on his back with several arms, collecting things from various spots on his body.

"What's up with this?" Joe wondered aloud.

"I don't know. He's trying to communicate something," Telisa said.

"He seems to produce this stuff out of thin air," Magnus said.

"His legs double as arms pretty well; he seem to use them however he wants," Telisa said.

"Maybe he's preparing a math lesson," Joe guessed. "That might help us understand his language."

The creature before them put down a small pile of stones, and set one of them forward on the ground between them. It was a tall intricate shape made of red cubes. Shiny touched the cluster once and then walked over to the center stack of cubes behind it. He touched it once in the same manner.

The humans just watched. No one said anything.

Once again, Shiny touched the small cube on the floor and then the large stack of equipment in the center of the room.

Then the alien put down several other small rock shapes. He placed one in front of himself and one in front of each of the humans. Shiny touched the rock in front of Telisa and then reached out and touched her lightly on the forehead. It was the first time he had made contact with her, and it shocked her.

"That scared me. I wasn't expecting him to touch me," Telisa said.

Shiny repeated the motion for Magnus and then Joe. Joe pointed his pistol at the alien but allowed it to touch him. A small gray sphere darted out from around Shiny's trunk and hovered directly between the alien and the barrel of Joe's weapon.

"Unreal!" Joe exclaimed. He pointed the weapon away.

The sphere moved away so quickly that Telisa couldn't follow where it went. Telisa realized that it was the same size and shape as many of the tiny balls of metal attached along Shiny's back.

"That was wild," Telisa said. "A defense system, I bet!"

"Impressive," Magnus murmured.

Shiny touched the stone in front of him, and then touched the smooth round part of himself that resembled a faceless head.

"These may be us," Magnus said, looking at his stone. "The shapes in front of us have four extensions like limbs, and his has lots of tiny ridges on it like a miniature of himself."

Joe nodded. "I think you're right. And I think the big red thing represents the stack of cubes in the center of the room." Joe reached out and collected his figure and placed it next to the red cube that Shiny had first placed out.

Shiny moved directly between Joe and the cache in the center of the room. Then the alien put its own facsimile between the miniature cube stack and Joe's shape.

"Yes, that's exactly what he's up to," Telisa said. She placed her own miniature on the ground indicating her position, and Magnus followed suit.

Shiny raised his first right arm.

"Yes!" Telisa translated.

Shiny took one of the cubic devices off the stack behind him. He set it on the ground next to him. Reaching into some of the silver covering near his trunk, the alien produced several small blue stones. He touched a blue stone with a pincer-like, three-fingered hand and then touched the thing beside him.

"Those stones represent the device beside him," Joe guessed. Telisa and Magnus nodded.

Shiny reached out and moved his marker to the side. He moved Joe's and Magnus's stones with him. Telisa's marker remained next to the main cache. Shiny placed a very small chip of blue stone at the other spot, next to his marker. Then he moved his marker again, still bringing the other two markers with him. He repeated this until eight of the small blue stones were placed.

"He's going to move around and place those things at different spots," Joe continued.

Then Shiny took Magnus's and Joe's markers. Joe's marker moved to one side and sat by itself. Magnus's marker moved back to the center where Telisa's marker had sat untouched. Then Shiny moved Telisa's marker in the other direction from where Shiny's and Joe's markers had circled. Magnus's marker was moved first to Telisa's stone and then beyond it. The final result was a wide dispersion of all the stones. No single stone remained next to any other.

"Weird," Magnus said.

"That about sums it up," Telisa agreed. "We think we understand what he's saying, but why does he want us to do this?"

"And what do these stone liquefaction tools have to do with it?" asked Joe.

Shiny retrieved all the stones and set them back to their original positions. Then he began again. He went through the same sequence, moving the stones exactly as he had before.

"I think a key clue is the way that Telisa is supposed to stay here until Magnus comes back through to get her," Joe said. "Shiny wants you here until the devices are all spread out."

"For what purpose? To keep the cache from disappearing, perhaps?"

"That's all I can think of. But then why won't it go away when you leave?" asked Magnus.

"Maybe he won't need it anymore, if whatever this is works. I'm wondering about those devices. What will keep them from disappearing?"

"Maybe he can sense them," Telisa said. "Maybe they emit something he can feel like when he sees through walls."

"Are we going to go through with this?" Magnus said.

"What choice do we have?" Telisa asked.

Joe nodded. "I think we should. He seems to understand this place better than we do."

The conversation lulled. Shiny collected the stones and moved through the sequence again.

"He really wants to make sure we know it," Magnus said wryly.

"Well, he has no way to verify that we are paying attention or to know how smart we are."

"We could help him out," Joe said. "When he finishes, I'll duplicate the movements of the stones myself to show him that we understand."

Telisa nodded. She thought that was a great idea. She found herself wishing that Joe was her real friend instead of a UNSF officer. She snuck a peek at him and saw that he kept his hand near the butt of his pistol, but he stood in a relaxed manner and seemed to pay more attention to Shiny than to Magnus and her.

When Shiny finished the next demonstration, Joe stepped forward and crouched down to replace the stones. Then he duplicated the moves. Shiny stood back and watched. Telisa noticed that the alien twitched slightly from time to time as if extremely impatient. Joe finished the sequence and returned to a standing position.

Shiny turned back to the pile behind him and started gathering the devices together. Telisa marveled at the odd way in which the alien seemed to flicker back and forth between inactivity and fervent motion. It was as if the creature stood in place to think and plan and then, like the flip of a switch, executed the plan without further hesitation.

"Just like that? We're going to do what he's demonstrated?" Telisa asked.

Magnus answered first. "I think he knows a way out. Since we don't have a plan of our own, I'm content to spend a day trying out what he wants."

"I agree," said Joe.

Telisa and Magnus went back to retrieve their packs at the edge of the room. As they walked back to rejoin Joe, Shiny finished his preparations and moved to one of the exits, waving his arm to encourage the others to follow.

"Here we go. I'll be back by to pick you up," Magnus said. He walked away to follow Shiny.

"Good luck," Joe said and followed Magnus out.

Left alone, Telisa sat down and awaited Magnus's return.

Chapter Fourteen

Telisa resolved herself to a wait that she estimated at about ten minutes, given the speed with which Shiny buzzed along. Everything had happened so quickly with the alien. Telisa could hardly believe that she had seen a live alien—even spoken with one, if you counted a lifting of its leg to say "yes" or "no."

She still held the small digging device that Shiny had given her. She rolled it in her hand, examining the faintly visible metal lace patterns around and inside the cubes. A real alien artifact. What fascinating things would she learn about Shiny's race by analyzing it? And once she had learned all she could from it, could it be sold? Such a piece might command a hefty price on the black market for alien technology. She could use the money to finance other expeditions.

But first, they would have to escape this place. She listened but didn't hear any sign of Magnus's return. Her gaze settled on Shiny's cache of objects in the center of the large cavern. It looked like a piece of art, made of hundreds of cubes laced together with delicate strands of molten silver. Yet whenever Shiny manipulated it, the cubes seemed almost malleable. Everything turned and glittered at his lightest touch, almost too fast for the eye to follow. What else was in that trove before her?

Telisa wanted to walk over and investigate it, but she realized that it would be dangerous to do that. A wrong move with some unknown device could kill. Or she might somehow disturb Shiny's plan, which she desperately hoped involved escape.

The minutes dragged on. She checked her link chronometer. Ten minutes came and went. Crazy thoughts of a fight in the caves ran through her head. What if Shiny had decided to separate the humans and kill them one by one? Telisa told herself that nothing had happened. She hadn't heard any shots or explosions.

At last Magnus jogged into the cavern.

"Oh, good. I was starting to go paranoid!" Telisa said

"Hi," he said. "Everything's going fine. Let's go this way," he said.

Telisa fell in after him. They moved through to the other side of the large cave and out a tunnel.

"When we separate, how long should I wait?"

"We can talk about that later, over the link," he said. "We should just concentrate on remembering the direction of the cache room. Since this place is unpredictable, we need to pay attention to that so we can find each other again."

Okay, Telisa said over the link. *Just checking to see if it works.*

I hear you, Magnus returned.

They moved for about fifty meters as straight as they could manage through the caves. Directly ahead, Telisa saw a smooth white corridor stretching straight away. Bright lights flooded down onto the passage and out into the caves toward them.

"Okay, you wait here. I'll move ahead until I'm well out of sight and contact you."

"Okay. Good luck," she said and patted Magnus on the back before he strode away.

Telisa turned back to look the way they had come and took out her stunner. She thought that the heading of Shiny's cube cache was slightly to the right of the tunnel that headed back in that direction. The tunnels would probably be different if they went back that way.

Telisa waited for Magnus's message. She wondered what would happen if Shiny's plan worked. Would the alien come back and get them? Where would he go? What would happen to the caves and the mazelike corridors?

I'm in position, Magnus's voice echoed in her head.

This is crazy, Telisa sent.

Crazy, but at least we're alive, he sent. *If we get out of this place, let's make a run for it. Joe may be telling the truth about letting us go.*

I want to stay and learn more about Shiny, Telisa replied.

The UNSF won't let us. The most we can hope for is an artifact or two in our hands and escape from this planet.

Telisa didn't want to hear that. But she thought Magnus was probably right.

***

Kirizzo moved slower than he had in recent memory. He estimated that the others were in their positions and now he walked away from the last observation pod, concentrating on all the ones he had set out. Only a fraction of his attention focused on the passage he moved through. Kirizzo felt his way forward almost as much as he used his vision.

He came to an obstruction of some kind. He waited for a moment, watching his monitors and waiting for a chance to glance forward. Kirizzo set up a rhythm of checking everything in order and inserted a peek at his current surroundings into the sequence.

The center of the passage ahead was blocked by a gray matrix of hexagonal cells. Kirizzo sensed that this backing substance was vacuous, with little more mass than air. He reached out and tore away a piece of the material in a single claw. For something so light, it showed great structural strength.

Kirizzo suspected the inert substance backed the entire complex. It filled out the volume of the installation when nothing could sense it. He took a risk and skipped looking at one of his modules. After a few seconds he peeked at its data again. Nothing had changed.

Everything had stabilized.

Kirizzo abandoned his observer modules altogether, ignoring their input. He savagely tore into the gray matrix with six or seven of his arms. His race had primitive roots as a burrowing culture, and he now returned to his origins with a vengeance. He cut through cell after cell, discarding the ragged fragments behind him as he dug forward.

Up ahead a large mass loomed. Kirizzo could feel it, a massive wall of dense material. He cut his way through. It looked like a smooth wall of strong metal. Kirizzo cleared away the base matrix from the surface, digging along the barrier.

There had to be an exit.

***

I've had enough, Magnus said over the link. *How about you?*

Yes. It's so frustrating! Let's go back and see if we can find Joe or Shiny.

Magnus appeared from the direction he had gone hours before. He ran toward her, looking more excited than she expected.

"Something may be up after all," he told her. "The doors and the halls are the same as on my way out."

"The same? Can you tell from such a short distance?"

"Well, I think something would have changed before, even for just a couple of hallways. Let's go back toward the cache and maybe we'll see more."

They walked away from the human-style area and returned to the dim red caves. The tunnel angled slightly left of where they wanted to go, as Telisa remembered. Then they jinked to the right through two caves and continued in the right direction.

"It does seem familiar," Telisa said. "Or is it my imagination?"

"I think it does. I'm hesitant to jump to conclusions too, but it does really look like whatever Shiny planned has worked. The tunnels didn't change."

Magnus led the way the last few meters into the large cavern with the equipment cache in the center. Everything looked the same as they had left it.

"It's all still here!" Telisa said.

"Minus Joe and Shiny."

"They may not be back yet. I hope we didn't leave too soon."

"I think it's okay. Shiny was careful to let us know what he needed; I think if we had to stay longer he would have figured out how to communicate that."

"Well, what now? If everything is frozen in place, does that mean we can search the whole thing and find the exit now?" asked Telisa.

"Maybe so," Magnus said. "You wanna go look for the exit now, or should we wait and see if Shiny and Joe come back?"

"I'm already back," came the familiar voice of Joe. Magnus and Telisa turned to see him walking around the cache to join them.

"And Shiny?" asked Magnus.

"I haven't seen him. Do you think he fooled us somehow?"

"It worked! The caves don't change anymore," Telisa told him.

Joe raised an eyebrow and looked around. "Well, this place hasn't changed."

"Or any of the passages on the way to where we waited. They always changed before," Magnus said.

"I wonder how it worked," Joe said. "We should try and find Shiny."

"Or the exit," Telisa said. "If the place doesn't change, we could map it all out and find out for sure if there's a way out or not."

"Okay. Let's take a look," Joe agreed.

"I'll do the mapping," Telisa offered. She accessed her link computer and set up a mapping program. She could see the map in her mind's eye;

effortlessly she added the cache room and its exits to the center of her new map.

"Ready?" Magnus asked.

"Yep, let's go," Telisa said.

The group walked down a side tunnel. They traversed several side caverns, moving slowly so that Telisa could map them. They worked their way through the dark caverns until coming across the human-style corridors where Telisa and Magnus had waited.

They found meeting rooms and a cafeteria with a group of vending kiosks along one wall. Telisa walked up to the machines and asked for a menu through her link.

"Furnam's Chocolate Squares?" Telisa read aloud, mocking the faux items it sold. "Anyone want a Sloozebar?"

"Food is food," Joe said. "We should break in and take some."

"We can do that later since things have stabilized," Magnus said. "Or even if they haven't, for that matter. We'd just have to look around for long enough and we'd find some, even if things are changing."

Joe shrugged. "Okay. I have enough for now. But I am a bit concerned about hoarding some more for the long term."

They left the cafeteria behind and moved down another unmapped corridor. The wall on the left was made of clear glass, displaying an abstract art exhibit. Telisa didn't have an eye for art, but the paintings seemed real enough until she read one of the names from a plaque.

"Talvent Checksparr? That's a crazy name. More fake stuff, I guess."

"How can you tell?" asked Magnus. "Artists sometimes have weird names."

"Grumbit Shalzpleen?" Telisa read aloud.

"Um, okay, it's fake all right," agreed Magnus.

The next corridor broke off in a T-shape. Magnus started to go to the right, but Telisa turned the other way.

"Over here. I need to check something," she said.

"Okay," Magnus said. "What's up?"

Telisa didn't answer, her face a mask of concentration. They walked forward another twenty meters, ignoring doors on both sides. On her mental map, the corridor they were in collided with a spot they had been in earlier.

"Damn!" Telisa barked.

"What's wrong?" Magnus asked.

"The map just overlapped itself. Something is wrong," Telisa said.

"Let's head back the other way and double-check. Maybe you entered a turn wrong," Joe suggested.

"I hope I did," Telisa said. "Okay, let's double-check."

They turned and went back the way they had come. After making the first turn, Joe shook his head.

"There were two doors in this hall before. Now there's three."

"But it stopped changing," Telisa said. "At least for a while."

"Whatever we did, it only lasted a while," Joe said. "The place has started working again."

"And there's no sign of Shiny," Magnus added.

Telisa shook her head. "I can't believe it. He's abandoned us."

Michael McCloskey

Chapter Fifteen

Kirizzo moved through a vast room filled with angular columns of gray metal that stopped just short of the low ceiling. Black plates embedded in the devices glowed with symbols in a funny violet color at the edge of his visual capabilities. He supposed that he saw only a fraction of the wavelengths that the creators had used to view the information.

His backside twitched slightly as he scanned the room with his mass sense, trying to find the next door. Kirizzo suppressed his curiosity about the devices in favor of his effort to escape to the surface. An oppressive feeling came over him, causing him to slow. Something was wrong. Kirizzo took another few steps forward. Ahead, below the floor, he detected something too massive for his senses. His head reeled. Kirizzo staggered back, retreating from the overwhelming input.

A few moments later he began to recover. The golden alien knew what he had encountered: a microscopic singularity. The intense gravity close to the event horizon would daze a Gorgala almost to the point of helplessness. The tiny black hole was probably used as a source of power for the energy-greedy complex. Matter could be tossed into it, and the superheated gases outside the event horizon would emit a small fraction of the energy released as high-frequency radiation that could be harvested by a sufficiently complex technology. Just holding the singularity in place took an advanced science. Without any support, the black hole would tumble into the center of the planet and consume everything until no planet remained—just a black sphere orbiting the star, a dark monster with a fat stomach lingering where its victim once lived.

Kirizzo took a different route, trying to avoid the dangerous area he had accidentally discovered. He skirted the outside of the large chamber and came across a circular opening in the side wall.

The tunnel reminded him of the entrance that he had scrabbled down, pursued by the Bel Klaven war machines. He entered it, moving through the tube. The inside was utterly dark, so he relied upon his other senses to find his way. It took a familiar twisting, inclined course up toward the surface.

He encountered a blockage at the end of the passage. Dirt and leaves completely obstructed the exit. Kirizzo dug through the matter efficiently, scooping dirt out of place and under him with his forelegs while several sets of rear legs flicked it far behind him. He burrowed a few meters down the tunnel before he sensed the surface, a vast low-density area only a few more meters above.

The surface light flooded into the tunnel around Kirizzo when he emerged. The light-sensitive bundles under his gravity-sensing bulb retracted slightly to protect the sensors from overexposure. Once his vision had adjusted, the shining searcher darted back into movement. He flitted through the dense foliage, taking his bearings. Kirizzo recalled the direction of his initial approach to the complex and took off, adjusting the tall plants out of his way with several limbs while the others carried him along.

Kirizzo thought about his flight through the forest as he traveled through one valley and into another.

The forest seemed calm and peaceful compared to the tumult of the day he arrived, lulling Kirizzo into a sense of safety in the heavy cover. He came to the hillside where he had landed and started a spiral search for his craft.

Although a lot of time had passed while Kirizzo was imprisoned—several revolutions of this planet around its star—he felt sure that even if his starship had been destroyed there would be signs. He wandered along the hillside, his legs stopping occasionally but his mass sensor bulb always moving to feel for anomalies underground.

It took Kirizzo a long time to find the first piece of metal. He detected a small triangular fragment, buried under a layer of dirt and leaves. Kirizzo recovered it and held the clue up in a single hand to examine it visually. The plate the piece had broken from had been shattered; tiny fracture lines crisscrossed the item.

This was what Kirizzo had feared. The Bel Klaven had destroyed his ship in their zeal to exterminate him so long ago. He froze in thought.

How, then, might Kirizzo make his escape from this planet? What had happened in the war between his species and the Bel Klaven? Had they succeeded in eradicating his race from the galaxy, or had others like him survived?

It seemed that the aliens trapped in the nearby complex might serve as Kirizzo's only way to leave the planet. He might be able to convince them to allow him onto one of their ships. From that point, it might be possible to return to a Gorgala stronghold, if any still existed.

With his new plans formed, Kirizzo returned to motion. His legs blurred and he ran back down the hillside toward the complex.

***

Telisa sat on the cafeteria chair to rest, opening her pack on the table in front of her. Across the table, Magnus and Joe moved in on a triplet of food kiosks in a predatory manner. They had tried to access the kiosks through their links, but the machines refused to function. The real versions of such machines back on Earth produced snacks for anyone who accessed the service through their link, and the cost would be charged to the customer's global account automatically. Magnus drove his knee into the plastic panels of the support column, putting white stress fractures into one of the panels and knocking it loose. Joe reversed his rifle and applied the stock to another vending kiosk in a sharp thrust. His attack broke out a large piece of the dispensing counter.

"Not exactly health food," Telisa commented as she counted up her remaining food packets from the ship.

"We might find some other stuff in those refrigerators back there," Magnus said, pointing back behind Telisa. "Go check them out if you want."

Telisa nodded and got back to her feet, leaving her pack behind. She had a craving for some real fruit, since the rations they had been eating, although tasty, had a texture that left something to be desired. She thought it odd that humans could travel through space to distant planets, but they couldn't come up with nonperishable food packets that didn't grate on the consumer after a few days.

Telisa opened up the first industrial-sized refrigerator and started looking through it. A couple of shelves were filled with milk containers. The lower shelves had dozens of square cakes on small white plates. Telisa removed the wrapping from one and took a close look. It looked like pineapple upside-down cake.

"Hrm," Telisa murmured. She closed the refrigerator and walked back toward Magnus and Joe. They had finished ransacking the machines. They each had a pack full of candy bars and snack packages.

"There's some cake in there. If we're going to eat it, it had better be now. It's not going to keep."

Magnus frowned. She knew what he was going to say before he said it.

"We should eat all of our food first. The food created here by the complex might harm us somehow."

Joe shrugged. "If it tastes like the real thing, it's probably of the right molecular makeup."

"There are a lot of things people can't taste that can kill," Magnus replied.

"But that would almost be intentional," Joe said. "Actually, our taste buds amount to a pretty sophisticated analysis system. If the food is off by any significant amount, it will taste different. If the complex creators meant to kill us, why do it by poisoning the food?"

Telisa thought that made sense. "I agree there's a possibility that it is poisonous and we wouldn't taste it. But compared to the other dangers of this place, I'm thinking it'll be small."

Magnus smiled. "Okay. Eat it if you want. You can be my guinea pig."

Telisa grimaced and turned back toward the refrigerator. She dug out a couple of the plates and brought them back to the table. She set one in front of Joe and kept the other for herself.

"Forgive me if I forgo the silverware," she said, picking the cake up in her hand. She noticed that Joe had made no move to eat his cake and stopped. She frowned at Joe.

"Wait a minute," she said. "You were the one who convinced me the food would be okay!"

"It probably is," Joe said. "But it would be a silly risk for me not to wait and see what you think it tastes like, wouldn't it?"

Telisa looked at Magnus. He smiled.

"Shit," Telisa muttered. She took a bite of the cake. It tasted just as she remembered it should.

"Tastes okay," she said. She set down the rest of the cake. "I'll wait a while. If there's something wrong with it, one bite may let us know without killing me."

"A wise decision," Magnus said.

Suddenly a sound echoed through the cafeteria. Telisa couldn't identify the noise, but she thought that perhaps it was a chair being moved or a door being opened.

Magnus reacted first, grabbing his slugthrower and dropping prone to the floor. Joe and Telisa followed his example quickly. Telisa managed to find her stunner within the next few seconds. She realized then, lying on her stomach and peering through the chair legs across the room, how much she had relaxed since the early hours in the complex when Jack and Thomas had been killed.

Telisa heard something else, another sound joining the thudding of her heart—the skitter of many feet. A glint of gold pierced the masking chair legs in Telisa's field of view.

"It's Shiny!" Telisa exclaimed.

Magnus remained in position and trained his rifle on the bundle of legs. The alien came to a stop several meters away and then stood still, as if waiting.

"I guess he could kill us now if he wanted, even though we have some small amount of cover," Magnus said.

Apparently Joe came to the same conclusion, as he had risen to his knees to get a clear peek at the creature.

"Looks just like Shiny," he called.

Telisa took a quick look and agreed. "He's waiting for us."

"He's still trapped in here too, then," Magnus said gloomily.

The alien waved its forwardmost arms rhythmically. It turned slightly and took a few steps away.

"He says follow him," Telisa said, recognizing the motions from before. Everyone slowly stood up and watched the creature.

Magnus and Joe exchanged glances. Magnus nodded.

The small group of humans followed the glittering, many-legged creature. After about twenty meters, the human corridor turned into the familiar reddish-crusted caves.

"He stole our environment from us again!" Joe shot out. "How does he do that?"

Telisa shook her head and kept following Shiny through the dim caverns. The footing altered randomly, causing her to slow down and walk carefully. She wondered where the alien was taking them this time. She half expected to see another room with a beautiful pile of red cubes in the center.

Instead they came to a gray barrier of hex-shaped cells. A hole large enough to walk through had been ripped in the center of the stuff. Shiny went into it without hesitation. Telisa walked up to the new material and felt it with her hand.

"Wild. It's like a giant wasp nest made of tough plastic."

"Another environ? Does that mean there's another alien of a different type?" Joe asked.

"I've never seen this stuff before," Magnus said. "Something different is going on. Let's keep up with him." Now Magnus stepped ahead of Telisa and followed after Shiny. Telisa smiled as she saw his skinsuit replicate the gray hexagons around him. He looked like a sim model without texture art, a generic human silhouette waiting to be painted. Telisa turned her suit back on as well, just in case.

They moved through a cramped passage in the tough material until coming to a hexagonal portal made of metal. When Telisa stepped through, she looked around and gasped.

"This is Trilisk stuff!" she announced, looking around the dark room. Columns of metal rose around them, bedecked with flat black panels and cubic clusters of metal that looked like art sculptures. She no longer had any doubt that Shiny wasn't a Trilisk; his technology had a different look and feel. She wondered if his race was as advanced as the Trilisks had been.

Telisa took out a flashlight and immediately started examining the column before her. Fuzzy violet symbols flickered on the flat panes of the column, but they hardly gave enough light for a detailed examination. As she fully focused on the machine, Telisa's foot nudged something on the floor. She turned her beam down to the ground and saw a metal object lying in the dust.

She crouched down and snatched up the item. It was about fifteen centimeters long and looked like a small double wrench, with a viewing panel embedded in each flat end. A hexagonal opening sat next to the view screen on one end, and a one-centimeter spike of metal protruded from the other end.

Joe distracted her. "Shiny is up to something unusual," he said.

Telisa surreptitiously dropped the artifact into a pocket of her camo suit and turned to look at the alien. One of the small spheres that moved around Shiny's trunk glowed gently, casting a feeble light onto the scene. Shiny opened a silvery pack lying on the ground in front of him. Telisa saw a collection of small green objects inside, like green charcoal briquettes.

"What's up?" Magnus asked, walking up to the others. He clicked his own flashlight off.

"He has some weird package full of green bricks or something," Telisa said. She pointed to the pack Shiny had unlimbered, then realized there might not be enough light for the others to see her pointing, especially with her camo suit on. She turned her thin light to wide beam and added its light to the area around Shiny.

Magnus and Joe stood with Telisa and watched. Shiny rotated his body and faced away from the open container. The curved end of Shiny's trunk dipped down and split open from the sides. A slimy, reddish interior was revealed.

"Oh, so gross," Telisa breathed. She unconsciously stepped back. Her light wavered.

"Uh! Is he all right?" Magnus asked.

A charred black rectangle slid out onto the floor next to Shiny's package of smooth green blocks. The black thing was similarly shaped to the green ones, although much smaller. As soon as the darker object was ejected, Shiny's body flexed and the opening fastened itself onto one of the green blocks. In seconds the entire thing had been consumed whole. Then the trunk closed up again, and the end of Shiny's body resumed its appearance of a curved beak or hook.

Joe stood as stunned as the others. "What did we just see?" he said. "Did it just defecate and eat from the same orifice?"

Telisa winced. "I think so," she said.

"If that's food, he has the whole rest of the pack. I wonder how long it'll last him?" Magnus said.

Joe shook his head and then took a long look around the giant chamber. "I'm going to try and find my way up," he announced. "I have to contact my superiors and report this complex and the alien. As I said, I only care about the big picture here, so I'll hold to my word and leave your presence here out of my summary, if that's what you want."

"Okay, leave me out," Telisa said.

"Same here," Magnus added.

"Very well," Joe said. "I'll be back soon."

Joe turned and moved away from the machines, headed toward a far side wall.

"We must get out of here now," Magnus said. "We won't have much time once he tells the UNSF about this place."

"But we're in the middle of a Trilisk complex! Who knows what amazing things are lying around this place!"

"Grab what you can. I'm going to follow him just long enough to figure out the way to the surface. Then we're out of here."

Michael McCloskey

Chapter Sixteen

Telisa looked at Shiny. She felt the need to speak even though the alien couldn't understand her.

"Unbelievable! Here I am surrounded by artifacts and now I have to leave in a matter of minutes!" The creature shifted, as if it took great effort to sit still and observe her.

Telisa moved up to the nearest pillar. She ran her hands along its surface, searching for loose items in the dim light. The smooth metal felt cool against her skin. The column bulged in many spots. Its surface meandered in a chaotic way, covered in knobs and extensions of all shapes and sizes. Telisa knew from previously studied Trilisk technology that the knobs would not move; most Trilisk artifacts had no manual controls of any kind.

"I wonder how they kept dust from accumulating on it?" she asked herself. Her hand found a depression, and she slid her fingers along it.

"Probably going to lose a hand doing this..." she commented. Her fingers wrapped around a ridge and she pulled a drawer-like container open. Instead of a hollow box, the device pulled out and then folded open with a small whir. An ovoid device glowed in the interior. It looked like a glowing egg with a metal net woven over it. Some other items sat next to the lit ovoid, revealed by its dim light.

Telisa pulled her backpack off and unzipped it. "Let's hope this stuff isn't super fragile," she said. She put the egg into a pocket and examined the other items. She saw a flat, square plate the size of her palm that had ridges on its edges as if it were made of dozens of layers of metal. She gently picked up the plate and felt for something else in the drawer. Her hand found a triangular piece of material identical to that of the plate, with the same ridges on its side. She slipped these things into her backpack and closed it up.

"Fantastic! We have to make the best possible use of our time," she said to Shiny. She moved to the next pillar without waiting for any response from the alien.

A scraping sound emanated from the floor nearby. Telisa jumped, turning back toward Shiny.

"Shit! Was that you?" Telisa asked. She didn't expect an answer. Another noise came from the other direction, several meters away from her and Shiny. A chill ran down her back, and she grabbed her flashlight again. Turning the device to wide beam, she swept the area.

Something moved along the floor. It left the swath of light rapidly, causing Telisa's heart rate to climb. Was she being attacked? Her other hand groped for her stunner in a moment of terror while the noises continued, bouncing off the pillars in the dark. Then her beam caught something in front of Shiny.

A small stack of devices had been created in front of the alien. As Telisa watched, a small silver sphere flew over and deposited another artifact into the pile. Telisa realized that the sphere looked the same as the thing that had blocked Joe when he pointed his weapon at Shiny.

"Wow! You're collecting stuff faster than I am!" Telisa exclaimed.

Shiny indicated the pile and moved several of his legs. He pushed one of the items toward Telisa and then backed off.

"For me?" Telisa asked. She watched the alien for a moment, then moved forward. The intriguing stack beckoned her, and the alien didn't move.

"Thank you!" she said, bending down to scoop the items into her backpack. "Thanks!" she said again. "I need to figure out how to say that so you understand."

Telisa continued to look for loose items in the room for a few more minutes, but it seemed that Shiny's scavenging efforts had retrieved most everything in the area; she found nothing else that wasn't attached to the other, heavier equipment.

The sound of footsteps alerted her to someone's approach. Telisa slid behind a pillar until she heard Magnus's voice.

"Telisa?" he called, walking carefully up to Shiny.

"Over here," she answered.

"There's a passage upward to the surface," he told her. "If we're going to lose him, we have to go and wait for Joe to come back through it. We'll hide near the entrance and when he walks back to this spot, we'll run for it."

"So soon?" Telisa moaned. "There are all kinds of amazing things around here."

"What've you found?"

"I haven't the slightest clue," Telisa said. "All kinds of stuff, maybe enough to discover something really amazing about the Trilisks!"

"That's great, but we have to go or end up on a prison asteroid chipping at ore veins," Magnus said.

"He could be back soon; I don't think it'll take very long for him to make a report."

"All right. Lead the way," Telisa said.

Magnus strode back the way he had come, with Telisa and Shiny following closely. They skirted to one side, and Magnus quietly indicated a circular opening in the wall that they were avoiding. They ended up beyond the entrance, standing behind one of the massive pillars.

"We have to wait here for him to return. When he comes out and goes looking for us, then we'll go up the tunnel," Magnus whispered.

Telisa noticed that Shiny waited with them in plain view of the entrance. He hadn't placed himself behind the column of equipment.

"Shiny," Telisa whispered. She performed the motions for "follow me," facing the alien and stepping slowly backward.

The creature watched her for a moment, and then took a few steps forward. Telisa walked farther back behind the pillar, continuing the hand motions.

"He'd better not give us away," Magnus said. "I'd rather not have to shoot Joe."

"No problem," Telisa said. "If he sees us, I'll give him a jolt with my stunner. He'll wake up later and we'll be long gone. What I'm worried about is, what if he doesn't come back quickly? He could be calling in reinforcements and waiting for them up there."

"Shit."

"What?"

"We have to stun him at least," Magnus said. "I just realized that he probably has vids of us in his link memory. We need to erase it."

"He may have already sent some if he's managed to contact the base."

"Yes. We should have shot him in the back before he left. So stupid," Magnus growled at himself. "We'll just have to hope that he hasn't done that yet. His link memory would take a lot of bandwidth to transfer. But he may have sent a summary."

Telisa sighed. Another risk for them to take. There had already been so many.

"Are you sure you've done this before?" she asked.

"Yes. But we never got detected on the way in before. And I wasn't trapped in an alien complex. That's why things are so screwed up this time."

"Well, I agree we should stun him, but it's probably not critical. Even if the link memory is erased, they can still work with him to come up with our visual profiles."

"Yeah. But it might slow them down, introduce some uncertainty. His memory might even be faulty. Maybe he spent all his time looking at you and he can't remember me."

Telisa smiled. "I'm going up closer to the exit then. I'll stun him the instant I see him."

Magnus nodded. "Sounds good." His Veer suit made him difficult to see, maintaining a near-black color that blended into the dark room.

Telisa crept around the side of the pillar and turned her flashlight down. She took the stunner in her right hand and moved until she stood with her back against the wall beside the tube exit. She turned her flashlight all the way off and waited for Joe.

***

Kirizzo watched from his position behind the pillar as the two humans observed the exit portal in front of him. Their behavior had been extremely odd. Kirizzo felt that perhaps a problem had arisen in the alliance the creatures had formed with each other. Perhaps he was about to witness a falling out among them.

The smaller human still carried the alien items that Kirizzo had gathered for it. Kirizzo hoped that this gift served to further convince the four-limbed creature that his presence would be beneficial. He would need any goodwill he could get when the time came to find transport off the planet.

Kirizzo felt a mass disturbance in the tunnel they watched. He decided to attempt to aid the humans again, to further demonstrate that keeping him around was to their advantage. Kirizzo moved behind the pillar so that he could not be seen, and he extended a single limb forward, pointing toward the doorway.

The larger human observed his motion and transmitted some information to the smaller one, whose primitive weapon was ready. Kirizzo predicted the ambush would succeed. Their outlines were obscured by the clever suits they wore that broke up their visual signatures. To creatures with no mass sense, Kirizzo decided this must go a long way toward disguising their presence.

Momentarily, the third one emerged from the tunnel. It seemed from its movement patterns that it did not suspect anything was amiss. Kirizzo watched as the newcomer walked into the pillar room, then fell to the ground, incapacitated. The other creatures moved forward to inspect their enemy.

Kirizzo felt surprised. Why didn't the pair take advantage of their position to destroy the third one? Perhaps the race did not eliminate others of their own kind but simply permuted their alliances from time to time.

Now the larger alien took a device out of his carrying shroud and applied it to the back of the head of the disabled creature. Kirizzo detected an EM spike and an electrical interaction between the device and the embedded equipment in the disabled creature's skull. Kirizzo thought perhaps the victors stole knowledge from the head of their enemy. Or at the very least, they were forcibly disabling their foe even further.

Once the electronic vandalism was complete, the larger alien motioned to Kirizzo and the smaller one. He moved toward the exit, with his body bent forward oddly. Kirizzo guessed this must be their battle posture. It did serve to shrink their silhouette, perhaps to reduce the possibility of being seen. He filed the observation away for future use and followed them toward the tunnel.

In the exit passage, the bipeds increased speed, lengthening their strides and pushing off strongly with each leg. Although they seemed rather ungainly to Shiny, his estimation of their balance did come up a notch. He kept up with them easily, working his many legs without conscious thought.

He emerged after them onto the surface of the planet. The weather was still calm above; a few motes of moisture floated in the sky under the yellow sun.

The spiny plants still looked strange to Kirizzo. On his home planet, life thrived on volcanic heat below the surface, not solar radiation from above.

The larger biped took only a moment to acclimatize to the surface conditions. Then they resumed running, heading off into the vegetation. Kirizzo hoped that some transportation had been cached away somewhere nearby. It would take a significant amount of time to go any large distance on foot. He wondered about the physical endurance of the creatures. They didn't usually seem to prefer moving so quickly, so would they eventually tire and slow to their more normal speed?

When they moved into the forest, the group did slow. It appeared to be more because of the inhibiting mass of spiny growth than any fatigue. The leader took out a sharp implement and raised it as if to clear a path but then hesitated. The pair moved their mandibles for a moment and then the larger human put it away. Kirizzo theorized that they didn't wish to leave an obvious sign of their passage.

They marched deeper into the forest. Kirizzo thought that if they had a vehicle here, this would be a sufficient distance from the site to avoid visual detection. Perhaps they feared some other form of sensor with a wider perimeter. Kirizzo continued to hope that faster transport would be forthcoming. The language barrier would have to be broken as soon as they had a chance, he decided.

Suddenly a large mass exploded into movement within meters of their position. Kirizzo turned his optical receptors toward the disturbance and caught a glimpse of shaking vegetation. Then a large creature burst from the leaves, headed straight for Kirizzo.

The creature sported a wide maw that bristled with spiky mineral deposits. Kirizzo realized that it would enjoy a considerable advantage if the opening were to be fastened upon any part of his own body. He maneuvered to avoid this, his many legs thrashing in the vegetation as he tried to flank the thing.

Kirizzo's move saved his torso from the jaws of the monster, but as the huge mouth clamped down it caught two of his legs. The thin brittle limbs snapped off near his body, spraying black goo on the spiny leaves of a shrub. Kirizzo felt the throb from each of those legs that his muscle sensors gave when the flexors in his body contracted completely.

The smaller of the two aliens worked its mandible and scrabbled for its weapon. The large alien had unlimbered its long projectile thrower and leveled it toward the thing that had bitten Kirizzo's two legs off.

The Gorgala readied a seeker projectile to destroy the threat, but he held his fire. His supply of weapons was limited. He scrabbled away at full speed, running around the base of a large plant.

The muzzle of the larger human's long weapon flashed. Kirizzo felt the ghost of rapidly moving mass pellets tunneling their way through the thing that fought him. Immediately its movements became erratic. Kirizzo continued to retreat, hoping that the wounds would render it inactive. He saw that the smaller biped used its weapon as well. It did not appear to be a projectile-based weapon; Kirizzo could not detect what principle it worked on. Perhaps it emitted radiation on a wavelength he could not detect.

The thing seemed to be mortally wounded. Like Kirizzo, it leaked its internal fluids out onto the fuzzy leaves on the forest floor, but it did not have attendant modules to tend to its wounds. The small spheres moved over to Kirizzo's severed limbs and began a temporary repair. Kirizzo realized that the bipeds had lost interest in the native creature and had moved over to see how he fared. Perhaps they did value his presence, since they watched the modules working carefully, or perhaps they were simply curious. Kirizzo indicated the previous direction of travel with one limb, urging them to continue.

***

"Do you really think he's okay to keep going?" Telisa asked Magnus.

"We don't really have a choice," he said. "Obviously we have no idea about his physiology, but we have to get back to the ship as soon as possible."

"You're right," she agreed. They stepped around the body of the awful creature that had bitten Shiny. The thing looked like a giant salamander, but it had moved like a tiger, bolting out of the cover and attacking without warning. Just looking at its mouth gaping in death made her shudder. She kept her stunner ready and scanned the forest. If another thing like that lurked nearby, it could kill them.

Obviously Magnus thought the same since he cradled his slugthrower in his hands and his gaze moved across the area warily.

They moved up the hillside and through to valley after valley, making good time. Without Jack and Thomas holding them back, Telisa thought they might make it in a single day, but when the light of day faded, twenty percent of the distance remained.

"We're almost there—let's keep going," Telisa urged.

"It'll be dangerous, but I agree," Magnus said. "I don't want to run into one of those monsters in the dark, but we need to leave now to avoid any kind of UNSF response to Joe's messages."

"And we'll take Shiny with us," Telisa said.

"That's insane. The government would hunt us down," Magnus said. "Our DNA is still back there, somewhere."

"Maybe it is, maybe it isn't," Telisa said. "Inside the part that shifted, the matter was being molded all the time. It may be absorbed. And I noticed that in the other room with the Trilisk columns in it, there was no dust. That means it gets cleaned somehow. Any hair or skin we left there might get removed."

"Well, it's still insane. But Shiny got us out of that place. So if he wants to come with us, I'm not saying no. Besides, maybe we can sell him," Magnus said.

"Uh!" Telisa started at the suggestion, ready to rant back at Magnus, and then she saw that he was smiling at her. It was a joke. "Of course we won't. Think what we can learn from him!"

"Yeah, we won't. But Momma Veer would pay a pretty penny for those floating things of his."

"We'd be arrested for selling something like that," Telisa said.

"In normal channels, yes," Magnus said. "But Jack knew some people. We might be able to work something out and keep out of prison. Maybe. With some work. It helps if you're selling defense systems and not armament."

While they talked, the light became inadequate. Telisa took out her flashlight and turned it on. Magnus attached a light to the end of his slug thrower so he could see ahead.

An eerie red light came from behind Telisa, illuminating the nearby leaves and tree trunks. She looked back and saw that Shiny had many glowing cubes.

"Like in the caves back in the complex," Magnus noted.

"Yes! That's interesting. He must come from an underground society, at least in its primitive beginnings."

"Wouldn't they make regular-shaped tunnels like humans do inside of buildings? The caves seemed...so primitive."

"The walls were irregular, but they weren't natural. His race probably doesn't have an aesthetic about regular-shaped rooms. It's not surprising, considering how different their technology looks."

Magnus grunted in response. They were working their way over the last rise into the valley where the ship rested. They worked their way through the forest for a few minutes in silence.

"Worried?" Telisa asked.

"Yes, but I shouldn't be," Magnus said. "If they detected the ship and they're waiting for us, we're already caught. Our lights will give us away."

"What about satellites?" Telisa asked.

"This planet isn't developed at all," Magnus said. "They don't have enough infrastructure in place to detect anyone anywhere. That's one of the reasons why we came here, because there's a lot to be taken and not a lot of resistance to taking it."

They came to a flatter area, and the vegetation thinned. Telisa knew they were almost to the ship. She could see a map and their location in her head via her personal link. Would a team of soldiers be waiting to arrest them?

They sped up, consuming the last of the distance in less than half an hour. At last the ship stood before them, and Telisa let out a sigh of relief. There were no lights or cordons of men. The forest remained silent.

Telisa could tell that Shiny was sizing the ship up in the red light.

"What do you think he thinks?" she said.

Magnus snorted. "He's probably thinking it's not safe to fly in that thing," he said.

"I can't tell for sure if he's more advanced," Telisa said. "He seems mysterious, and his modules are impressive, but he may have been there a long time, collecting knickknacks. And maybe his technology is better than ours in some areas and worse in others."

"Yeah, or maybe we're primitive worms and he's barely tolerating us," Magnus retorted. The ship's entrance port activated and lowered a ramp for them.

"Ship says we haven't been detected," Magnus reported.

Telisa remembered that she could link in again. It felt reassuring to link in and see the ship's resources available to her, like coming home. She had never before gone as much as a day without being able to link into nearby services.

They walked up the ramp, and Shiny followed without hesitation.

"Looks like it'll be a flight for three," Telisa said.

Chapter Seventeen

"We must be crazy. Trying to smuggle away a live alien from the UNSF," Magnus said. He sat in a chair, eyes closed. Telisa knew he preferred to close his eyes while running the ship interface.

"How could we turn him away after he helped us escape from that place?" Telisa demanded. "It's obvious he wants to go with us. Would you rather he get captured and prodded by those UNSF monkeys?"

"Hey, careful there. I used to be UNSF, y'know." Sounds reverberated through the ship, signaling their takeoff. Telisa hoped that Shiny wasn't getting into trouble where they had left him in the cargo bay. Hopefully if he could survive trapped in a mysterious Trilisk complex, he could make it in the bay. Telisa thought she should get back there soon.

"Be ready to get in a pod," Magnus said. "I don't know if they considered us important enough to have called any ships back before they heard Joe's report. We might be in for another rough ride."

"What're you worried about? You can defeat their scanners, right?"

"We can probably get away from this planet. Probably. But now they're going to be hunting for us everywhere. They don't have the funds to search for every handful of smugglers that sneaks away with an artifact here and there. But this is huge. They'll spend a lot of money to recover Shiny."

"You think they'll know where to look?"

"They won't be able to ID this ship, at least not unless the scout ship is back in-system. It might have scanners advanced enough to get a good look. But those ships are expensive, there's only a few of them, and one of them already spent its time here. They'd only send it back when Joe gives his report, and it probably isn't here yet."

"Where should we go?" Telisa asked. She realized that she was still very new at this smuggler stuff, and now she was in way over her head.

"Let's just stay in space for a while," Magnus suggested. "I want to know what we've got in Shiny. I also need to scan the ship carefully, in case the UNSF managed to mark us somehow. Why don't you talk to Shiny—see if he's a willing passenger, for starters."

Telisa loved that idea. She could forget about the UNSF for a while and study the alien and the artifacts.

"That sounds great! I need to scan the artifacts, and I'll try to talk with Shiny some more while I'm at it."

"I'll concentrate on getting us out of here. Remember what I said: be ready to run for a shock pod."

"What'll Shiny do? We don't have any pods for aliens."

Magnus grimaced. "We'll try our best. Maybe we won't have to go for the pods."

"Okay, maybe I could show him one."

"I wouldn't. If he went in there, he'd probably panic."

"A human would, if they didn't know what was going on. But I think he's pretty smart. He knows we don't mean him any harm."

"Your call. Just make sure you get in a pod if I say so."

"Okay." Telisa turned and headed for a cargo bay where she could catalog her hoard of artifacts. She used her link to ask the computer where the scanning equipment rested and got an odd notification.

"There's something wrong with my link. It's not working right," Telisa said, turning back toward Magnus. "And the ship's computer is complaining about it too. It says I'm hogging storage."

That got Magnus's attention.

"Hogging storage? Have you been recording a lot?"

"Hardly anything," she said.

Magnus remained quiet for a moment. Then he cursed.

"Damn!"

"What's wrong?"

"Something's up with your link," Magnus said, his eyes still closed. "It's been compromised somehow."

"What?"

"Give me a minute. I have to fire off some comp tasks and then I can talk more."

Telisa waited. Now she felt more tense. Something wrong with her link? Was it the complex? Trilisk tampering? Or had Shiny somehow damaged it?

At last Magnus opened his eyes. He looked at Telisa for a moment in a way that scared her.

"What? What's going on?"

"I've discovered a UNSF snoop program running on your link."

"What! You mean they've tapped me? Those fu—"

"It must have run out of space in your local cache. We spent all that time in the complex, and you didn't link to anything. Usually the spy program gathers information and uploads it at public links. But we've been isolated from public links for a long time now."

"So everything we know, who we are, and what we've found…"

"Including Shiny, will be uploaded next time you connect to a public link," Magnus finished for her. "We have to clear this out before we enter any port. It may even be sophisticated enough to detect public ports in range and upload all by itself."

Telisa bit back a scream of rage. The UNSF…the ones who had taken her father from her, the ones who tried to control everyone's lives, had been recording her life from a secret program placed into the link hardware at the base of her skull.

"Those bastards," Telisa lamented. "They recorded everything. Probably down to every request for the local time. Wait a minute—that means they know about my employment with you, Thomas, and Jack! If they know it all, why'd they let us leave?"

Magnus shook his head. "No, you had a sleeper. It wasn't active when we hired you; believe me, we checked."

"You checked? You scanned my link? How could you?"

"We had to. It wouldn't be safe not to. Look, we didn't record anything of yours. We just checked to make sure you were clean. That's all. I promise."

Telisa took a deep breath. What Magnus said made sense. They would have to check things like that to keep from getting caught in a society in which people could be unknowing spies for their government.

"That isn't the only unusual thing going on with the links," Magnus said. "Since Shiny came on board, he's been trying to emulate our link's handshake codes to connect to the ship's computer."

"Really? He's trying to break in?"

Magnus shrugged. "From his point of view, it's probably not so much trying to break in as just trying to communicate. Obviously he's detected the data we transfer on the link frequency, and he's trying to speak the same language. But our ship's computer is rejecting him."

"You should give him an account. We need to learn to talk with him somehow."

"Okay. But I want to restrict his access. He seems to be on our side, but he is an alien, after all. Until we understand him better, I'll keep an eye on it."

"And my problem?"

"We can work on that once we're out of the system," Magnus said. "Link up with me and we'll poke around through Thomas's programs and see if we can find something to clean up your link."

***

Once on the vessel, Kirizzo turned his resources toward learning to communicate with his hosts.

Kirizzo worked for several subcycles on the problem. He had been recording and cataloging their movements for some time now, but had not had the chance to analyze the data in depth. He began this analysis once it became obvious that he would have a lot of time available.

He realized that the movements the creatures made were too simple. They could not encode enough information for a meaningful dialog. He pondered the meaning of this new discovery.

Either the aliens were much more modularized than his race and could function with very little interaction, or else they were using other means to augment the transfer of information.

The first idea did not fit what he had observed of the creatures. When the time came to break off the alliance with the third one, the original two had quickly organized a plan and acted in a coordinated way to leave the other behind. That implied that they had exchanged a plan. A slight chance existed that the two had done this kind of thing many times and didn't have to communicate much to select a plan, but that seemed unlikely.

Kirizzo decided to examine the second possibility in more detail. How could they be exchanging information?

He scanned the radiative emanations of the environment and picked up several frequencies being used for information transfer. This examination revealed that the humans had artificial means of communication much like himself, via small devices embedded in their bodies. He monitored these frequencies and started a group of experiments to try and inject his own transmissions into the system to learn more.

Once again the bandwidth proved to be low. Hardly any information passed at the frequencies where he detected activity. But it might be that their devices just weren't exchanging anything right now.

When he jumped in on the channel and sent some transmissions of his own, he followed the protocol but lacked the one-time link codes that the others used. They worked on a principle of using passcodes to connect, but each passcode was good for only one use. He didn't have enough samples to try and crack the pattern. For now, it seemed all he could do was eavesdrop on the coded messages.

Still, this system was a more modern veneer added onto their original state in nature. Kirizzo wondered if effective communication was required before any civilization could become advanced. It would have taken a long time for the race to become coordinated with an extremely limited mode of communication. He doubted his race would have been as successful without their original communication system based on limb movement.

That meant that they might be able to exchange information using senses that Kirizzo lacked. They could have been using media that escaped Kirizzo's attention the whole time. The idea that their primitive base language used movement exclusively, as his race did, was probably a bad assumption on his part.

In order to make further progress, Kirizzo would have to learn about the senses utilized by the creatures. These natural "primitive" capabilities would be what they used in their simplest forms of transferring ideas.

Kirizzo moved through the large chamber to which he had been directed. The walls were monotonously regular, almost perfect in their boring rectangular theme. He found this style to be gratingly dull, but he had expected as much after seeing their simulated environment in the alien installation.

Artificial radiation streamed down from above. The obvious deduction here was that the creatures could sense this light as Kirizzo could. He worked his way further around the many storage containers that littered the area. The wall had an embedded device in it, shielded by a metal grille. He scanned this area and analyzed the function of the site.

The system placed in the wall converted electronic impulses into movement with a network of wires and magnets. The resulting vibrations could conceivably range into frequencies beyond the ability of his mass sense to detect. A possibility occurred to him. An experiment was in order.

Kirizzo couldn't move his legs fast enough to emulate the vibrations the device produced, but he could reproduce them with one of his defense modules. The defense module was capable of extremely quick interception, and its drive could cause the module to vibrate rapidly if he told it to change directions back and forth very fast. He instructed the device to drop into contact with the floor and utilize its movement system to buzz at high frequency.

Kirizzo experimented with the setup, starting at a low frequency that he could sense with his mass detection. As he increased the speed of movement, the disturbance quickly left his range. He instructed the module to continue in ascending frequencies up to its limit. When he sensed a larger mass approaching, he became distracted from the experiment.

One of the aliens burst into the room. Kirizzo saw that it was the smaller one, brandishing a primitive weapon. He immediately stopped creating the vibrations, concerned that perhaps he had broken some taboo of their culture. The alien seemed to calm, lowering its device. Had he alarmed it?

Kirizzo repeated the experiment and watched the alien. It showed obvious alarm as the module vibrated again, raising its weapon and stepping back. It sensed the movement of his module.

It appeared that these creatures used an even more sophisticated movement sensor than Kirizzo was naturally capable of. This revelation shocked him a little, since he had thought the creatures devoid of nonvisual motion sense altogether. But the evidence here suggested that they could detect movements at a much higher frequency than Kirizzo could, a rate of millions of vibrations per subcycle.

Did it detect the movement of the sphere or the ship's deck? Or the resulting movement of the molecules of the atmosphere? It could even be the high-frequency impact of the shock waves on its outer integument, Kirizzo realized. Either way, it was a fascinating method of information transfer.

The breakthrough gave Kirizzo the tools he needed to begin analyzing the alien language. Unfortunately, it meant that they might not be able to communicate without artificial help. Still, being able to understand the creatures would aid in achieving his next goal.

Michael McCloskey

Chapter Eighteen

Magnus closed his eyes and linked into his virtual cockpit. Display screens and controls came into being all around him.

He turned to a display on his left and reviewed the status of his launch decoys. The *Iridar* had dropped five of them as it descended over the continent. Each drone now awaited his command in distant parts of the land mass. The devices would simulate a takeoff of his ship and hopefully distract any waiting UNSF trap to the wrong vector.

Magnus activated the drones and sent them off. At the same time, he brought the *Iridar*'s engines to full power and prepared for his own takeoff. He routed power to temporary storage pools for more drones, the EM warfare pod, and weapons.

The core of the *Iridar* held its greatest miracle: the gravity spinner. Although the spinner took most of the energy consumed by the ship, it was well worth it. The spinner allowed generation of artificial gravity during voyages, as well as faster-than-light travel. Magnus started the spinner last. He locked down the ship and brought the *Iridar* up from the planet by using the spinner to cause it to "fall" upward. The ship's thrusters kicked in, adding to the speed. He couldn't fully engage the spinner so close to the planet without causing vast destruction.

As an afterthought, Magnus turned to a new virtual panel and created a new account on the ship's system. He left a pointer to the flight information console. If Shiny found his way in, he could monitor their progress through that. Magnus thought it might help to keep the alien calm during their escape.

He watched on several displays as they made their way up through the atmosphere. Several ghost images of the *Iridar* climbed up from the planet. Magnus saw the ones generated from his launch drones as well as several other electromagnetic fakes thrown up by the EM module. The module scrambled many useful frequencies to confuse things for the enemy, as well as watching and interpreting the planetscape for signs of other ships and facilities.

Magnus looked at a control on one of the virtual boards before him. It activated at his thought. One of the launch drones exploded. The screens lit up with the EM pulse of its destruction, playing havoc with Magnus's readings. He launched two other EM bombs to add to the noise. He wanted to blind as many satellites as possible to cover their escape route.

The *Iridar* left the atmospheric envelope of the planet. Magnus cut the thrusters to preserve fuel and let the spinner accelerate them. He dropped off some missiles in their path. In a few minutes they'd activate and move to kill a group of satellites over a different part of the planet. It would look like they were trying to blind another part of the network. The ship operated very stealthily, but it never hurt to overlap the protection. Magnus wrapped their escape in deception after deception. If someone could figure out their route, he hoped it would be many days from now.

He relaxed a notch and watched the displays for a while. As he'd hoped, they hadn't had to use any of the crash pods. They were a last resort for when a spinner failed. The UNSF had weapons that would disable a spinner, and the resulting g-forces could smash a crew around inside their vessel.

Magnus wondered about Shiny. He checked the alien on a surveillance viewer to make sure things looked normal. The creature seemed quiescent.

The mercenary looked over the screens as the *Iridar* moved farther out. The planet behind him remained noisy. He selected a frequency from the comm display and packaged a message. His equipment would make the transmission look like noise; only someone searching for the agreed-upon pattern would be able to recognize and descramble it.

"Hawk, I'm leaving the target system. I'm golden. We'll get back to you in a few weeks," Magnus sent.

"This is Hawk. I read you. Noisy, though. Hah, your noise coder must be workin' too well."

"I'm surprised to get a realtime link with you, Hawk," Magnus said.

"Hello to you too, Vulture," Henman replied. "Yeah, well, my ship's been dispatched toward target system. Something about some smugglers. You wouldn't happen to know anything about that, would you?"

"We're out now. But A and B are dead. As you know, we blew the approach so it's noisy on the way out."

"Shit, sorry to hear that. You guys had a rough ride. The Unies want you bad, though, whatever you did. They're throwing a lot of hardware your way."

"Well, we're a little more golden than I can express. I'll have to lie low for a while. We'll figure out a way to get you your cut, just like always. Hey, they may have gotten a few traces of us back there. If you can snoop around and make some of it go away, it would help."

"Sorry, no way. Not on this one. If they got anything on you, it'll be impossible for me to make it disappear. Not without giving myself away. It's one thing to clean logs that no one looks at anyway or to make a random security pic go away, but this is different."

"I understand, Hawk."

"So have you spaced your VIP yet?"

"No, not this one. VIP's the real deal, very capable. I think there's a lot of potential."

Henman laughed. "What, you've fallen in love with your passenger, have you now? C'mon, Vulture, keep your head for god's sake. She's just some spoiled brat who you're hot for."

Magnus frowned. Henman was being a little too specific. Even though he believed no one could listen in, he preferred being more nebulous while in the thick of it.

"Seriously, VIP's working out well. Held it together after we lost A and B. Don't worry… there's only a few of us to split the load with."

"I suppose. I really hope this one doesn't bite you, though. You're so damn trusting. I've tried to set you straight a hundred times. You're gonna get us screwed if you're not careful. And I don't mean by that eye candy you hired, either."

"Don't worry. I'll be in touch."

Magnus cut the connection. He felt anger rising in him at the way that Henman assumed things about his judgement. He changed course to avoid any chance that their conversation would give away his escape vector.

A calmer part of himself considered Henman's accusation. Had he really let his primitive drives take over when it came to Telisa? He did have some kind of impulse to protect her that wasn't fully logical.

He also found Telisa's presence to be somewhat distracting at times. During training he remained as professional as possible, but he found it difficult to ignore her youthful attractiveness. Grappling proved to be the most frustrating, when he could feel her entire body struggling against him.

Magnus let out a sigh and ripped his thoughts away from the grappling. They'd made it out of the system, so his next task would be cleaning up Telisa's link.

He considered the source of the link spy program. He decided that Jack might have been behind it just as easily as any active UNSF agency. Magnus had been aware that they were monitoring her link for hours after the first meeting, just in case she had decided to run to the authorities. But he hadn't known of an invasive modification to her link at that time.

Magnus had already isolated the entire link. Now he copied over its storage to the *Iridar*'s computers and sterilized the original. He performed a hardware scan to make sure that the link hadn't been modified except for its programming. Everything checked out. He still needed to install a fresh link kernel and start everything back up. Telisa would have to set up a lot of things, but at least she'd have her link back soon.

He set a dissection routine to work on the program to see what it could find out. It quickly found a catalog of the visual records it had been storing. He realized that he could find out how long they'd been recording without waiting for the routine to complete. He could just browse through them and see when they started.

Images of Telisa's recorded sight flashed through his mind's eye. Magnus stopped the progression periodically, trying to determine how long the link had been active. He caught a flash of the redly glowing caverns, a vision of himself standing in a corridor. He flipped through more recordings.

The next hop stopped. The image showed Telisa standing naked before the narrow mirror in her ship's quarters. Magnus blinked and moved forward again. He felt a familiar desire rising but shoved it back. It would be despicable to spy on her this way.

He thought about what Henman had said. If Telisa had a hidden agenda, this would be the way to find out. But it didn't make sense; if she worked for an agency, they wouldn't have the program hidden from her and she wouldn't have brought it up to Magnus. She must be unaware of whoever had tried to use her vision against her.

He found that the images started after a few days into space on the *Iridar*. He decided that made sense; presumably she could be monitored any of a number of other ways while on civilized planets. He archived the recordings and left them for Telisa to see, then turned off the virtual displays and sat for a moment in darkness.

"We've dodged some bullets, haven't we?" he told himself. Magnus wondered how many more were headed his way.

Chapter Nineteen

The *Seeker*. A sleek gray cylinder with sensor bulbs every few meters along her surface. Joe saw the green circle of the United Nations Space Force emblazoned on the hull. The ship extended almost two hundred meters from end to end. Although not as large as a battle cruiser, the vessel probably embodied the pinnacle of UNSF science. The ship's complex sensors and analytical capabilities enabled it to catalog new systems and assess them for suitability as colonies or detect traces of alien civilizations.

Joe had never seen a UNSF scout ship in real life. The ship looked the same as it had in VR sims, but knowing it was real had some impact. He found it hard to believe he would be going aboard. He had been ordered to report directly to Captain Relachik.

Information came cheap, and terabytes of data traveled between here and Earth every day, but exploration ships were another matter. He had studied the latest specs on the ships last night. He could clearly see the two turrets mounted 180 degrees apart at the bow of the ship. Unlike an old Earth navy ship, no barrels projected from the turrets.

Joe knew the *Seeker*'s main armament consisted of its sublight transport mechanism, a long tube running through the center of the entire length of the vessel. The accelerator could eject charged mass at relativistic velocities either forward or backward to provide thrust to move the ship. As a weapon, the tube could be used essentially as a railgun that was aimed by pointing the entire vessel. Joe had also learned that a spread could be given to the salvo, calculated to arrive with different concentrations depending on the range and nature of the target. The two lasers mounted in the front turrets provided a more flexible secondary weapons system.

The ship could not produce enough power to use these weapons continuously. The lasers discharged from superconducting storage banks under the turrets, and the fusion reactors that powered the *Seeker* could fire them at their designed maximum intensity three times an hour if the accelerator remained quiescent. The railgun could operate continuously, although its power could also be augmented with stored energy to impart higher velocities to its particles.

The ship rolled away from Joe's view as his shuttle spun to match the *Seeker*'s rotation. The ship maintained a spin around the central accelerator tube to simulate gravity for the crew when the gravity spinner wasn't running. He knew that the matching maneuver meant the trip neared its end; soon he would be aboard the *Seeker*.

He regained his seat and strapped back in. Only one other passenger shared the shuttle ride up from the surface of the planet, a taciturn officer whose name Joe couldn't recall. The other man hadn't left his seat the whole flight and seemed lost in a mental interface, so Joe hadn't attempted conversation.

The shuttle computer indicated that the docking had completed. Joe tried to use his link to access the ship's services to find out what time it was on board, but the *Seeker* computers denied him. He didn't possess clearance for even the most basic services yet.

A small acceleration made itself felt in the shuttle. A distant clunk occurred, more felt than heard. Joe took a deep breath and waited.

"Clear for disembarkment," came the pilot's voice in his head. Joe rose and stepped toward the exit. The other officer moved more slowly, so Joe left him behind. He didn't have any patience—he wanted to get on board the starship as soon as he could. He stepped through the hatch and came to a ladder. He would climb "up" toward the hollow spine of the *Seeker*, through her hull.

Joe started up the ladder. He glanced up and saw the cold black sphere of a security monitor looking down at him from the top of the tunnel. He wondered if a robotic weapon had locked onto him with an infrared laser sight. No point in dwelling on it, he decided. He came to the top and found himself in a small receiving room. There were three doors and a flat black plate in one wall before him. Two of the steel doors were closed; the third headed past a check station manned by two soldiers. Joe stood uncertainly.

The other officer who shared his flight walked straight forward to enter the body of the ship. Joe started to follow, but one of the enlisted men stepped into his way.

"This way, sir. I'm afraid you're not cleared for a straight boarding."

"Very well," Joe said, altering his course.

"I'll have to request that you turn your link off, sir. For just a few minutes."

Joe didn't like that, but he obeyed. The man led Joe through one of the side doors and into a scanning room. He pointed to a seat underneath some heavy equipment, and Joe sat down.

"This only takes a second. Sit very still, please."

Joe waited while the soldier walked behind a screen and stood staring at the wall. Joe recognized the absent look as that of a person accessing a virtual interface in their mind's eye. Joe didn't move. He couldn't detect any activity, but the man nodded and opened his eyes again.

"Okay. I need to ask you a few questions, sir. They are required if you are to be allowed on board—captain's orders, sir."

"Okay, I'm ready," Joe said.

"I'm sorry, sir, I'm not ready. Please wait a moment," the soldier said. He stared off into space for long moments, then focused his eyes back on Joe.

"You joined an organization when you were a young boy, age of seven," the crewman said. "Please relate the details of that."

Joe's eyebrow rose. "When I was seven? Is this a joke?"

"Answer the question, please. When you were seven, what organization did you join?"

Joe took a deep breath.

"I joined a junior chess club," Joe said.

"And how many people were in it?"

Joe thought for a moment. If he got the answer wrong, what would they do?

"There were over ten people…we had six games going sometimes…so about twelve people, maybe a few more."

"And who had the highest rating that year?"

Joe thought again. He could remember that.

"It was Cory Russell."

The man nodded. "That's acceptable, Lieutenant Hartlet. You may proceed through the lock on your right."

Joe stood carefully, leaning to avoid striking his head on the machinery near the chair. He went to the door and opened it. The man wasn't following him, but he kept his blank look.

Joe stepped through and found himself in a tubular hallway with a flat metal grate placed as a walking surface. He saw tubes and wiring arranged in neat rows under the grating. He wondered how he would find his way and automatically asked his link to provide directions before he remembered that it had been deactivated. The link connected. A map of the ship came up in his mind's eye.

Joe grunted. His access had been granted. He requested a route to the captain's office and saw it light up in green. Then he set off.

The interior of the ship felt comfortable. The air smelled fresh and the temperature was perfect. Wide, smooth glow mats on the ceiling provided a generic illumination that remained constant as he moved along.

The passage branched, and Joe ended up in a busy corridor running the length of the ship. He received a few curious glances, but no one spoke to him. He thought the crew probably knew one another well enough that a newcomer stood out. He wondered how much they knew about what had happened to him.

After a minute he arrived in a small waiting room and the computer gave him a message to wait. He regarded the uncomfortable-looking seats and had resigned himself to selecting one when his link gave him the signal to enter.

Joe stepped into a small, Spartan office. The captain sat back in a chair in one corner, looking off into space. Joe could see he was one of those men that looked as fit after forty as they had at twenty. The captain had short grey hair cut close to his skull. His face looked rough, his nose slightly bent to one side. Joe figured some sparring partner had probably gotten a good shot in on it years ago.

"Lieutenant Joe Hartlet, reporting for duty."

The captain absorbed this silently and regarded Joe. He looked to the side for a moment. Joe thought the captain must be accessing files. Then the captain stood and acknowledged Joe's existence.

"At ease. I'm glad you were able to make it here so quickly. Tell me about the alien, lieutenant. I've read your report, but I want your gut feeling about the creature. Did it feel threatening to you? Dangerous?"

Joe wavered for a moment, caught off guard by the question. "Um, I didn't feel any…malignance, but I believe that it could have killed me at any time."

"But it did use you for some sort of scheme to escape the complex. It may have had other reasons for leaving you unharmed than compassion or respect for life."

"Maybe, sir." Joe tried to sound skeptical.

The captain smiled. "You think you understand its basic drives. I could sense that in the report. It's a common mistake, lieutenant. People look at someone else and they make assumptions. It happens between people, and with aliens. But if there's one thing we've learned about the Trilisks, it's that aliens don't think like people. And so maybe this Shiny doesn't either."

Joe nodded. "May I ask a question, sir?"

"Go."

"When I boarded, I went through an extensive decontamination procedure, and they asked me some odd questions. What was that all about?"

"The report states that you've been exposed to Trilisk technology. Precautions have to be taken. We don't fully understand the capabilities of the Trilisks, and very troubling incidents have occurred in connection with artifacts of that race."

"I understand, sir." Joe wanted to ask about the "incidents," but he knew that he wouldn't be cleared for it.

"In fact, it's so bad that the request to pick you up was almost denied. I managed to convince my superiors that your personal viewpoint would be valuable enough to warrant this risk. While we're on the subject, I should tell you: The computers are going to be monitoring you very closely. If you do anything that you shouldn't, you may meet with lethal resistance. That's because of the possibility you have been suborned by an external power."

The captain pointed to a small black module in the center of the glow pad on the ceiling. Joe hadn't seen it when he came in. He wondered what array of weapons was pointed at him.

"I'll try to move carefully, sir."

"That would be wise."

The captain stared off into space for a moment. Joe knew he was accessing a mental interface. He imagined talking to the captain often included such pauses, as the business of running the ship interfered with conversation.

"Your link got erased by the smugglers, but I've reviewed the profiles you've created since then," the captain continued.

Joe's link indicated that the captain had sent him a pointer. He accessed the information and saw a picture in his mind's eye. It was the female smuggler from the planet. She looked younger in the pic, but it was definitely her.

"That's one of them, all right," Joe said. "How did you nail that one so quickly?"

"News from Earth," the captain said slowly. "Someone important went missing…they failed to attend a funeral where they were expected."

Joe thought the captain's voice sounded odd. He looked almost crestfallen. Joe was impressed at the intelligence network of the space force. One girl went missing from a funeral and they linked it to this smuggler already?

"I'm ordering you to clear that pic from your link," the captain said. Another pause came. "That girl is the brat of a high-up in the world cabinet. You are not to mention this conversation to anyone. You understand? It will be handled quietly."

That explained it, Joe thought. His eyebrows rose.

"Yes, sir, I understand. Not a word."

"Good. Don't be surprised if the DNA snoopers down at the installation turn up empty, either. At least officially. And don't ask about it if you like your career in the force."

Joe nodded.

"I assume that you're here to ensure that no more smugglers get to the planet," Joe said. "Now that we have discovered a site with active Trilisk technology, will the government be stepping up its presence on the planet?"

"No. We're leaving the planet immediately to pursue the two smugglers you met and the alien that you called Shiny."

Joe stared for a moment, shocked.

"How can we do that, sir?"

"That, lieutenant, is need-to-know. But it should be obvious to you that the UNSF doesn't share all of its capabilities with everyone," Captain Relachik said. "We'll have a decent chance at recovering the alien."

"That's fantastic, sir! I hope I can be of some assistance. If nothing else, they know me, and I might be able to keep the trespassers and the alien calm when we close in."

"That will be important. We have the Trilisk facility, but it's clear from your report that the alien you met, who we suspect left with the smugglers, is of a different race. Its civilization may still be active just beyond our frontiers. We need more information, and I intend to get it."

Michael McCloskey

Chapter Twenty

"You know, he's working the computer resources I gave him pretty hard," Magnus told Telisa. They sat on mats in the cargo hold across from Shiny, surrounded by bags of equipment and training hardware.

"Right now? I thought he was still working on making noises."

Shiny's small sphere module buzzed against the floor again, parodying her voice.

"Riyyyyyt Neow? Rieeeeyt Now?"

"I think he can do lots of things at once. Or at least he has computers with him that can."

Magnus closed his eyes to check. Telisa kept her eyes on Shiny, considering the alien's silvery equipment around the trunk of his body. She supposed that part of it did comprise a computer or an alien analog of one.

"That makes sense. It's a natural progression from where we are with our links," she said.

After mentioning the links, Telisa felt a loss for hers again. Once the spy program had been detected, Magnus had shut it down so he could clean out the tampering. The entity she had queried every few minutes for her entire adult life now stayed completely silent. Her mind felt empty without it. At least down in the Trilisk compound, the link had responded to her queries with polite error messages and explanations. Now she felt lonely in her own skull.

"Thaaaat makzzzz senzze," buzzed the device.

"He must be trying to correlate this with our readable files. It's too bad that we can't link up to a net source without giving away our location, or we could download some language tutorials for him. He'll have to make do with our local file cache."

Telisa knew that the ship had large stores of knowledge that it kept to allow the most common inquiries to occur without having to ask for external data. It wasn't surprising that there was little information about language, though, given that no one had accessed that kind of data before they had left Earth.

Telisa stood up and carefully walked forward. She pointed to herself and spoke slowly.

"Telisa."

"Telllizzza."

Telisa pointed at Shiny. "Shiny," she said.

There was a pause. "Shhhhineeee," the device whined.

Telisa pointed back at herself.

"Tellizzza."

She smiled back at Magnus, but his eyes were closed.

"Shiny just queried the dictionary for several hundred possible phonetic spellings of Shiny and Telisa," he said.

"He can match the phonetic breakdowns with the words? How could he know that?"

Magnus shrugged. "There must be some kind of probabilistic approach. He hears what we say…he sees what we do and tries to match them up with the images in the dictionary. Then he can make and test assumptions about the phonetic symbols and—"

"So we think it's possible. I knew it would be difficult; he must have a lot of help, or else he's a major brain train," Telisa said.

"To an alien, it wouldn't even be obvious what part of the information in the definitions represents the phonetic structure," Magnus said. "Just figuring that out could take a while. Just converting the compressed binary data of the dictionary into characters would take us some time to work out."

"And he had to figure out what the image data format was. And which data were images. And what it meant...I guess he could have cheated and looked at how one of the wall imagers worked," Telisa said.

"Well, he's ahead of where we thought. He probably made a breakthrough when we went through the names of everything in the cargo hold and showed him the imagers. A lot of the pics must have matched up with stuff in the dictionary. Not to mention all the image notations that must be in the ship's data cache. Probably everything we looked at for weeks before leaving Earth is in there."

Shiny shuffled about briefly and then faced them with twitching legs.

"Greeetingz. Hellllo."

"Hi Shiny!" Telisa burst out. "Hello!"

"Queeeery. Question. Request."

Magnus and Telisa exchanged amazed looks.

"Ask. I'll answer," Telisa said.

"Destination. End point. Terminus."

"Uh, nowhere. I mean, unknown," Telisa said. "We're thinking about it. Someone may be looking for us wherever we go."

"Request."

"Request away, Shiny," Telisa said.

"Destination. Allocate. Set."

Magnus frowned. "He has a suggestion for where to go?"

"Hrm. I don't imagine he wants to go anywhere we're familiar with."

"Destination. Suggestion."

"He does have a course plot," Magnus reported, holding his eyes closed. "It is beyond the frontier. If a human scout ship has been there, then it's been kept secret."

"Shiny, what's there? Is that where you're from?"

Shiny twitched again on one side and didn't answer immediately.

"Why should we go there? Can you explain?"

"Destination. Safe. Haven. Sanctuary."

Magnus frowned again. "Odd. I guess he knows that we're being chased?"

"I don't know. Does he mean safe for us or safe for him? Or both?"

"War. Conflict. Battle. Shiny. Safe."

"Oh. So you will be safe there. Or us too, if whoever you're fighting finds us."

"Shit," Magnus interjected. "What if he's fighting the UNSF? Could they be fighting a secret war against Shiny's race and we don't even know about it? This could be bad. If we take him to one of his planets, we could be killed."

"Let's try and find out more," Telisa said. She tried to access her link again and failed. "Dammit. I keep forgetting my link is off. Driving me nuts."

"I can fix it up. But this is pretty distracting."

"Of course. I understand, I didn't mean that it was your fault."

Magnus stood up. "Let me go take care of that now. I need to make sure that I don't overlook anything or else they may end up in control of it again. I'm going to go into my quarters and work on it for a while."

"Thanks. I'll keep him company while I examine these artifacts."

"See if you can figure out why he's obsessed with our destination," Magnus said.

"Will do."

"Wheel do," buzzed Shiny.

Magnus turned to go, but Telisa called after him. "Magnus?"

"Yeah?"

Telisa gave a weak smile. "I really appreciate this. I appreciate everything. I know that this hasn't gone the way we planned, but I'm glad you're here."

"Kinda rough for your first sortie, huh? Fifty percent casualties," Magnus said. "I'm glad you're here, too. You're tough and smart—we'll get through this just fine."

He turned and left the bay. Telisa went over to her bags of tools and set out a small work area on the metal bay floor.

"Let's figure out what these things are, Shiny," she said.

"Investigate."

"Yeah, investigate. And try not to get killed. This is why I'm making the big bucks, Shiny. Messing with artifacts can be dangerous business. Not to mention landing on forbidden planets and taking them in the first place."

"Caution. Balance. Curiosity."

"Hrm, yes, you understand, don't you?"

Telisa carefully took out an artifact, a small double-wrench-shaped link of metal. It had flat panels of some dull gray material on one side, one panel on each end. A hexagonal opening lay next to the panel on one end.

Telisa found a container that would hold the artifact and set it nearby. She looked through her scanners and picked one that did a passive analysis of electromagnetic fields. She knew from previous results with Trilisk artifacts that an active scanner could trigger something inside the device, causing it to perform one of its functions. That could be good or bad, depending on what its function was and whether or not it could hurt someone.

"Let's start out safe," she said. She turned the passive scanner on and looked at the inside of the wrench object. There appeared to be two solid blocks of what were called "Trilisk ultradense cybernetic blocks" by researchers, one at each end, connected by a series of filaments. The cybernetic blocks were truly black boxes to human investigators. No one had figured out how they were built or how they worked, but each such block was theorized to be capable of receiving mental instructions from alien brains and performing tremendous amounts of computation.

"It has two ultradenses," Telisa said. "Nothing surprising there. Standard Trilisk fare so far. Who knows what it does?"

Automatically she tried to access the scanner's wireless infodump through her link and failed. "Shit," she mumbled.

"Excrete," Shiny said.

Telisa chuckled. "You haven't mastered figures of speech yet. I guess you're not so stunningly on top of things after all. Not that I can brag. Without my link, I'm not going to be able to get at half the information these scanners can give me."

Telisa stared at the wrench for a moment longer. Why two ultradense computing blocks for one small device? Why was it shaped like a human double wrench? A lot of Trilisk artifacts had the gray plates which could emit radiation, the supposed viewing panels on them. This tiny device had two of them, presumably one for each block of cybernetic material.

"Well, maybe I'll just do an overview of everything we have, since my link isn't working," she said. Shiny had no comment, so she put the wrench object into the foam-lined container she had chosen. She taped an ID number to the outside of the plastic box and set it aside.

"Next artifact," she called out, as if processing a line of customers.

"Neeeext artifayct," mimicked Shiny. "Function. Investigate. Theorize."

Telisa smiled and took the next item out of her backpack. It was the glowing ovoid thing, like a slightly yellowish egg with a weave of silver netting wrapped onto it.

"Let's see what's inside this thing," she said.

"Caution. Warning. Device. Active," Shiny said.

"It's on? How do you know? What is this thing, Shiny?"

Shiny didn't answer. The legs on his twitchy side jumped again briefly. Telisa turned on the scanner and looked down at the display. The world melted and suddenly became horribly wrong, twisted into an unrecognizable form. Telisa felt that she must be dying—she couldn't feel her body, take a breath, or see correctly. Yet there were sensations, input that she found non-sequitur for a moment. Then came the thoughts, invading her mind at first, and then blending with it.

Jangar looked out through the clear panel across a barren, rocky landscape to the far towers. His vision was highly focusable, and the far image shot forward at his will, expanding to a clear view of the distant dwellings. Now he could plainly see the devastation visited upon the surface by the methane-breathers' assault.

His body twitched, and he stepped into a new stance to let another of his sides take a look. Jangar's thoughts became more abstract, losing the details of the image he had seen from the original stance. This was the death site for three thousand of his race, yet Jangar bared his auditory sensors in a smile. A small price to pay for the success of the retribution fleet.

Their final revenge, to be inflicted by the assembled home fleet of Body Riken, had passed through two days before the assault here. The carapace-lacking methane-breathers still would not know of its approach. His mouth tentacles writhed at the arrogance of the creatures, to think that his race could be toyed with! Jangar's only misgiving was that he was not among the Body's finest, even now cutting deep into the methane worlds. The fleet would be ruthless, of course. The methane-breathers' worlds would be totally destroyed, made useless forever.

An alarm transmission triggered in the OTHER. The enemy was attacking again! Jangar switched his focus and the OTHER took control. The view dimmed as his primary legs propelled him down the corridor, heading for the vertical translator. While the OTHER had focus, the submerged parts of him made acceleration estimates and reveled in the knowledge that revenge would be enacted.

"Five Holy Entities," Telisa gasped. "That was high-voltage stuff!" She cradled her head in her hands. The experience had been overwhelming, stepping into the consciousness of another being. A nonhuman creature, with a body beyond description, feelings that she had never felt before. Telisa felt faint. Without warning, she fell forward and vomited, barely managing to miss her backpack and the scanner. She lay to one side, breathing heavily while her stomach tightened and her heart pounded away.

"Shiny…that was awful…and wonderful all at the same time. It was so powerful."

"Device. Active. Caution," Shiny repeated.

"Yeah. Active. No kidding," she said.

"Partial view. You have two parts in three."

"What? You mean the other? That thing had three parts, first one was looking out the window and I could see every tiny detail, enough to make my head hurt. Then he stepped…turned, or something, and just started thinking about what it all meant, and the details became more distant. But there was some alarm or something, then the whole recording washed out, like I was feeling it all secondhand."

"Two parts in three. Brain sections. Telisa with two. Trilisk with three."

"Uh, wow. I guess our name for them was better than we realized. We call them Trilisks because the discoverer of the initial ruin decided that they must have been trilaterally symmetrical."

"Yes. Trilisk, three parts. Three stances. Three facings. Three minds."

"Yet I could feel the others, some kind of underlying togetherness…like the way my two hemispheres are connected!"

"Similar. Analog. Comparable."

"Well, what about you? You could understand the Other? How many lobes do you have?"

"Twenty."

"What! No way! Twenty…hey, you have forty legs?"

"Yes. Twenty nodes along central connection. Analog of human spinal cord. Twenty lobes. Generic. Nonspecialized."

"Generic? They each do the same tasks equally well? Wow. But the Trilisk brains were super specialized…more so than human left and right hemispheres, I think. One did way more abstract thought than the first one. But the Other…I don't even know what it could be specialized to do."

"Yes. Trilisk specialized. Telisa understanding perhaps beyond Shiny. Brain is partially specialized. Right lobe, left lobe. Alien. Fascinating."

"Yeah. Fascinating is an understatement."

Michael McCloskey

Chapter Twenty-One

Telisa catalogued the other items, scanning and tagging them one at a time. Each of the things had an ultradense block that she could see through the passive scanner, except for one artifact, a flat, square plate the size of her palm that had ridges on its edges as if it were made of dozens of layers of metal. It seemed as inert to her eye as it did to the passive scanner.

Telisa tried to activate her link recorder to take some notes. Her link gave no reply. She sighed and summarized aloud anyway.

"That's fourteen Trilisk items all together," she said. Shiny seemed attentive. "So far I only have a clue about one of them. It appears to be some sort of communication device, or maybe a memory recorder of some kind. What's astounding about it is it can actually translate from an alien consciousness to experiences that my brain can understand. Well, partially understand, modulo my 'missing' third lobe. Although it seems already that the…feelings, or senses, that the alien had are fading from my mind."

"Trilisk. Ancient. Enigmatic," Shiny buzzed.

"Very enigmatic," she agreed. Telisa pried herself up from her sitting position on the deck and started to put things away.

"You're enigmatic to us too, Shiny," Telisa said. "You and your forty legs and your little spheres."

"Thirty-eight legs," Shiny corrected.

"I'm sorry. I forgot," Telisa said. "We'll figure out how to grow them back, I'm sure."

"Probable."

"Who are you at war with, Shiny?"

"Conflict, combat. Waged against race you cannot name. Humans have not coined term."

"What're they like? Why do you fight them?"

"Competition for limited resources. No optimal cooperative solution. Optimal solution, my side wins."

An insistent tone interrupted her from the conversation. Her link awakened and responded to her first query with the current time. Telisa smiled and sighed in relief.

"Yes! It's so nice to have a link back! Sorry, Shiny, gimme a second."

Telisa queried for the date and received it. She asked the link for her blood sugar and it replied. It told her how long she had been awake and a list of other personal links within range. She scrolled through a list of local services offered by tiny computers placed throughout the ship. Once again, a huge amount of information was back at her fingertips—the temperature of hot water in the ship's reserve, the number of rations stored in the galley's cabinets, and the volume of the forward hold.

She could even see three-dimensional images of the ship in her mind's eye. Telisa asked for an overview of her position and saw a tiny red figure, herself, sitting in a transparent green technical drawing of the ship. She queried for directions to the pilot seats and saw the route light up with a red line.

"Ha! My link works! Sooo wonderful! How did humans ever live without links?"

"Link dysfunction. Query. Source, cause, root?" buzzed Shiny's tiny sphere.

"Yes...oh, ah, the cause. Hrm, well, the government, that is the UNSF...you know what that is? The government thinks that I'm a danger because I'm a xenoarchaeologist who won't join the space force. But I won't join because they take everyone's rights away, and my father chose the force over my family when I was a kid. Or maybe it's because I joined a group of smugglers. I don't know; all I do know is, they control everyone too much, and they won't let me live my life the way I want to...the way I need to."

"Human government. Oppressive, bureaucratic, inefficient. Corrective course: decouple control of structure from organization being structured."

"Hrm. Yeah, since when did the government ever make itself smaller or reduce its own power? Not since the last revolution. Maybe us humans will get it right next time...if we ever manage to get control back again."

"Government, humans apply cyclical evolution strategy. Yes, improve framework on next iteration."

"Anyway, Magnus cleaned it up and it's so nice to have it back...I bet you'd miss your computers or whatever all that stuff you have attached to your body is, if it were turned off...but now I need to go back and look at the artifacts all over again!"

Telisa unpacked the scanner and linked with it to check out its memory of the items that she had examined. She had just brought up the first readout when she heard footsteps approaching on the deck.

"All better?" Magnus asked.

Telisa looked up at her last human companion. Magnus stood straight, in his Veer skinsuit as always, regarding Shiny.

"Much. Thanks!" she said. "I've been looking at the artifacts and chatting with Shiny. By the way, one of them is a memory recorder or something like that. I picked it up and suddenly it was like being in a sim except I had an alien body and alien senses."

"Amazing what we could learn. Plus, if we can ever sell those things…"

Telisa nodded. "We'd be set for life. Except for the minor detail of being hunted criminals."

"Jack was better about that sort of stuff, but he taught me a thing or two. We'll have to think everything out carefully before we head back."

"I suppose we need to talk about where we're eventually going to go," Telisa said.

"We need to hang low. There're a few smaller frontier ports I know that we may be able to get supplies from after a while without going through too much security. On the other hand, that's what they'd expect us to do."

"Policy. Statement. Destination. Control. Modification."

"We have to go hide, Shiny. We must control the destination. We're in danger, we may be hunted. By the UNSF," Telisa said.

"Shiny. Destination. Modification," Shiny's device said. Telisa tried to make sense of this for a moment.

"Telisa." Magnus said it gently. Telisa turned to regard Magnus.

"Yes?"

"Shiny has control of the ship. He's changed our course."

Telisa's mouth dropped open. She tried to speak, but only an odd grunt came out. She took a deep breath.

"Control of the ship? He just learned to speak a few hours ago."

Magnus shrugged. "In some ways, he had to master the computer systems to get that far. What I didn't expect was his ability to find and exploit security holes in our systems. I'm convinced that he has very powerful computers of his own at his control."

"Yes, part of his amazing equipment there on the trunk of his body. Shiny, where are we going now?"

"Stronghold. Sanctuary."

"Well, it sounds good enough if you put it that way. One of your worlds?"

"Outpost. Existence uncertain," Shiny droned. "War. Conflict. Damage probable, destruction possible."

"Okay, now it's sounding less safe," Telisa said.

"Come with me, let's talk alone," Magnus suggested.

"Query. Magnus, Telisa, communicate. Exchange privileged information?" Shiny asked. An awkward silence ensued.

"Uhm, we're going to go mate," Telisa said. "Y'know, copulate. You can look that one up."

Magnus's eyebrows rose. He smiled and offered his hand, which Telisa took, and they marched out of the cargo bay.

As soon as they left the bay, Magnus raised his finger to his lips, signaling silence. Telisa nodded her understanding. He led her to the forward most g-damper pod. Telisa crawled into the tube. Magnus pulled the slugthrower off his back and slid in next to her. He smelled good, and Telisa realized she hadn't been in such a private situation with a man in a long time. She smiled.

"We really ought to figure out what to do about Shiny," Magnus said. "He seems nice, but I wonder if he's dangerous. We've been over-anthropomorphizing him."

Telisa tore her eyes away and forced herself to think about Shiny.

"We have to take control of the computers back, lock him out somehow. It occurs to me that we didn't even ask him to relinquish control. It just kind of freaked me out—I haven't really absorbed everything yet."

"We could always try to blow a hole in his head," Magnus said.

"Seems extreme. Is he threatening our lives?"

"I guess that depends on where we're really going. I don't know if attacking him would work…those little spheres that follow him around seem to protect him. I think we both doubt he'll just give control back, since he took it away without asking."

"I wonder if he knows he's being rude, or if he cares," Telisa said.

"You mean maybe it's acceptable in his society to take over someone else's ship? Sounds unlikely."

"Shiny's an alien. Who knows what kind of codes of behavior he follows? Speaking of which, I just got a dose of just how alien is alien."

"What do you mean?"

"That Trilisk artifact I accidentally activated. It was sort of like a VR sim, except I was an alien. I mean, in more than just form, but in frame of mind, feelings, senses, everything. It wasn't like anything I've ever experienced before. Shiny told me that I couldn't quite experience it right because the recording was for a creature with three brain lobes, and he said he has twenty!"

"If he's capable of behavior that inexplicable to us, then he could kill us at any time. We have no way of knowing if he even values our lives. There are just too many unknowns."

"All right. You work on getting control back, and I'll grill him about where we're going and what he means to do with us. He may not tell me the truth, but it can't hurt to try. We can save the blowing-him-away stuff for later."

Magnus nodded and stared at her for a moment.

"We should probably do some of that mating stuff," he said. "Just to throw off suspicion, of course."

Telisa laughed. It seemed like they never had time to be alone, ever since things had started going wrong. How many times had she daydreamed of a moment like this since she met Magnus?

"Good idea," she said and pulled him closer.

Michael McCloskey

Chapter Twenty-Two

Hours slipped inexorably into days while the *Iridar* traveled through the void. Telisa puzzled over her artifact collection while Magnus prodded the computer system, trying to learn what limits Shiny had placed on their controls.

Telisa found herself daydreaming about Magnus again, despite her attempts to remain focused. Since their encounter in the crash pod, they had grown much closer. She relived their experiences in her mind's eye, pleased to know that even though their situation remained dire, she had him to share it with. The uncertainty of their future made the relationship all that more intense. Everything that had seemed important in her past life suddenly seemed so trivial, so silly.

An odd twitch in her chest brought her out of her reverie. The artifact she held had done something she could feel. It looked like two horseshoes welded together side by side and felt like dense plastic. Her notes from earlier said that the passive scan had revealed an ultradense block and a single gray panel on one side, presumably some kind of visual feedback mechanism that worked in the wavelengths usually associated with Trilisk artifacts.

The lights in the bay flickered.

"Desist. Refrain," Shiny buzzed.

"What was that? The artifact did it."

"Energy emission. Disruptive."

She looked at the latest scanner buffer in her mind's eye to see if it had recorded anything unusual. In the data she saw an electromagnetic spike, an event that had induced a current through her body. It had lightly shocked her. In fact, it had almost been enough to reset her link.

"Now how did that happen?" she asked herself. She carefully set the object back down into its holding container. If the thing could shock her, it might be potentially lethal, even though the current she had experienced had been small.

The scanner didn't reveal any recognizable power signatures from the device. Either it didn't have any power cells, or its surface blocked her scanner from detecting them.

"I'm sorry, Shiny, did that hurt you?"

"Disruptive," Shiny said.

Telisa looked at the alien again. She'd actually started getting used to Shiny—even the eerie front end of his body that had struck her at first as being a faceless head. She realized that she still didn't understand very much about how his body worked.

"Shiny, did you look up anything about our bodies in the computer?"

The backside of the alien flinched again. Nerve damage, the alien had said. She wondered how severe it was.

"Cache contains rudimentary data," Shiny said.

"Ah, yes. I'm used to a cache that can retrieve more from the outside system. But we're isolated here on the ship. I guess you don't know quite as much about us as you'd like. And I'd like to learn more about your physiology, as well. Do you see things?"

"Yes. Collect visual data."

"Where…where are your eyes?"

Shiny's front leg indicated the tiny fibers under his wide head at the opposite end of his body from the hook Telisa now thought of as his mouth.

"Oh, wow, those little things? Hrm. Do they allow you to see through walls?"

"No. No human analog of mass sense."

"Mass sense? You can detect mass?"

Shiny swung his head side to side in a now familiar motion.

"Yes. Relative motion required."

"Amazing...I envy you that one, I must say."

"Hearing, smell, these inputs are advantageous as well. I do not possess them by nature."

"Then how do you know what I say?"

"Artificial detection. My attendants. Just as I speak with them."

"Those tiny spheres that float around you and attach to the silvery part of your back?"

"Correct."

"Hrm, so you can't hear or smell. Interesting. Magnus had guessed that you had some kind of ability to sense things through walls." Telisa became nervous as she thought of the attack on Thomas and Jack. Would Shiny do something bad if she told him they believed he had killed their friends?

"Collected data, created theory to explain Shiny actions?"

"Yes...it was when we were attacked. The attack seemed very much like you or another of your race was behind it." Telisa winced, hoping she hadn't said something dangerous. Would the alien deny it?

"Memory. Recall. Encounter before alliance. Competitive status and resulting conflict."

"Competitive? Why did you assume that we were in competition, Shiny?" Telisa asked in a quiet, shaking voice.

"Preventative measure. Avoid attack."

"Then why did you assume we'd attack you?"

"Your race. Attacked Shiny before. Projectile barrage. With war machines."

"Oh. I'm sorry we had the…misunderstanding then. My race…we don't all share the same goals. Magnus and I would never attack you. Do you understand?"

"Alliance. Cooperative relationship. Optimal at this time."

"Yes, that's optimal," Telisa said. But she had caught his words…*at this time.*

***

Every fourth day was grappling day on the ship. Telisa arrived in the gym area early, carrying a workout bag.

She broke open the recloseable top, took out a spray bottle of artificial skin, and gave the tops of her feet a quick layer. Telisa found that she tended to bleed all over the mat from tears in her feet if she didn't strengthen the skin there. Magnus's feet were covered in thick calluses that prevented the problem. When she'd asked about it on the voyage to Thespera, he told her it had taken years to thicken the skin on the tops of his feet.

Magnus came in. He stripped off his Veer skinsuit, leaving him in thin black stretchy pants. Telisa stole a look and smiled. Training days like this were one of the rare times he could be observed out of the protective suit.

"Hi. How's it going with Shiny?" he asked, grabbing a pair of white gi pants out of his pack.

"Oh, he's been pretty helpful pointing out a few details about the artifacts. The big thing is just having my link back. It's hard to use any of our equipment without one."

"Yeah. We're pretty dependent on the links."

Telisa could tell from his tone that he was thinking about the disadvantages of depending on their links in combat.

"What's it like, grappling with the skinsuit on?"

"Close to the same. But elbows and knees don't hurt, even with a lot of weight behind them. It's harder to get a choke or a joint lock, but it's still possible. It's mostly just that the little things that make you uncomfortable aren't there. So you can't train with one or your stomach won't harden up right, for instance."

Telisa nodded. She took a VR hookup out onto the floor and lay down on the mat. They each usually went through about an hour of virtual lessons and practice before warming up for real and doing some grappling against each other.

"See ya in a few," she said and hooked in.

Telisa found herself in a beautiful training building made of glass and wood. Light streamed in from outside, a bright sunny day on a tropical island. Palm trees were visible through the giant windows, swaying in a breeze that couldn't be heard.

Telisa faced herself on a matted floor. For weeks she'd been fighting herself, overcoming her own weaknesses. Each time the computer upgraded her virtual opponent with her own tricks and added new ones. Telisa learned the new tricks and shored up her weaknesses by fighting the model of herself.

She stepped forward and grabbed the enemy at neck and arm. They stepped around each other, pushing and pulling, trying to throw each other off balance. Finally Telisa stepped inside and tried to trip her opposite. The attempt failed, and she got thrown off balance but managed to twist so that they both fell onto their sides next to each other.

Telisa tried to wrap her leg over her opponent's legs, but unexpectedly her mirror image grabbed her foot and then moved back from her to twist it. The pain rose rapidly. Telisa tried to ignore it, but something snapped in her foot, so she tapped her opponent's leg, indicating submission. Her replica released her foot, and Telisa pulled it back and massaged it. It didn't seem broken despite the snapping sound. She decided it must have been a tendon sliding over a bone ridge. The foot felt sore.

"Legs, huh? That's cheating," she said, even though she knew it wasn't true.

"Breaking an opponent's foot would be a desirable outcome," the computer replied.

Telisa shook her head and started again. By the end of the session, she'd figured out that it helped if she pulled herself toward her opponent, trying to bring her leg close and grab onto her enemy. But applying the same hold to her duplicate's foot eluded her.

She cut the link and returned to the real training area. Magnus sat nearby, involved in his own training session. Telisa took a drink of water and stretched until Magnus finished.

"Okay, let's hit it," Magnus said. He rolled forward onto the mat and stopped before Telisa. They started on their knees, grasping each other at neck and elbow. The combat proceeded as a familiar ebb and flow of forces, bringing Telisa alternately forward and backward. Telisa knew that pitfalls existed in either direction. If she went off balance toward Magnus, she could be brutally pulled down and find herself in a lock with an arm choking her head. If she were thrown back too far, then Magnus could take a top mount.

After a few moments Magnus decided to force the issue. He pushed forward and to one side, sending Telisa reeling away. He dashed to her backside. Telisa rolled to face him, although he had passed her legs and now held a superior position over her, pinning her on her back. He kneeled with his knee pressing down into her stomach, making breathing difficult. Telisa concentrated on defense, keeping her arms up to protect her head and neck.

He pressed forward mercilessly, pressing his other elbow against the side of her jaw. Telisa growled at him in pain and frustration. She pushed his elbow away, but he brought it back a few seconds later, pressing again. Telisa ignored the pain and grabbed at his legs instead, rolling toward him. She fishtailed her body out from underneath him, pushing away with her arms.

Magnus slid smoothly back over her and brought his leg around, taking a top mount. He grabbed one of her arms and pried it back. Telisa knew she didn't have long before he would apply a lock to it. She wrapped one of her ankles over his and threw him to one side with her hips, rolling with the motion.

Now Magnus lay on his back underneath her, but his legs still trapped her. She slipped her knee along the inside of his leg to pry it back, passing his guard. His powerful arms came forward to take hold of her gi, preventing her from mounting him. Telisa faked an attempt at attacking one of his arms, threatening to apply a lock.

When Magnus responded to the danger, she changed her tactic and shot her other leg over his knee, taking a full mount. She settled onto him, keeping her center of gravity low to make herself hard to throw off.

Telisa tried to control one of his arms again, but Magnus was too strong. Her thin arms, although toned, seemed inadequate to take control of his heavier limbs. Under her mount, Magnus presented her with his stony elbows, keeping her from his throat. She stilled for a moment, breathing steadily.

Vaguely some part of her became aware of the hardness of his groin cup under her pelvis, reminding her of other things she had experienced in the crash tube with her opponent in similar positions. She relaxed, molding more of herself against him.

Magnus sensed her subtle change in mood. He opened his elbows and allowed her to press his arms back over his head. She felt a flutter of a noncombative emotion in her stomach.

"Let me show you a new hold I've thought of," Telisa said, bringing her face close to his.

Magnus looked into her eyes. "By all means, instruct me."

Michael McCloskey

Chapter Twenty-Three

"Hi. Are you making progress?" asked Magnus.

Telisa turned to see him walk into the bay. She smiled and pointed out the horseshoe device. "Some."

"So these can be dangerous, right? That's why the space force makes it illegal to have them." He winked at her to let her know he wasn't trying to justify their policies.

"Yeah. Well, I could be more careful in a real lab. This is the artifact I shocked myself on," Telisa said. "It still has some juice, even after all this time."

"I wonder how?"

"Search me. I don't know what the power source is. My scanner isn't showing that it has any power at all. It should be dead. But it just generated quite an EM spike."

"Broadcast power, maybe," Magnus suggested.

"We left the planet a long time ago. You're not suggesting that it could have such a range…?"

"No. I don't know. We could try to hook up a circuit to check it out more carefully," Magnus suggested. He chuckled. "It might be easier to study when your body isn't part of the conductor."

Telisa smiled. "Yeah, that sounds like a great experiment. Let's set it up. I wonder how much power the thing has left? Of course, we might end up using the last bit of energy it needs to work; then we'll never figure it out."

"Well, right now there's something else up. I came down here to tell you…we've arrived."

"Where?"

Magnus shrugged. "What Shiny called the sanctuary, I guess. Some kind of space station or outpost. Here, I'll point you at our sensor data."

Telisa's link received a location to find what Magnus saw. Telisa closed her eyes and saw the ship's sensor output interface in her mind. She flipped through the accumulated scans, seeing images and three-dimensional models in her mind's eye.

The base extended well beyond the size of the *Iridar*, shaped like three identical spheres anchored together in a triangle with thin filaments of material. The entire assembly shadowed a rocky moon in its orbit around a nearby planet.

"It's not really rotating. I wonder if Shiny's race has mastered artificial gravity," Telisa said.

"I'm betting there is. They have to have gravity control or else the whole base would eventually collide with the moon. I think it's paired with the moon, kept at a constant distance with some kind of force link."

"Shiny's probably been gone for a while. I hope they welcome him back…and for that matter I hope they welcome us, too."

"I assume that Shiny will be going over there soon. Question is, will we be going over there?"

"We could stay here, but I'm tempted to follow. There might be more artifacts, and we could meet more of his kind, see if they are at all interested in us."

"They might just flush us out the airlock, of course," Magnus said.

"Yes, they might. But Shiny hasn't seemed openly hostile. Despite his recent takeover."

He shrugged. "All right. As we've said, he could have killed us already. Let's follow him and see what we can learn. But make sure your link logs the way back. I assume this time, the stupid tunnels won't switch around on us."

"Funny—it makes sense that they won't now, but I half expect them to," she said.

Magnus nodded. "We've learned not to take that for granted anymore. At least for a while."

They walked over to the equipment bags they had taken with them on the previous sortie.

"I already restocked the food and water. And added a little more, this time," Telisa said.

"Can never have enough of that canned rations crap," Magnus added sardonically.

Shiny marched into the bay, his many legs flicking nervously.

"Lead the way, Shiny!" Telisa said.

The alien stood in place for a moment. One of his legs twitched periodically, making a slight scraping sound.

"Why do you do that, Shiny?" Telisa asked.

"Brain damage. Leg moves sometimes," Shiny answered.

"Wow. Sorry to hear that. At least you have nineteen other brains!"

"True. Correct."

"We can go onto your base, can't we?" Telisa asked.

"Egress. Entrance. This is allowed," buzzed Shiny's generated voice. The statement ended the moment of inactivity. The cargo bay doors activated, filling the space with the sound of the hatch mechanism.

"Shit! Shiny, you're not depressurizing the bay, are you?" Telisa asked, her voice wavering near panic.

Magnus bolted across the bay, motioning to Telisa. "Go for one of the pods!" he called.

"Pressure, present externally," came a broken sentence from the alien.

Telisa stared at the growing opening of the bay doors and realized that there was no screaming wind of depressurization. Instead of the darkness of space, a soft white light filtered in from the outside.

Magnus stooped and put his hands on his knees. "You're a laugh a minute, Shiny," he said, his voice strained.

The doors reached their maximum dilation, and the mechanical sounds stopped. Shiny moved out, heading straight down the lower door, which formed a ramp to the outside floor.

"We're inside the station, I assume," Telisa said. She checked the sensor feed through her link and saw that she'd guessed correctly. She saw their position within one of the large spheres that formed the body of the base.

"Should we follow him or what?" she asked Magnus.

They walked side by side to the edge of the bay, staring out into the alien room. It looked like a natural cavern, lined with pockets of the now-familiar formations of dull beige shapes littered with green rods. Shiny was just disappearing down a side corridor.

"Ah, I guess not," Magnus said. "Unless you want to sprint after him."

"Yeah. He's in a hurry or something," she said.

"It's just like back in the Trilisk installation," Magnus noted. "All this cave stuff is going to look alike."

"Yeah. I'm using my link to map it. This stuff might be a little different. Before it was a poor copy—remember the reports we read in the fake office place? This should all be real."

They walked down the bay ramp, looking in all directions. Telisa walked up to a bank of cubes.

"It all looks connected. Shit, don't any of these aliens have a civilization where they keep a lot of junk lying around?"

Magnus laughed. "So you can take anything that's not nailed down?"

"Exactly."

"Well, as things get more advanced…stuff just starts getting smaller and more remotely activated…for all we know, there's furniture embedded in the floor, factories waiting in every wall, who knows what."

Telisa stared at the intricate blue panel. She didn't dare touch anything since it was a complete mystery.

"Where are the other Shinies? Aren't they curious about the new visitors?" she wondered aloud.

"I'm getting a little nervous," Magnus admitted. "Let's go see if we can catch up with him, since there isn't anything just lying around for us to collect."

Telisa nodded. She led the way, heading out the tunnel that Shiny had raced down a minute ago.

"Well, we won't have any trouble finding him," Magnus said. Telisa looked at the floor where Magnus indicated. She saw an intricate trail of tiny footprints, each little more than a round impression the size of a thumbnail.

"Hrm. I would expect some sort of automated cleaning system in a place this advanced."

"Maybe it was shut down to save power, or because there aren't any other Shinies here right now," Magnus guessed.

"Or maybe they just like living with this dirt or sand on the floor. We removed dirt from our inside environments. This sandy stuff looks pretty clean, though. It may be sterile."

They followed the trail through three chambers and a long, rough corridor before finding Shiny. The alien worked on a bank of cubes at a feverish pace. Several of his legs held blocks of the material that laced the walls, and his attendant spheres danced in and out, fusing things together almost faster than the eye could follow.

"Shiny, where are the others of your kind? You aren't the only one here, are you?"

Shiny swiveled around and spoke with an orb that buzzed against the wall. "Singular. One. Only."

"There's only one of your race?"

"One, here, sanctuary. Others, elsewhere, distant," Shiny said.

"Is it unusual that others aren't here?" asked Magnus.

"Unusual. Unexplained. Mysterious," Shiny said. The many legged alien turned back and skittered down the passageway. Telisa and Magnus jogged after, trying to stay close.

"Hey Shiny, are there any...pieces of equipment around here that aren't attached to the walls? I want something to bring back with me. Is there something here that you wouldn't miss?"

"Telisa maintains objective: collect artifacts," Shiny said.

"Yes! That's me. You're getting better at speaking our language all the time," she said.

"Collect artifacts. Begin. Commence. Select alternate location."

"Hrm, ahhh, so you mean, take what I want...just don't take it from what ya got here, huh?"

"Affirm. Correct."

I will ask Telisa desist, cease, if critical equipment is confiscated.

The voice came to Telisa in her head, across her link. It was the smooth voice of a man. Telisa glanced around.

"Whoa...who is that?" Telisa asked.

"Who's talking?" Magnus asked. "My link says it's...Shiny. I guess that's why some of the authentication information is missing."

Abandoned primitive methods. Now communicate through your more advanced system.

"Umm," Telisa wondered if she should complain. "Shiny, could you use your real voice? I mean the way you used to speak, well, I've associated you with the buzzing voice from your...helper spheres."

I will comply.

This time the voice in her head sounded like the buzzing voice Shiny had used with them before. It sounded much better to her than the strange man's voice, which Telisa didn't want to think of as coming from Shiny.

"Thanks, Shiny," Telisa said.

"Yeah, that's a lot better. It sounds like you really sound. Well, I mean like you…never mind," Magnus said.

"All right, then. We have permission from an owner. Let's take a look."

Magnus laughed and nodded. "Lead the way."

Telisa consulted the maps in her head. "Let's move deeper into the sphere."

They chose a corridor at random and walked through the fine sand. Telisa couldn't see any real difference between these caverns and the ones they had encountered while trapped underground on Thespera Two. The light came from the exposed cubes hanging from walls or rising from the floors.

They took a side branch, looking for a more interesting room.

"Too much of this stuff all looks the same to me," she said. "I think a human station would offer more variety."

"A human city would," Magnus said. "But the insides of the *Iridar* look pretty much the same throughout."

"Hrm, yeah, I guess so."

"When did you first become obsessed with alien artifacts?" Magnus asked.

"Well, that's a change of subject," Telisa said, but she was secretly pleased. "Let's see. I remember one time when I was a kid poring through my dinosaur books. My father brought home a Talosian water compass. At first he let me play with it, and I remember being amazed by the thought that it had been created by creatures that weren't people. He told me stories the few times a year that he showed up after that, and I became hooked. I sought out artifacts in museums and traveling displays wherever I could find them."

"You haven't mentioned your father before," Magnus said carefully.

"One day years later, he showed up and took the Talosian back to the government. He told me to forget about the artifacts until I joined the space force. I was upset but I didn't grow apart from him until later, when I joined a civil rights group in high school."

Telisa became silent for a moment. They both realized at the same moment that a noise like rushing water came from a branching in the corridor on their right.

"What's that sound?"

Magnus shrugged. "Stop. Before we go check it out, tell me what happened with your father."

Telisa sighed. "The government kept taking rights away. They made it illegal for us to own artifacts. They stopped telling us about the new discoveries. They kept information about aliens from the academic community. At the same time, I was starting to get a mind of my own, and I became ashamed that my father was part of the force. I rebelled against my mother and I gave my father the riot act, until he exploded. He hit me for the first time ever, and told me I wasn't his daughter. It was the worst argument of my life."

Magnus listened carefully.

Michael McCloskey

"Sounds to me like you're strong and independent. Got a head of your own. Your father and your mother would be proud of you now, if they only knew."

"A smuggler? Running around with an alien behind his back? I don't think so. I told my mother I was going on vacation in the Mediterranean. She's separated from him, now. At least I still visit her now and then."

"But they would have to be proud of your resourcefulness, and the fact that you're a survivor. You're stronger now than before, tougher."

They shared another moment of silence. Telisa heard the background sound again, like a distant waterfall.

"C'mon, enough talking about that shit. We're on an alien space outpost!" Telisa said.

They walked toward the noise. Telisa wondered if the sound emanated as noise from speakers, like a radio tuned to an empty frequency.

They came into a larger circular chamber, with hundreds of cubes lined up along the walls. The sound came from a large hole in the wall that ejected a steady stream of sand into a bay that ran along half the circumference of the room. The sand flowed evenly through the bay until leaving from another portal in the wall on the other side from where it entered.

Telisa laughed. "It's Shiny's version of an escalator, or a conveyor belt," she said.

Magnus raised an eyebrow. "Hrm. Yeah, I suppose it could be. Or maybe it's a system that cleans the sand."

"We should dive in and take a ride."

"Not so fast. What if it's a garbage disposal? What if you jump in and you can't stay above the sand? You could suffocate."

Telisa bent down onto her knees and peered down the tunnel. "It doesn't look dangerous from here…but I suppose you're right. Who knows where it ends up going?"

"There could be machinery under the surface that could chop you up into little pieces. I wouldn't even stick my hand in it. But we should toss something in and see where it goes."

"Something bright that we would see easily if it comes back around."

Telisa took out her pack and rummaged through it.

"Well…"

"You have something?" Magnus asked.

Telisa looked up sheepishly, holding a small piece of red fabric in her hand.

"What's that? Oh," Magnus said, and smiled. He had realized it was a bright red pair of undersheers. "Let's hope it doesn't gum up the works. An advanced alien outpost, brought to its knees by a sexy undergarment."

Telisa tossed the undersheers into the flow and they watched it get whisked away into the exit tunnel. They waited for the red fabric to reappear in the stream for several minutes, but they didn't see anything but the smooth flow of the tiny tan particles.

"I have a new idea," Telisa said. "This could be a Shiny restroom. When they regurgitate those bricks, they could throw them in here to be taken away and…recycled, or whatever."

"Well, we can ask Shiny about it later," Magnus said. "Let's keep looking."

"Sure thing," Telisa said. "Oh wait. Or if our links can connect, we could ask him right now." Telisa connected with Magnus sent a message to Shiny.

Shiny?

Present. Listening. Ready.

Magnus and I have found a room…there's a lot of sand moving around, sand like on the floor. We're curious, what is it? A transport system, or does it clean the sand…or is it a restroom?

There was a pause.

System you inquire about fulfills all of those functions.

I see. Thank you, Shiny.

The connection was dismissed.

"Ah…all of those. Well, there we go," Telisa said.

Magnus grimaced and shook his head.

"That's…well, alien."

Chapter Twenty-Four

Two days later, Telisa trudged back up the ramp into the *Iridar*. The weight in the sack she carried caused her to slow and wobble.

Magnus greeted her with his slugthrower leveled.

"Another batch!" she announced. "You gonna shoot me?"

He lowered the weapon. "I asked you to announce each arrival with your link," he said sourly.

"Sorry, I forgot. Besides, half the time my link can't get through to yours."

"Okay. Looks like you found some more building blox."

"You make'em sound like toys. But they're not. They're the entire basis for an advanced technology."

"You sure? Maybe we just helped Shiny knock over a giant alien toy factory!"

"I don't think so. They've been in all the caves we believe make up Shiny's preferred environment. Imagine a system where they can make any electronic controller they need from these basic blocks. They would be produced cheaply, interconnected, and programmed to perform whatever task they're needed for."

"Hrm. If they're all computing components, then they must have a hell of a distributed system."

"These blocks, or tinker toys or whatever you want to call'em. The ones with the rods placed into them are emitting electromagnetic waves at frequencies that are related to the length of the rods."

"Ah! So the components talk to each other without wires."

"Yep. Just like a lot of our stuff does…except I think Shiny's race has progressed farther along those lines. I've detected at least fifty separate wireless networks used by these components. And here's a crazy thing. I took the antenna or whatever it is out of one component and put it into one that didn't have one…and that component started talking on the network. So I think any of these modules with holes in them can speak to each other if they're given an antenna, or whatever the green rods are."

"That's weird. That's like attaching a radio to your toothbrush and all of a sudden it starts talking to the house computer, offering cleaning services to your guests."

"Yeah. I think each of these modules may be generalized. They each may be their own small computer, programmable. When you give it an antenna it links to the network to see what you want to tell it to do. So it's more like you hooked a radio to your jacket and the house told it the toilet needs cleaning and so the jacket transforms into a scrub brush and the house sends a bot to grab it and start scrubbing!"

Magnus shrugged. "Ha. Sounds possible. A giant distributed system composed of everything from your toaster to your supercomputers. It's a good theory, anyway. But we need to crack their protocols. Then we could try telling a fresh component to be something…maybe just copy an existing one. Test it out."

"Do you know how hard it is to figure out a protocol from scratch, just looking at the waveforms coming from these things at a given frequency? And what if only part of the data is on each frequency?"

"Shiny did it to us in a short time."

"Yeah, maybe we should ask him how to do it."

"We should. For now, start simple. Work your way up from there. I'd start by assuming that each frequency is a signal with an isolated stream of information on its own."

"All right, well, I'm going to need your help. We need to get the *Iridar*'s computers recording these signals." Telisa dropped her collection onto the rubberized deck.

"Okay. But I have some areas I want to show you first," Magnus said. "I think there's been a fight here. That may explain why the other Shinies are gone."

"You think that they were defeated but the base was left intact?"

"Well, depends on what you mean by intact," Magnus said. They walked together back down the lock and out into the caverns of the base. Telisa referred to the maps in her head, looking at the layout of the parts of the base that she had explored. Although the caves seemed to be naturally formed, the map gave away the order with which the oddly shaped rooms had been puzzled together to fill the available space. Telisa believed that Shiny's race preferred the aesthetic impression of natural caverns, but in fact they were anything but natural.

Magnus took her to a section she hadn't seen before, near the hull of the base sphere they occupied. Telisa saw blackened sections of wall. The sand below their feet remained pristine.

They came into another smooth-walled room. The deck had been pierced by a giant metal spike. A thin ovoid door in the side of the spike had been left open. The opening was larger than man-sized.

"I think this was an attack site," Magnus said. "This spike pierced the outer hull and delivered something bad into the station."

"It didn't depressurize the area," Telisa noted.

"I'm not sure. Maybe it did at the time but it's since been repaired. Or maybe the attackers didn't want to depressurize the inside. They may have wanted it intact, or even been after capturing live prisoners. Who knows?"

Telisa peered inside the giant canister. Something about it felt creepy, and she kept her distance. The inside surface held striations that she couldn't make sense of. It reminded her of a crash pod.

"This could be anything," Telisa said. "Maybe it's supposed to be here."

Magnus led her around the spike and into the next room. The smooth walls held black scars and fragments of metal. Two heaps of trash littered the floor.

"So much for the cleaning system," Telisa said.

"Maybe Shiny's race would only repair it if the damage is more than cosmetic."

"I suspect there is damage here that caused the system to break down."

"That may be so. Look at what this is."

Telisa walked closer. She saw that the pile closest to her had a silvery harness lying over a large husk or skin of something as large as herself. She saw fragments of legs lying jumbled all around it.

"This is an…alien corpse. One of Shiny's people!"

"So is the other one. And this shrapnel in the walls indicates an explosion. These black marks are burns from some kind of energy weapon."

"How come they're just here? I haven't seen this in the other parts of the base."

"It's all over in this section. This spherical piece of the base. So maybe you're right, this sphere may have been damaged beyond easy repair. Or no inhabitants were left to order the repair."

Telisa remembered that the base consisted of three large spherical parts. She realized that she hadn't explored this one yet.

"They must have fought here. This sphere may have some special importance."

Magnus nodded. "The power systems are here, I think. I checked it out for artifacts, but I think most of the equipment here is inside the walls, hard to dig out or too large to take back."

"Well, what I wanna know is, what was in that spike?"

"I have some clues about that, too," he said. He walked further into the caverns. Telisa followed him past several more battle sites. Only the sand of the floor remained untouched. Everything else had been charred or broken. Telisa counted three more piles of rubble that she believed to be corpses of Shiny's race.

Magnus stopped and pointed ahead.

The burned out hull of a large machine lay in the corridor, blocking the way. Long metallic tentacles curved around the wreck, ending in sharp looking hooks. The surface of the thing sported several equipment bulbs that Telisa imagined were sensor pods or weapons ports.

"A war machine," Telisa said.

"Yes. Something pretty bad if it could do this to Shiny's people."

"Or if it caught them by surprise. We don't know how warlike they are. I wonder if they were prepared for this kind of attack."

"Knowing Shiny, they were prepared for anything. But who knows."

They walked over closer to the machine. Telisa touched one of its tentacles, feeling the cool metal. Then she moved over and looked at one of the pods, viewing it through a gash in the side of the machine. She tested its mount, trying to dislodge it.

"Stop. I'm not sure that's a good idea," Magnus said. "It looks a bit like the heavies the space force battlecruisers carry, except for the tentacles."

"What's wrong? If we could get a sample from this race too, we'd be in even better shape. Something from yet another science and culture."

"What you might get, is ripped to shreds." Magnus stepped around the mass and viewed it from the far side. "We don't know anything about its weapon systems. It may have live ordnance, or it might be set to self-destruct if we poke through it."

Telisa sat back, frustrated. "How in the hell is a girl supposed to make a living if she can't even grab a choice alien weapon or two without dying?"

"Join the space force, then use expensive scanners and robots to poke through the stuff for you," Magnus answered.

"That's what we need, some robots. Then we could send them in to grab all the good stuff for us."

"Yeah, well, you know that we can't get anything bigger than a cleaning robot back home."

Telisa ground her teeth. The world government and its rules. She had managed to forget about that for a while, since she had left civilization. If they had any real robots, they would have to be custom-built and kept secret.

Robots had become widespread until their power became evident. Just as the world government had restricted lethal weapons in the hands of civilians, they had expanded the rules to cover ownership of robots. Secret groups with control of dangerous robots were routinely rooted out and exterminated by the space force.

"Then we should build our own and keep them out in space, like the rich corporate executives do."

Magnus shrugged. "I think Thomas had some plans along those lines. But it takes money. We needed to bootstrap ourselves with a few good hauls first, before we could come up with the kind of credit that it takes to establish a cache of our own in deep space."

Telisa sighed. *Shiny, does it bother you if we ask more questions?*

Mild disturbance. Ask. Query. Begin.

Uh, do you have any robots here?

Affirmative.

Can we see them? Can we have one?

Magnus laughed.

"Hey, it can't hurt to ask, can it?"

Magnus shrugged.

263

Affirmative. Affirmative.

Telisa's link brought up an image of the sphere they were in drawn in three dimensions. It spun in a confusing way, peeling off layers and finally exposing a highlighted path through the base.

Thank you, Shiny.

"I think he just sent me a map to them, but it's a little more…three-dimensional than we're used to."

"Well, he offered us a robot, so let's go check it out—if you can tell which way to go," Magnus said.

"Yeah, definitely," she said, making a face. "I think it's this way."

They moved through the caverns with a new purpose. The route took them through the rest of the ruined base sphere and to its far outer edge. When they entered the final chamber, the light inside increased as several of the glowing cubes lit up. A wall on their right seemed to melt away, revealing a smooth-walled oval-shaped bay. Three tall walking machines stood inside, towering over Telisa and Magnus.

"Wow," Telisa muttered, walking forward to touch one shiny leg. The machines had eight slender support legs, each about as tall as the two humans. The bodies of the constructs were the size of a compact autocab.

The machine Telisa had touched whirred to life. Telisa stepped back. Magnus crouched and pointed his slugthrower at the machine. The body slowly lowered until it hovered less than a foot above the sandy floor.

Now Telisa could see that a clear cockpit dominated the top of each machine. The top of the lowered robot slid open.

"I guess it can take a pilot or a rider as well," Magnus said.

Telisa peered into the machine. The inside had forty tiny metal buttons arrayed around the circumference. A single metal rod rose from the center with a tiny stirrup or chair at the top.

"You think Shiny could fit in there?" Telisa asked.

"I don't know. I think if he were curled up he could. There's a button for each leg."

"I'd assume he would use a neural interface rather than buttons. But I guess it might be a backup control system."

Magnus shrugged. "The important question is, how are we going to get this into the bay?"

Michael McCloskey

Chapter Twenty-Five

Captain Relachik stared at the alien base in an artificial world painted in his mind's eye by the ship's sensors. The general shape of the base was known, but the interior remained mostly blank. Only a few outer regions and corridors were part of the view, places where a few teams had attached sensor drones and managed to report back despite the alien EM scrambling.

"Download what we have to orient the ARs," Relachik said aloud and simultaneously transmitted over his command link. He wondered if he was about to commit his child to death. The assault robots were not known for their finesse. "I want the alien and the smugglers alive, if possible. Make sure the controller teams are on top of that."

There, maybe I've given her a chance.

"Aye, sir," came the reply from the officer next to him, Colonel Baker. Baker handled the AR teams and would coordinate with the *Seeker*'s assault shuttle crews to deliver the deadly arsenal that the scout ship held in her metal belly.

"Prepare to launch within the hour," Relachik ordered. So far the encounter had been a stalemate. The scout ship's sensors were almost blinded by the amazing electronic warfare capabilities of the alien base, but they had managed to figure out that the outpost had been damaged in some previous battle.

Send Lieutenant Hartlet into operations, he ordered over the command link and walked into a glassed-off side room of the bridge.

Most of Relachik's officers now believed that the base they had found had been crippled to the point where it had no external weaponry it could bring to bear on the *Seeker*. Relachik wasn't so sure. He thought that they might be right, or perhaps the aliens weren't so hostile as to attempt to destroy the *Seeker* on sight. He also knew that his daughter had been seen consorting with a live alien, a shock that took a while to fully absorb.

His daughter. Telisa had been more on his mind these past few days than at any time since her childhood. Part of him wanted to forget about her. She had chosen her own path. But he couldn't ignore the fact that she was his daughter. He'd try to save her now. Then, he'd hunt her down next time he got back to Earth, and try to set her straight. But she'd gone so wrong this time…was she beyond saving? He ground his teeth in frustration.

Joe Hartlet came in and saluted. The captain returned his salute and pointed him at a chair.

"Are you ready to join the action, lieutenant?"

"Yes sir. We're making an incursion on the alien base?" Joe asked.

"We're conducting a probe. To gather information, learn more about the base. Ideally we'll find the alien, and perhaps the smugglers, and bring all of them aboard the *Seeker*."

"I have reason to believe it'll be very dangerous. In my report—"

"Yes. It may be dangerous, but this is vital to our future. These aliens may have technology that we need to learn more about. Having the first live alien ever would of course come in handy as well."

Relachik watched Joe consider objecting further.

"I can guess what you're thinking. But given that the base is not responding to our efforts to communicate, and appears largely inactive, we think it may be deserted. And you've already come under hostile fire in the installation."

"But that could have been from some other alien culture," Joe said. "I don't know who it was that destroyed my escort. Also, given the programming of the robots, it could have been a misunderstanding."

Relachik steepled his fingers and leaned back.

"It's a moot point. The order has been given. The UNSF is prepared to accept the risks to this ship and the marines in order to learn more about an advanced technology in the hands of a race that could still be in existence."

"I see, sir. Then I hope we can find some valuable items or information."

"You've been assigned to Major Franks' personal squad. They've targeted a sector of the base that looks particularly promising," Relachik said. He sent Joe's link a pointer, indicating the area on their electronic master map of the outpost.

"Will I have any responsibilities with regard to the...combat effectiveness of the unit?"

"No. Which isn't to say you won't be armed...but the assault robots bring to bear more than ninety percent of a squad's firepower. Your primary task is to lend us any additional thoughts your particular perspective may offer on the base, since you have been in this creature's environment before. Assuming, of course, that the theories you put forth in your report prove correct."

"Of course I welcome the opportunity to accompany the probe."

"There'll be more than one boarding party. Someone'll come up with something."

***

Telisa and Magnus found Shiny sitting still in a twisty cavern . Telisa thought it looked like the alien was thinking or busy with a mental interface. The familiar leg twitch revealed the gold and silver statue of an alien as alive.

"Hi Shiny. We managed to load your robot into the bay. Thanks for letting us study it."

Shiny responded through their links.

No problem. You're welcome. You owe me one.

Telisa laughed. "Yes we do. Can we ask you some questions about what attacked your base? We'd like to take some samples of the technology, but we're afraid it might be dangerous."

No time. Collection not feasible. Others in proximity.

"What? Others of your race?"

Humans. Companions. Allies.

"Other humans are here?"

UNSF Seeker, transmitted Shiny. *Leave. Rejoin.*

"Holy shit! The *Seeker*?" Telisa asked.

"You know the ship?" asked Magnus.

"That's my father's ship. The bastard is probably here to exterminate Shiny and anything vaguely alien." She took a deep breath. "Then he'll throw us in the brig and bring us back to Earth in chains."

Telisa. Magnus. Rejoin humans. Shiny, leave. Separate.

"Now wait just a minute," Magnus said, raising his voice slightly. "Those guys are after us because we took off with you. If not for us, you'd be their prisoner by now."

"Well, mostly for that reason," added Telisa, thinking about her father. What would happen if she were captured by her father's ship?

Corrective action. Abscond. Retreat. Flee.

Telisa's link received an external pointer. She accessed it and saw a scanner interface from the *Iridar*. She saw that the *Seeker* had arrived as Shiny claimed. Assault shuttles were disembarking assault robots and electronic warfare teams from the scout and forcing their way into the base at several points. A message came through to *Iridar* from the *Seeker*.

"This is the UNSF transmitting to suspected smugglers aboard unknown vessel. You are to surrender immediately. All contraband will be annexed by the UNSF and you will be held pending charges. Repeat, surrender to UNSF personnel or risk being killed."

"Holy shit! They're going to be swarming in here in a matter of minutes!" Magnus said. Telisa realized that he was examining the same data that Shiny had sent to her link.

The pointer continued to feed more data. Telisa saw hundreds of red points indicated in the three spheres of the base.

Defenses. Weapons. Resistance, Shiny said. A path lit up in green in Telisa's mental image of the base. *Retreat.*

"The path leads back to the Iridar," Magnus said. "But what I don't get is, are those defenses going to be gunning for us, too?"

Telisa. Magnus. Access allowed. Flee.

Shiny turned away and scuttled down one of the side passages.

"Where are you going?" Telisa called out, but no answer came.

"The map says we need to go this way," Magnus said.

"Should we go? What's going to happen to him?"

"I don't know. Y'know what, we can't make his decisions for him. This is our chance to leave. And we still have shitloads of artifacts. If we can get the hell out of here, we might still make it."

Telisa shrugged. "Okay. Let's get outta here!"

She grabbed Magnus's hand and they ran. "Good luck, Shiny!" Telisa yelled back at the receding alien. Then they were loping through the dim tunnels, passing the mysterious clusters of glowing cubes.

***

Joe strode out into the familiar cavern-like area on the far side of the lock. He wore a stiff new Veer skinsuit and had a military-grade scrambler slung over his shoulder, though the weapon was of cheap government issue.

"Link up," the squad leader said. Joe's link asked for connect permission from the group's interface and he gave it. A window opened in his mind's eye, showing him the disposition of the squad. Joe tried to split his attention between the mental display and his natural senses, but had a moment of difficulty.

"It's a little awkward at first, but believe me, it's helpful when you get used to it," the marine next to him signaled.

"Second nature after a while, right?"

"Exactly. Just stick with me, we'll watch out for ya."

"This look familiar?" the squad leader asked Joe.

"Yes. The cubes are banks of equipment of some kind. The caverns tend to be the same size, seemingly random variations…"

"Weapons? Defense systems?"

"I have no idea," Joe said. "But both of my robots were destroyed quickly and they only managed to get a couple of shots off."

The leader nodded and signaled for the group to move out. Joe watched half the time in his mental interface, trying to get used to the added input to his brain without stumbling around. Joe felt immensely nervous as they started into the complex, waiting for all hell to break loose. Presumably if this incursion was unwelcome, a superior technology like Shiny's could make it very bad for them.

After a few minutes of moving through the caverns, Joe's link signaled the presence of another network in range. He checked its source. For a moment he thought the aliens had brought up a network to talk with them. Then a message came through to his link.

"You lied to us. You said you would let us go."

Joe checked the sender and saw that it was unidentified. But he could guess who it was.

"Tam? I was willing to let you go. But not the alien. I wouldn't have paid any attention to you if you hadn't kidnapped the alien."

"Kidnapped? Shiny followed us. We had no choice—how could we turn him away after he helped us escape from that place? We don't even know how the installation worked; for all I know we would have died in there without his help."

"Who are you talking with, Lieutenant? Our networks aren't operating in here; we're completely scrambled. Is it the renegades?"

Joe found it difficult to think of Mark, Tam, and Shiny as renegades. But it was an accurate enough term now.

"It's them. Tam and the other one."

"You're sure? The link frequencies are all scrambled…how could you be reaching her?"

"Yes, I'm sure."

The comm officer nodded and then retreated back into himself. Probably alerting the entire fleet, Joe thought to himself. The rest of the squad stopped and kneeled against the walls of the room, waiting for information from the *Seeker* about where the signal was coming from.

"We're having trouble with the telemetry," the officer said. "This place is screwing with all our ECCM. It doesn't make any sense that they're coming through to him."

"This is Joe. I'm here for the alien, true, but the captain of the *Seeker* also wants us to bring you back to safety. How is it that you can talk to me? A huge chunk of the EM spectrum is completely trashed in here."

"We're doing just fine. Besides, Shiny isn't here right now. I don't know how we can talk to you...Shiny said something about giving us access."

"He said? Well, where are you? And where is he?"

"If you can only get us or the alien, which one are you supposed to bring back? If I were you, I'd be looking for him instead."

"We're getting you both. Look, this could get dangerous. Just come turn yourself in before someone gets hurt. Is the alien with you?"

"No. Good-bye, Joe." Telisa cut the link.

Joe shrugged to the members of the incursion team. "She won't cooperate. Somehow she has the help of the alien, I don't know how, but apparently he made it so her link still works."

The comm officer shook his head. "These links use a limited set of frequencies; you can't just jam one and leave the others alone—"

"Well, the alien can," Joe said. "I don't know how."

"We'll see how much it can do with bullet holes in its ass," came a comment from somewhere in the squad.

"Enough arguing. Back to the old-fashioned way," the squad leader announced. He pointed to an exit. "Sims on point, that direction."

Joe's nervousness increased again.

Michael McCloskey

Chapter Twenty-Six

Kirizzo searched through the many chambers in the base by accessing the system interface. Data flowed into the cybernetic parts of his body and became part of his memory. Kirizzo accessed the new information as if thinking of events that had occurred seconds ago. He now knew that hundreds of alien war machines were in the base with him, moving in from three access points. Well behind this force, teams of the aliens themselves came in, forty-one of them in all so far.

He considered the advantages of their presence. The aliens seemed to be of an inferior technology level. It seemed they had little to offer in comparison to his own civilization. Still, they would have access to large amounts of natural resources and perhaps information that could be useful. They might even know of others of his kind, or of the disposition of his enemies.

On the other hand, the aliens posed many problems where they were. Kirizzo faced potential malfunctions in base equipment while the aliens were milling about. If they sought to capture him at an inconvenient moment, his aims could be impeded. There even existed a chance that their weapons, although primitive, could harm him. And since they were so primitive, it seemed unlikely that they could be successfully resisting any of the foes of his race.

Kirizzo decided to activate the automated defenses against the intruders. He calculated a fair chance that the aliens might overcome the defenses through sheer numbers, based on his combative interactions with them in the Trilisk installation. But it was the best he could do for now; he decided to concentrate on gathering what he would need for leaving the base in a fast ship that could take him home as quickly as possible. Almost as an afterthought, he left a few automated entities to make sure that the ones he had dealt with would remain unimpeded. He had developed a rapport with this tiny faction, and he decided to keep that investment intact in case he required their cooperation later.

***

An almost imperceptible shudder came through the floor.

"What? What happened?" Telisa asked.

The only answer came a moment later. A spray of projectiles impacted the cavern in a random pattern, sending one or two ricochets nearby. Telisa and Magnus threw themselves onto the smooth floor. Nightmare images of the deaths of Jack and Thomas raced through Telisa's mind.

"Shit! They're trying to kill us!" Telisa snarled. "Those are human weapons!"

"They're probably moving in after us. But I don't understand why they're firing lethal rounds at us. I'd expect an ultimatum first, at least."

"My father's a hard-core soldier."

"Shiny's base must be messing with their weapons. Those rounds should have been able to lock in on us. It's a miracle they missed. Actually, now that I think about it, they might not be firing at us.

They must be firing blind, or they would have hit something in particular."

"See if you can guide me back. I'll try and discourage any pursuit," Magnus said. He slid the slugthrower off his back and discharged a staccato burst of rounds down the sloped tunnel. The sound stunned Telisa, slamming into her ears painfully. She had realized abstractly that the military slugthrowers were loud, but she hadn't understood just how loud they really were until she experienced it in person. Magnus released a tangler grenade from his suit and set it on the floor. It rolled away, accelerating down the tunnel, seeking prey.

She rolled away from the opening and slightly down the hall so she could regain her feet without becoming a target. Shaking her head in a useless attempt to rid her ears of pain, she regained her concentration and linked with the *Iridar*. She brought a map of their path up in her mind.

"Up ahead and to the left," she said.

Magnus put his back against the wall beside her. "If their scanners are working, they'll know exactly where we are. I'll have to stay back periodically. They'll see that and be wary, thinking I'm preparing traps or making a counterattack."

"I don't think their stuff is working at all," Telisa said. "The bullets missed us, remember? I bet they can't see anything and the robots are almost useless."

Telisa felt fear thrilling through her. She was at once excited and terrified. *I wonder if the end of my life is here*, she thought.

Magnus nodded. "We can risk it. Hug the wall. If their rounds are blind, they'll be more likely to pick you as a target of opportunity if you're standing in the middle of the room than if you become part of the wall."

Magnus's level voice calmed her. She leaned back against the cool wall of the cavern. It made her feel a little safer. She started shuffling in the direction of the ship, scraping along the irregular side of the passage.

She laughed a little as she looked at the stunner she gripped in her hand. She hadn't remembered drawing it from her hip. The tiny nonlethal weapon was made to protect people against muggings, not to fight off assault robots. It occurred to her that it might not even work against any robot, even a household cleaning robot.

"Magnus, does this stunner work against robots?"

Magnus shrugged next to her. "It can't be good for them. But I doubt it would do anything against a space force assault model. But keep it out; there are probably marine teams behind the robots."

Telisa nodded, but she was still thinking about the robots. Then she remembered that she had brought the double-horseshoe artifact with her to show to Shiny.

"Remember the artifact that we fired up? It generates a huge EM spike locally," she said. "I bet that would get a robot's attention."

"Yeah, maybe. Once we're back to the ship, though, we should just leave."

"No, I have it with me!"

"What? Why isn't it on the ship?"

"I was going to ask Shiny about it today."

Magnus shrugged. "Couldn't hurt to keep it ready."

Telisa slipped the artifact out of her pack. She zipped the carrying container back up and slid it over her back. Telisa dropped the plastic holder on the floor and held the device in her hand. She held it by one arm carefully.

"Okay, let's keep going," Magnus prompted.

"Wait. I hear something."

A high pitched whine rose and fell. Telisa caught a glimpse of something in the air. She blinked. Whatever it was, she couldn't sense it anymore. It reminded her of a hummingbird.

"Some of those tiny orbs like Shiny had," Magnus said. "They headed past us."

"What—"

A cacophony arose from the tunnel ahead. At first it sounded like a pile of garbage being emptied from a large container. Then the thunder of slugthrowers erupted and drowned the rest out. Magnus pulled Telisa down. They hugged the floor for a moment, listening and cowering. Telisa understood now that these were the sounds of a battle.

The orbs are fighting the Seeker's assault robots, right?

Must be, Magnus replied on the link. Telisa was glad for the link conversation, since her ears rang so terribly she wondered if she'd ever hear again.

At last the noise slowed then stopped. Telisa lay on the sandy floor, breathing rapidly.

We need to find another route, I guess, she said on the link.

No. This is perfect. The orbs have made a hole in the forces ahead of us. We might be able to get through to the ship if we hurry.

281

I don't know. We don't want to be in the thick of the fight.

"Too late. We *are* in the fight," Magnus said aloud. Telisa felt relieved she could hear him despite her ringing ears. "Those orbs are formidable. They've probably taken the assault machines out. Keep going straight for the ship."

They moved through a narrow room with two adjoining passages. Magnus stayed close and covered the entrances with his weapon, but he didn't shoot again. Telisa chose the passage that she believed would take them closer to the *Iridar*. Any moment she expected a shiny war machine to appear and attack them. Telisa wondered if such things only shot people, or if they had giant whirling blades to slice victims up like in the horror vids.

They came into another room, filled with something unfamiliar. Broken space force equipment lay strewn all over the floor. Telisa saw green shapes mixed in amongst the carnage. She realized the green objects were uniformed bodies on the floor. Pieces of human were strewn about, splattered in blood. It didn't look real in the colored light of the cubes. Telisa made a confused noise.

"Shiny must've taken them out," Magnus said. "It's an assault controller team. They would have set up right after the robotics came through."

"Can't the robots be controlled from the *Seeker*? Or even fight on their own?"

"Yes. But teams like this are deployed for redundancy. They can also add flexibility to the machine's strategy."

"Shiny killed all these men. He didn't seem so violent with us. He never did anything—"

"We never waved guns in his face and tried to capture him. We never invaded one of his bases. Put one of these on," Magnus said, indicating a dead man who was still mostly in one piece.

Telisa stared in confusion for a moment. Then she realized he meant the corpse's skinsuit. She walked over to the smallest of the dead assault controllers, hopping over the wreckage of some equipment. The devastation was so severe that Telisa couldn't tell what any of it had been. She got a closer look at the man. Blood poured from a hole in the suit, right above his heart. She avoided looking at his face. She didn't want to remember what he looked like.

"Lot of good it did him," Telisa said, but she started to work the opening clasp at the man's neck.

"Just don't take a direct hit," Magnus said. "It works pretty well against the nerve scramblers, too. Of course Shiny's weapons…will probably still kill us."

"He must hate us now."

Magnus shrugged. "Maybe. We have more important things to worry about than our popularity."

Telisa unzipped the dead man's suit. She felt a shiver run down her spine as the head flopped to one side and a stream of fresh blood trickled out of one nostril. She exhaled and shook off a wave of nausea.

"Sorry, pal, but you don't need Momma Veer anymore," she whispered. She wrenched the arms out of the skinsuit and then realized that the boots would have to come off first. While she struggled with the operation, Magnus picked over the bodies, taking a couple of grenades and a few electronic devices.

"Can't they trace us with that stuff?" Telisa asked.

"Yes they can. And they can trace us without it as well, unless our theory about the countermeasures is right. Just hope that they're after Shiny a bit more than us. Truth is, this may be it. The *Seeker* is a formidable ship, and its crew is elite."

"Joe also said something about the EM spectrum being noisy. More evidence that they're running blind."

Telisa finally got the suit off the corpse and slipped into it. The flexible garment felt thick yet soft. Her legs fit well, though being a man's suit, it compressed her breasts somewhat. She sealed the front with a slide zipper and anchored the front flap over it.

"How's it feel?" Magnus said. Without giving time for an answer, he skipped forward and punched her swiftly in the solar plexus.

Telisa's eyes grew wide, but then she smiled. The blow felt like that of an old man, a barely noticeable impact across her entire torso.

"Very nice! Spreads the kinetic energy."

"Yep. Course I wouldn't go jumping off any buildings, if I were you."

"No problem. Wow, maybe we can get out of here!"

"Maybe."

"Anyway, like I was saying, I think that Shiny has scrambled their stuff. If they don't have links, they probably don't know where we are."

"That would explain why they fired at us after the tremor; they were firing blind in response to an attack," Magnus said. "That could be good, in a way. If they don't know where we are, we'll have a chance."

"Drop your weapons on the floor or I will fire," a synthetic voice commanded.

Magnus tensed. Then he dropped his slugthrower. Telisa slumped in defeat, letting her stunner fall from her hand.

They turned slowly toward the voice. Telisa scanned through the cavern, trying to figure out where the voice came from. She saw only dead bodies, shattered equipment and the alien blocks.

"There," Magnus pointed.

A black optical palette and the barrel of a projectile weapon resolved themselves to Telisa. She blinked. Part of a robot lay on the floor. Roughly a third of its surface had taken on the color of the cavern wall. Another part of it was colored like a green USNF uniform. Earlier, Telisa had mistaken it for a piece of human corpse. The rest of it was the silver and white of metal. Telisa had thought this part of the robot was just a shattered equipment case.

"Holy shit," she breathed. Even though she could see the thing now, she felt it must somehow be damaged. The parts she saw didn't move, and the robot's head remained at the level of her knees.

"It's damaged," Magnus said. Then his voice continued in her link.

It's hurt. It might be bluffing.

"Stand against the wall and do not speak," the machine ordered.

Telisa grabbed the wrench-shaped artifact in the middle as she had done when it shocked her. She felt an odd sensation in her hand. The fine hairs on her skin were standing on end. This time she resolved to hold onto it longer. It might shock her, but she felt desperate to try and take out the robot.

Her hand burned. It twitched. She felt herself losing control of the muscles in her arm.

I hope this doesn't—

A loud snap sounded in the cavern. Telisa staggered, dropping the artifact to the floor. The smell of burning electronics came to her nose. Telisa got a signal in her head that meant her link was resetting. She realized with a sinking feeling that she had just sacrificed her link memory. All her link pictures of the base and Shiny were gone.

"Cover your face!" Magnus said urgently.

Telisa obeyed as he snapped up his slug thrower and thrust its end onto the optical palette of the damaged robot. The thing didn't move. The bark of the slug thrower smashed into Telisa's ears. She felt a spray of metal fragments hit her arm, but through the suit it felt like a light splatter of rain.

"Okay, let's move it," Magnus said. Telisa glanced at the remains of the battle machine as she turned to follow. Smoke rose from several places on its body. A ragged black hole occupied the space where its optical sensors had been. Eerily, its skin continued to mimic the wall and the uniforms around it. Telisa suppressed a shudder and ran from the room.

Chapter Twenty-Seven

Telisa loped along behind her companion, trying to suppress the nerves that quickened her breath and tightened her guts. *Hard to think straight with this much adrenaline,* she thought.

The firm feel of her Veer skinsuit made Telisa feel stronger, helping her keep some of her fear in check. Vaguely she knew that it was a false confidence, especially with a gaping hole in the front, but on some instinctual level it calmed her.

Magnus turned toward her and put a finger over his lip. Telisa caught her breath as best she could, nodding at him. They crouched just behind a sharp corner and Magnus took another look.

There's three of them up here, Magnus sent on his link. *Moment of truth. Do you want to take 'em out by surprise or try and spare their lives at the risk of our own?*

Telisa grimaced and buried her face in her hands. What should they do? She made a quick decision.

Let's try a nonlethal attack...if that goes sour, then we kill them.

Good enough. Remember, they have Momma Veer, too. If you use that stunner, hit 'em in the face with it.

Telisa nodded. She held her stunner in sweaty, shaking hands. They stood up and Magnus counted off in his link.

One...two...three!

Telisa and Magnus bolted around the corner. Telisa saw that the intersection had large green equipment crates in it that had been set up as

makeshift cover. The soldiers were only partially
visible behind the three-foot-high containers.

As the marines first noticed the two loping toward
them, Magnus yelled out.

"Don't shoot, we're human!" he exclaimed. The
marine facing them leveled his weapon for a second
and then pointed it away as Magnus' words sank in.
The delay caused just enough time for Magnus to step
up to the nearest crate and swing his slugthrower like
a bat over the top of the obstacle. It struck the face of
the soldier who hesitated. The man fell back out of
sight.

Telisa sprinted past the first crate and shot her
stunner at a second guard. Her target shrieked and fell
back. Telisa took a blow on her back, as if someone
had taken a club to her. Vaguely she realized she'd
been shot but her suit had protected her.

She swung around but didn't see the third man.
She decided he must have taken cover behind a crate.
She heard the whine of a grenade and almost
panicked. An instant later she saw that the first man
she had stunned was up on all fours, trying to clear
his head.

Telisa kicked the kneeling man in the face,
sending him reeling back. Blood burst from his nose,
but Telisa didn't stop for a second. She whipped her
stunner back in line and shot him at point-blank
range, in the face, where his suit couldn't protect him.
He made an odd sound like a jungle bird in distress
and then fell back, unmoving.

The sharp crack of Magnus's slug thrower
assailed her ears again, making her heart jump. She
half expected to feel slugs or flechettes ripping

through her flesh. The loud popping sound of a tangler grenade going off erupted into the small space of the cavern.

Telisa realized she could still move and breathe, so she hadn't been the target of the grenade. She saw someone struggling on the ground wrapped in grey goo, a surreal sight in the reddish illumination of the cavern walls.

"Magnus?" she called out.

I'm caught, he replied through his link. *There's another one we didn't see. No time. He'll call for help.*

Telisa realized Magnus probably spoke through his link because his mouth had been immobilized by the grey glue of the tangler grenade. He could be suffocating even now.

She peeked up over the crate in front of her, holding her stunner in one hand and her backpack in the other. She picked a crate across the way at random and hurled her backpack over it, then sprinted around the crates on the other side. She came across the remaining man just as he glanced in the other direction, alarmed by the noise of her backpack smashing across the top of the equipment container. He lay prone behind a low crate with a rifle in his hands and two more grenades sitting on the ground in front of him. He had a full combat helmet on. Her stunner wouldn't work on a man with full head protection, she thought.

Telisa dropped her stunner and slapped down across his back. She snaked her right arm around his throat and pulled back with all her might. The man thrashed for a moment, but Telisa kept her weight on him and wouldn't let him roll out from under her. She felt the thick Veer suits between them. The suit's collar was keeping her choke from working.

"Frick!" she cried out in frustration. The man under her started fumbling with one of the grenades in front of him. She released her choke and batted the grenade away before he could set it. Free of her arm, the man bucked violently to one side and freed himself. They scrambled to their feet, but Telisa regained her balance first. She grabbed the man around the helmet in both her arms, pulled his head down, and drove her knee full force into his chin.

The blow would have broken his jaw or nose and stunned him at the very least, except for the full face helmet. Instead, the helmet popped off under the strike. His helmet hadn't been strapped on! Telisa realized that she had given up her stunner too quickly.

"You bitch!" snarled the soldier. The man glared at her from under a thick brow. He had a lot of stubble on his face. His neck looked thickset.

One of his fists stuck out quickly and rocked her world. Telisa covered up, stunned and hurt. She knew if she could keep from getting hit for a second or two she might regain her wits. The man tackled her, but she automatically rolled straight back with it and got her legs under him, throwing him clean over her as her back struck the sandy ground. She spit out a mouthful of blood and scrambled for the stunner.

She heard the man coming back from behind her as her hand closed around it. He grabbed one of her feet and pulled her toward him, yelling in rage. She rolled to see him dropping over her, his fists balled to pummel her to death. Telisa shot him straight in the face.

The man stiffened and fell to one side. Before she realized she was doing it, Telisa brought her elbow around and smashed him in the face again. A trickle of blood ran from the edge of his mouth.

Telisa shook like a leaf. She struggled to catch her breath without coughing on her own blood. She staggered back up and shot the unconscious man in the face again for good measure.

Then she realized Magnus still needed her help.

"Magnus!" she called out. *Magnus!* she sent on her link.

I*t's about time,* he responded. *Sounds like you got him.*

Telisa wobbled over to where he struggled in the thick adhesive.

Is it dry yet? she asked, staring at the mess. How would she get Magnus out of it?

Yes. Cut my legs free, and we'll run for it.

Telisa took out her knife and stabbed the thick substance where it joined Magnus' feet. The stuff was tough. Her knife struggled with it.

How can you breathe?

I covered my nose at the last instant. There's a reservoir of air in front of my face. There's only a few air holes, though.

Telisa freed Magnus's legs and pulled him to his feet.

Frick, you weigh a ton.

I'm glad you got that guy, whatever you did. Good job!

Telisa spat more blood out of her mouth. *He wasn't so tough.*

She cut at the glue that covered his face. She quickly realized that she couldn't tell exactly where the grey goo stopped and his hand and face began.

Find one of the holes and make it bigger. It's hard to breathe in here.

Telisa buried the point of her knife in a small hole on the side of the glob around Magnus' head and twisted, trying to dig into it. After a few moments she managed to make it a little larger.

"There's gotta be some solvent around here somewhere," Telisa said. "All these crates and crap lying around."

This is going to take too long. Others may come. Just lead me back to the ship. I can fly it through my link then we can clean this up later.

Grimly, Telisa decided he was right. The adhesive covered him in massive lumps and scraping it off with the knife was slow, dangerous work. The soldiers would have a solvent for it somewhere, but how long could she afford to stumble around looking for it?

"Okay, here we go," she told him. Telisa muscled Magnus forward, guiding him past the crates and out into a new corridor. Telisa felt her back crawl, knowing that if anyone was left behind them she'd take a bullet in the back of her head.

They trod through another couple of rooms. Each time, Telisa took a look at the room from the entrance to see if any enemies awaited them. Then she ran back and pulled Magnus through it. Telisa saw that his slugthrower had been glued into the whole mess.

As nonlethal weapons went, she decided the tangler grenade was as good as her stunner in many ways.

"We're almost there!" Telisa yelled, checking the map in her head. "Just sprint for it!"

Magnus increased speed, running recklessly and trusting that Telisa would point him correctly. They swung violently into the bay where Shiny had set the *Iridar*.

The ship looked just as they had left it.

Okay, here's the ramp coming up in three, two, one.

They scrambled up the back ramp. The two almost stumbled despite the warning as the surface angle rose sharply under their running feet.

Close it up, I'm getting us out of here, Magnus said.

Telisa used her link to close the loading hatch. She took one last look at the reddish caverns they left behind as the huge metal door closed.

Telisa linked into the ship and requested the location of the tangler solvent. Magnus fell to his knees, but the ship started to life under them.

Don't try to fly us out of here until I get that stuff off your face.

Okay, I'm just getting ready.

Telisa took a large silver can out of one of the black equipment bags where the ship's inventory said it would be. She accessed its directions. She skimmed the warnings, then started spraying the substance onto Magnus.

The mixture bubbled and a chemical odor filled the air. A glob of the glue fell off Magnus, revealing his red face. He took a deep breath of air and then coughed. She stopped spraying for a moment and let the air clear.

"Better?"

Magnus coughed again. "Yes…thanks. Can you get my hands?"

Telisa worked to free his hands of the blobs of adhesive. Magnus started to regain his normal color. He saw the blood on her face.

"Thanks. Are you all right?"

She nodded.

"When we get outta this, I want to hear what happened while I was down."

"Sure thing. How can we escape?"

"Let's just hope the *Seeker* is busy. If they decide the alien is on this ship, I guess we're going to be chased again."

"Shiny has to escape, too. I bet he jams all their sensors."

Magnus shrugged. "We'll find out soon. The bay doors have opened for us!"

"How did the *Seeker* get here, anyway?"

Magnus shrugged. "That, I don't know. I've scanned for latchers but I didn't find any."

"What are latchers?"

"Tracking mechanisms. They attach to the hull and serve to point out the ship to UNSF forces. Most latchers will show up on special UNSF scans, and they often transmit information about why the ship was marked. Very useful against smugglers."

Telisa nodded. "Hrm, let me guess. Stay near a crash pod?"

"Yeah."

***

Captain Relachik listened in on the comm traffic from his units in the alien orbital. The first wave of retaliation from the incursion had been severe, but after that the defenses behaved as if overwhelmed. A lot of men had died at the hands of enemies unseen. Slowly, the defensive equipment they faced had been identified and destroyed by sheer numbers. This was exactly the opposite of the way elite soldiers were meant to be used. Usually they enjoyed electronic superiority to the enemy, which allowed them to fight on their own terms.

"Can we support squad seventeen with ship's weapons? They're close to the outer hull," he asked.

"There's a lot of noise out there. We'd almost have to eyeball it," responded his weapons officer. "It might be worth a try if they're gonna buy the farm otherwise."

"Can we be sure we won't blow the whole damn base up?"

"No way to be sure—"

"Then no. Dispatch our last reserve shuttle to back them up. All our teams are either under extraction or turtling up. We'll hold as is until we can get them out of these hot spots."

Relachik cursed. If the *Seeker* were a UNSF battle cruiser, he'd have more powerful robotic forces at his command that were harder to destroy—although, since the robots were affected by enemy countermeasures like the rest of their equipment, their effectiveness would be greatly reduced.

"Captain, I think a vessel has detached and is maneuvering for an escape vector. It has a blocking screen up."

"It's probably only the smugglers."

"I agree, sir. Given the countermeasures exhibited by this base, I'd have to say that it's not the same technology."

Captain Relachik furrowed his brows and let out a heavy sigh. "Let them go. We have to stay and get our men out of there alive."

"The alien—"

"Yes, the alien may be with them. Or now, even more than one. But we have men in there, and we can learn a lot about them from capturing this base."

"I'll launch a spread of shark's teeth with tracker warheads," suggested the lieutenant.

"No. Hold that," the captain ordered. He hesitated. "Firing the latchers may be interpreted as firing on the alien base. It might retaliate."

The lieutenant blinked. Captain Relachik knew what the lieutenant was thinking. Just a second ago, his commanding officer had been talking about firing directly on the base to help squad seventeen. Now he was afraid to launch on another target just because it might be interpreted as an attack.

"Yes sir. I thought the analysis indicated the base's external weaponry had been disabled in a previous battle, sir. You sure we shouldn't try and tag'em for later?"

"The aliens are still strong enough to disable this ship with electronic warfare. So far we haven't threatened to destroy the base. For all we know, they could interfere with the flight computers, cause our gravity spinner to blow. The smugglers are not worth the risk."

Relachik's tone brooked no further discussion. He knew he'd have a hard time covering for this decision later. But for now, he was going to let his brat daughter escape harm.

The lieutenant at the console nodded. He closed his eyes, accessing a mental interface.

"Looks like the ship has fled the area, sir."

"Maybe next time, lieutenant."

Michael McCloskey

Chapter Twenty-Eight

"I guess the question is…what now?" asked Telisa.

"We have to figure out how to get back to civilization without getting caught and shipped off to a mining colony."

The *Iridar* drifted through the void of deep space. Out here in the vastness between the stars, no one could locate or disturb them. A morbid thought came to Telisa as they sat in the tiny kitchenette of the ship: what if the scout's gravity spinner failed, and they were forced to drift forever in the nothingness? Would anyone ever even notice they were gone?

"We need to modify the ship's exterior a little, in case they managed to burn through the stealth system," Magnus said. "The *Iridar* has a good optical wavelength scrambler, but who knows what the UNSF has these days? If they've made something that can defeat the scrambler since the war, you know a scout ship like the *Seeker* would have it."

"Maybe I'll just call up my dad and ask him."

"Heh. Yeah."

"Okay, so you have to take that part, because I don't know the first thing about space suits."

Magnus shrugged. "Time we changed that. We have the VR, with a training module for space repair. We'll run you through it, and I'll show you what to do."

Telisa swallowed. "Out there? If I screw up, I'll float off into space, or decompress or something, and I'll be dead."

Magnus laughed. "After what you've been through, this isn't going to kill you. You'll keep your head. I know it."

Telisa smiled. "Okay. I'll try it. So we both change the exterior of the ship."

"And maybe do a visual check for latchers."

"Okay. Then we have to stash the artifacts."

"Hrm. Yeah, that might be a good idea."

"I'm sure it is," Telisa said. "When we first show up, they may be searching ships trying to find us. But if they don't know who we are, or what the ship is, they might try searching but give up if they don't find the artifacts. So we need to stash them for a while. Maybe even only bring them back a few at a time, I don't know."

"We may have to give up our identities," Magnus said. "No one will know Thomas and Jack are dead for a while, but the fact that they're gone may eventually lead to investigation."

"Does anyone know they died? Did we mention it to Joe? And their bodies…once they died, I wonder if their bodies were dissolved away once we walked out of range."

"Let's hope their bodies and any trace of our DNA was dissolved. The UNSF is going to go through that base with some sophisticated equipment." Magnus shook his head. "If only it had been a few artifacts in some cave or something. They never would have bothered to waste the resources to find us, if they even knew we were ever there. But with an alien, the complex we were trapped in, and Joe…we may just be doomed."

"I'm not going to give up and neither are you," Telisa said. "They have a lot of other stuff to worry about, too, and it's going to take them time. We're a small part of it. Shiny is what they're going to care about. The Trilisk stuff is what they'll care about."

"Maybe."

"Well, what else is there to do…you have the ship's logs to clean up?" Telisa said.

Magnus let his head droop. "That's the big one. It's going to take a long time, and it sucks."

"Well we have time. Take a day off," Telisa suggested with a smile. "You deserve a rest."

"Well, I was thinking…about a crash pod inspection."

"What?"

Magnus winked at her. "Team crash pod inspection."

Telisa moved closer. "Oh, *team* crash pod inspection. Yes, I think one of those is in order."

Michael McCloskey

Epilogue

Kirizzo examined the data from his survey of the planet below. His vessel collected more data every minute, but the preliminary analysis was almost irrefutable.

Kirizzo's home planet lay dead, destroyed by a thorough application of heavy weapons from orbit.

He sent down drones to salvage what he could. It might be possible to retrieve useful supplies from the ruins of the planet. Close range scans showed the enemy had been Bel Klaven. The war machines had dropped onto the planet after the original barrage to dig the remaining Gorgala out of their tunnels. All evidence indicated this had been a year-long campaign, involving millions of invaders.

For Kirizzo, this revelation came as a life-altering event. New goals would have to be conceived, new plans laid to attain them. In some small way he was responsible for the carnage below, by allowing himself to be trapped in the Trilisk complex rather than returning in a timely manner with important Trilisk secrets. But now he could use what he had learned of those secrets to make a new life.

The Gorgala contemplated the aliens he had encountered, the soft ones with fat ugly bodies. Their primitive civilization looked more appealing in light of this new data. Perhaps they could offer Kirizzo the resources he desired.

He wondered where they had traveled to. There had been some sort of confrontation between the ones he had traded with and the others who were hunting them. Would it be dangerous to contact any of them without learning more first?

Kirizzo searched his download of the information he had gleaned from the computation tools of the aliens. Some of the data included star charts and astronomical reference material. And, of course, he had exacting records of the core replication elements of the individuals he sought.

With a little work, he should be able to find them again.

***

A hooded figure moved through the lock, passing smoothly under the security scanner. A brief disruption of the feed caused the nearby controller to review the data. It initiated a weapons scan which came up negative. The DNA of the latest few entrants ran through the matcher again but nothing seemed out of order. The discrepancy was logged.

Inside, a well dressed gentlemen waited at a long table in an empty warehouse room. The newcomer walked in and removed her hood.

"Ms. Vorauche?" asked the man, coming to his feet. He looked well manicured if slightly overweight, with brown hair and a thick moustache.

"Mr. Franklin," Telisa responded.

"Well, the item is quite a find. I would of course ask where you got such an amazing artifact, but I guess I know better."

Telisa shrugged. "The artifact itself will have to be enough."

The man nodded. "It is enough. Mystery enough all by itself. And I am paying quite enough for it, as well."

"Well you know, high demand…"

"Limited supply. Yes. We can thank the space force for that."

Telisa thought of her father for a moment. She wondered where he was. Then she reached into her jacket and brought out the device. It was a glowing egg with a thin covering of silvery netting.

"Be careful; it has a memory recorded in it," she said.

"Yes! Actually, I can't wait to see it myself."

"It is as I said. Very powerful. You won't be disappointed, even though you don't have a third brain lobe to receive the full experience."

The man took the artifact into his hands and examined it. After a moment, his eyes stopped moving, and he froze. She listened to his breathing for a few moments while he experienced the memory. Then he blinked and came out of it.

"Fantastic. Amazing. Unbelievable," he muttered. "And I hope we may do business again, if this is any indication!"

"Then we have a deal, Mr. Franklin," Telisa said, offering her hand.

The man took her hand in his own doughy appendage and shook it vigorously. "Excellent. A wonderful item it is. Being a xenoartifact smuggler must be very lucrative, and twice as exciting!"

Telisa smiled. "It is, Mr. Franklin. It is."